# A Beautiful Possibility

## Edith Ferguson Black

## CHAPTER I.

In one of the fairest of the West Indian islands a simple but elegant villa lifted its gabled roofs amidst a bewildering wealth of tropical beauty. Brilliant birds flitted among the foliage, gold and silver fishes darted to and fro in a large stone basin of a fountain which threw its glittering spray over the lawn in front of the house, and on the vine-shaded veranda hammocks hung temptingly, and low wicker chairs invited to repose.

Behind the jalousies of the library the owner of the villa sat at a desk, busily writing. He was a slight, delicate looking man, with an expression of careless good humor upon his face and an easy air of assurance according with the interior of the room which bespoke a cultured taste and the ability to gratify it. Books were everywhere, rare bits of china, curios and exquisitely tinted shells lay in picturesque confusion upon tables and wall brackets of native woods; soft silken draperies fell from the windows and partially screened from view a large alcove where microscopes of different sizes stood upon cabinets whose shelves were filled with a miscellaneous collection of rare plants and beautiful insects, specimens from the agate forest of Arizona, petrified remains from the 'Bad Lands' of Dakota, feathery fronded seaweed, skeletons of birds and strange wild creatures, and all the countless curiosities in which naturalists delight.

Lenox Hildreth when a young man, forced to flee from the rigors of the New England climate by reason of an inherited tendency to pulmonary disease, had chosen Barbadoes as his adopted country, and had never since revisited the land of his birth. From the first, fortune had smiled upon him, and when, some time after his marriage with the daughter of a wealthy planter, she had come into possession of all her father's estates, he had built the house which for fifteen years he had called home. When Evadne, their only daughter, was a little maiden of six, his wife had died, and for nine years father and child had been all the world to each other.

He finished writing at last with a sigh of relief, and folding the letter, together with one addressed to Evadne, he enclosed both in a large envelope which he sealed and addressed to Judge Hildreth, Marlborough, Mass. Then he leaned back in his chair, and, clasping his hands behind his head, looked fixedly at the picture of his fair young wife which hung above his desk.

"A bad job well done, Louise—or a good one. Our little lass isn't very well adapted to making her way among strangers, and the Bohemianism of this life is a poor preparation for the heavy respectability of a New England existence. Lawrence is a good fellow, but that wife of his always put me in mind of iced champagne, sparkling and cold. " He sighed heavily, "Poor little Vad! It is a dreary outlook, but it seems my one resource. Lawrence is the only relative I have in the world.

"After all, I may be fighting windmills, and years hence may laugh at this morning's work as an example of the folly of yielding to unnecessary alarm. Danvers is getting childish. All physicians get to be old fogies, I fancy, a natural sequence to a life spent in hunting down germs I suppose. They grow to imagine them where none exist. "

He rose, and strolled out on the veranda. As he did so, a negro, whose snow-white hair had earned for him from his master the sobriquet of Methusaleh, came towards the broad front steps. He was a grotesque image as he stood doffing a large palm-leaf hat, and Lenox Hildreth felt an irresistible inclination to laugh, and laughed accordingly. His morning's occupation had been one of the rare instances in which he had run counter to his inclinations. Sky blue cotton trousers showed two brown ankles before his feet hid themselves in a pair of clumsy shoes; a scarlet shirt, ornamented with large brass buttons and fastened at the throat with a cotton handkerchief of vivid corn color, was surmounted by an old nankeen coat, upon whose gaping elbows a careful wife had sewn patches of green cloth; his hands were encased in white cotton gloves three sizes too large, whose finger tips waved in the wind as their wearer flourished his palm-leaf headgear in deprecating obeisance.

"Well, Methusaleh, where are you off to now? " and Lenox Hildreth leaned against a flower wreathed pillar in lazy amusement.

"To camp-meetin', Mass Hildreff. I hez your permission, sah? " and the negro rolled his eyes with a ludicrous expression of humility.

His master laughed with the easy indulgence which made his servants impose upon him.

"You seem to have taken it, you rascal. It is rather late in the day to ask for permission when you and your store clothes are all ready for a start. "

"'Scuse me, Mass Hildreff, " with another deprecating wave of the palm-leaf hat, "but yer see I knowed yer wouldn't dissapint me of de priv'lege uv goin' ter camp-meetin' nohow. "

Lenox Hildreth held his cigar between his slender fingers and watched the tiny wreaths of smoke as they circled about his head.

"So camp-meeting is a privilege, is it? " he said carelessly. "How much more good will it do you to go there than to stay at home and hoe my corn? "

The eyes were rolled up until only the whites were visible.

"Powerful sight more good, Mass Hildreff. De preacher's 'n uncommon relijus man, an' de 'speriences uv de bredren is mighty upliftin'. Yes, sah! "

"Well, see that they don't lift you up so high that you'll forget to come down again. I suppose you have an experience in common with the rest? "

"Yes, Mass Hildreff, " and the palm-leaf made another gyration through the air. "I'se got a powerful 'sperience, sah. "

"Well, off you go. It would be a pity to deprive the assembly of such an edifying specimen of sanctimoniousness. "

"Yes, sah, I'se bery sanktimonyus. I'se 'bliged to you, sah. "

With a last obsequious flourish the palm-leaf was restored to its resting-place upon the snowy wool, and the negro shambled away. When he had gone a few yards a sudden thought struck his master and he called, —

"Methusaleh, I say, Methusaleh! "

"Yes, sah, " and the servant retraced his steps.

"What about that turkey of mine that you stole last week? You can't go to camp-meeting with that on your conscience. Come, now, better take off your finery and repent in sackcloth and ashes. "

For an instant the negro was nonplused, then the palm-leaf was flourished grandiloquently, while its owner said in a voice of withering scorn, —

"Laws! Mass Hildreff, do yer spose I'se goin' ter neglec' de Lawd fer one lil' turkey? "

His master turned on his heel with a low laugh. "Of a piece with the whole of them! " he said bitterly. "Hypocrites and shams! "

"Evadne! " he exclaimed impetuously, as a slight girlish figure came towards him, "never say a single word that you do not mean nor express a sensation that you have not felt. It is the people who neglect this rule who play havoc with themselves and the world. "

"Why, dearest, you frighten me! " and the girl slipped her hand through his arm with a low, sweet laugh. "I never saw you look so solemn before. "

"Hypocrisy, Vad, is the meanest thing on earth! The pious people at the church yonder call me an unbeliever, but they've got themselves to thank for it. I may be a good-for-nothing but at least I will not preach what I do not practise. "

"You are as good as gold, dearest. I won't have you say such horrid things! And you don't need to preach anything. I am sure no one in all the world could be happier than we. "

Her father put his hand under her chin, and, lifting her face towards his, looked long and earnestly at the pure brow, about which the brown hair clustered in natural curls, the clear-cut nose, the laughing lips parted over a row of pearls, and the wonderful deep gray eyes.

"*Are* you happy, little one? " he asked wistfully. "Are you quite sure about that? "

"Happy! " the girl echoed the word with an incredulous smile. "Why, dearest, what has come to you? You never needed to ask me such a question before! Don't you know there isn't a girl in Barbadoes who has been so thoroughly spoiled, and has found the spoiling so sweet? Do I look more than usually mournful to-day that you should think I am pining away with grief? " She looked up at him with a roguish laugh.

He smiled and laid his finger caressingly on the dimpled chin. "Dear little bird! " he said tenderly; "but when this dimple captivates the heart of some one, Vad, you will fly away and leave the poor father in the empty nest. "

Her color glowed softly through the olive skin. She threw her arms around his neck and laid her face against his breast. "You know better! " she exclaimed passionately. "You know I wouldn't leave you for all the 'some ones' in the world! "

Her father caught her close. "Poor little lass! " he said with a sigh.

The girl lifted her head and looked at him anxiously. "Dearest, what *is* the matter? I am sure you are not well! You have been sitting too long at that tiresome writing. "

"Yes, that is it, darling, " he said with a sudden change of tone. "Writing always does give me the blues. I think the man who invented the art should have been put in a pillory for the rest of his natural life. Blow your whistle for Sam to bring the horses and we will go for a ride along the beach. "

Evadne lifted the golden whistle which hung at her girdle and blew the call which the well-trained servant understood. "Fi, dearest! " she said, "if there were no writing there would be no books, and what would become of our beautiful evenings then? But I am glad you do not have to write much, since it tires you so. What has it all been about, dear? Am I never to know? "

"Some day, perhaps, little Vad. But do not indulge in the besetting sin of your sex, or, like the mother of the race, you may find your apple choke you in the chewing. "

Evadne shook her finger at him. "Naughty one! As if you were not three times as curious as I! And when it comes to waiting, —you should have named me Patience, sir! "

Her father laughed as he kissed her, then he tied on her hat, threw on his own, and hand-in-hand like two children they ran down the veranda steps to where the groom stood waiting with the horses.

## CHAPTER II.

A month full of happy days had flown by when Evadne and her father returned one morning from a long tramp in search of specimens. A delightful afternoon had followed, he in a hammock, she on a low seat beside him, arranging, classifying and preparing their morning's spoil for the microscope. Suddenly she turned towards him with a troubled face.

"Dearest, how pale you look! Are you very tired? "

"It is only the heat, " he answered lightly. "We had a pretty stiff walk this morning, you know. "

"And I carried you on and on! " she cried reproachfully. "I was so anxious to find this particular crab. Isn't he a pretty fellow? " and she lifted the box that her father might watch the tiny creature's play. "I shall go at once and make you an orange sherbet. "

"Let Dinah do it and you stay here with me. "

"No indeed! You know you think no one can make them as well as I do. I promise you this one shall be superfine. "

"As you will, little one, —only don't stay away too long. "

He lay very still after she had left him, looking dreamily through the vines at the silver spray of the fountain. The air had grown oppressively sultry; no breath of wind stirred the heavily drooping leaves, no sound except the rhythmic splash of the fountain and the soft lapping of the waves upon the beach. He closed his eyes while their ceaseless monotone seemed to beat upon his brain.

"Forever! Forever! Forever! "

A spasm of pain crossed his face as Evadne's voice woke the echoes with a merry song. "Poor little lass! " he murmured. Then he smiled as she came towards him, quaffed off the beverage she had prepared with loving skill, and called her the best cook in all the Indies.

"Has it refreshed you, dearest? " she asked anxiously.

"Immensely! Now you shall read me some of Lalla Rookh, and after dinner I will set about making a Mecca for your crab. "

Evadne stroked the dainty claws, —

"Poor little chap! So you are a pilgrim like the rest of us. I wish we did not have to go on and on, dearest! " she exclaimed passionately, "why cannot we stand still and enjoy? "

"It would grow monotonous, little Vad. Progress is the law of all being, and seventy years of life is generally enough for the majority. You would not like to live to be an old lady of two hundred and fifty? Think how tired you would be! "

She laid her cheek against his upon the pillow. "I should *never* grow tired, —with you! "

The evening drew on, hot and breathless. Low growls of distant thunder were heard at intervals, and in the eastern sky the lightning played.

Evadne watched it, sitting on the top step of the veranda, her white muslin dress in happy contrast with the deep green of the vines which clustered thickly about the pillar against which she leaned. On the step below her a young man sat. He too was clad in white and the rich crimson of the silken scarf which he wore about his waist enhanced his Spanish beauty. A zither lay across his knees over which his hands wandered skilfully as he made the air tremble with dreamy music. Mr. Hildreth paced slowly up and down the veranda behind them.

"What is the news from the great world, Geoff? I saw a troop ship signaled this morning. Have you been on board yet? "

"No, sir, I have been looking over the plantation with my father all day, and only got home in time for dinner. "

"You chose a cool time for it! " and Mr. Hildreth laughed.

Geoffrey Chittenden shrugged his shoulders. "When Geoffrey Chittenden, Senior, makes up his mind to do anything, he has the most sublime indifference for the thermometer of any one I ever had the honor of knowing. But the ship only brought a small detachment, I believe; she will carry away a larger one. The garrison here is to be reduced, you know. "

"Yes, it is a mistake I think. Will Drewson have to go? He has been on this Station longer than any of the others. "

"Yes, his company has marching orders for Malta. He told me last night he was coming to take leave of you next week. "

"Our nice Captain Drewson going away! " Evadne exclaimed, aghast. "Why, dearest, he is one of our oldest friends! "

"The law of progression, Vad darling. "

"How I hate it! " she cried, while her lips trembled. "Why can't we just live on in the old happy way? You will be going next, Geoff, and the Hamiltons and the Vandervoorts. Does nothing last? "

Her voice hushed itself into silence and again Lenox Hildreth heard the soft waves singing, —

"Forever! Forever! Forever! "

"Oh yes, Evadne, " Geoffrey said with a laugh: "we are very lasting. It is only the unfortunate people under military rule who prove unreliable. Let me sing you my latest song to cheer your spirits. I only learned it last week. "

He struck a few chords and was beginning his song when a low groan made him spring to his feet. Evadne passed him like a flash of light and flew to her father's side. He was leaning heavily against a pillar with his handkerchief, already showing crimson stains, pressed tightly against his lips.

They laid him gently down and summoned help. After that all was like a horrible dream to Evadne. She was dimly conscious that friends came with ready offers of assistance, and that Barbadoes' best physicians were unremitting in their efforts to stop the hemorrhage; while she stood like a statue beside her father's bed. She was absolutely still. When at last the hemorrhage was checked the exhaustion was terrible. Evadne longed to throw herself beside him and pillow the dear head upon her bosom, but Dr. Danvers had whispered, —

"A sudden sound may start the hemorrhage again, —the slightest shock is sure to. " After that, not for worlds would she have moved a finger.

The day passed and another night drew on. One of the physicians was constantly in attendance, for the hemorrhage returned at intervals. Just as the rose-tinted dawn looked shyly through the windows, her father spoke, and Evadne bent her head to catch the faint tone of the voice which sounded so far away.

"Vad, darling, I have made an awful mistake! I thought everything a sham. I know better now. Make it the business of your life, little Vad, to find Jesus Christ. "

Again the red stream stained his lips, and Dr. Danvers came swiftly forward, but Lenox Hildreth was forever beyond all need of human care.

\* \* \* \* \*

A week passed, and day after day Evadne sat by her window, speaking no word. Outdoors the fountain still sparkled in the sunshine and the birds sang, but for her the foundations of life had been shaken to their center. Her friends tried in vain to break up her unnatural calm.

"If you would only have a good cry, Evadne, " Geoffrey Chittenden said at last, "you would feel better, dear. That is what all girls do, you know. "

She turned upon him a pair of solemn eyes, out of which the merry sparkle had faded. "Will crying give me back my father? "

"Why, no, dear. Of course I didn't mean that. But these things are bound to happen to us all, sooner or later, you know. It is the rule of life. "

"'The law of progression, '" she said with a dreary laugh. "I wish the world would stop for good! "

When the clergyman came she met him quietly, and he found himself not a little disconcerted by the steady gaze of the mournful grey eyes. He was not accustomed to dealing with such wordless grief, and he found his favorite phrases sadly inadequate to the occasion. There was an awkward pause.

"Dr. Danvers says your father told him some time ago that, in the event of his death, he wished you to make your home with your uncle in America? " he said at length.

Evadne bowed.

"Well, my dear young lady, you will find it in all respects a most desirable home, I feel confident. Judge Hildreth holds a position of great trust in the church, and is universally esteemed as a Christian gentleman of sterling character. "

The grey eyes were lifted to his face.

"Shall I find Jesus Christ there? "

"Jesus Christ? " The clergyman echoed her words with a start. "I beg your pardon, my dear. The Lord sitteth upon his throne in the heavens. We must approach him reverently, with humble fear. "

"That seems a long way off, " said Evadne in a disappointed tone. "There must be some mistake. My father told me to make it the business of my life to find him. "

"Your father, my dear! Oh, ah, ahem! "

An indignant flash leaped into the grey eyes. Evadne rose and faced him. "You must excuse me, sir, " she said quietly. Then she left the room.

And the tears, which all the kindly sympathy had failed to bring her, at the first breath of censure fell about her like a flood.

## CHAPTER III.

Judge Hildreth sat with his family at dinner in the spacious dining-room of one of the finest houses in Marlborough. He was a handsome man, with a stateliness of manner attributable in part to the deferential homage which Marlborough paid to his opinion in all matters of importance. His wife, tall and queenly, sat opposite him. Two daughters and a son completed the family group. Louis Hildreth had his father's dark blue eyes and regular features, but there were weak lines about the mouth which betokened a lack of purpose, and the expression of his face was marred by a cynical smile which was fast becoming habitual with him. Isabelle, the eldest, was tall and fair, except for a chill hauteur which set strangely upon one so young, while her firmly set lips betokened the existence of a strong will which completely dominated her less self-reliant sister. Marion Hildreth was just Evadne's age, with a pink and white beauty and soft eyes which turned deprecatingly at intervals towards Isabelle, as though to ask pardon for imaginary solecisms against Miss Hildreth's code of etiquette.

The covers were being changed for the second course when a servant entered and approached the Judge, bearing a cablegram upon a silver salver. He ran his eyes hastily over its contents, then he leaned back heavily against his chair, while an expression of genuine sorrow settled down upon his face.

"Your Uncle Lenox is dead, " he said briefly, as the girls plied him with questions.

"Dead! " Mrs. Hildreth's voice broke the hush which had fallen in the room. "Why, Lawrence, this is very sudden! We have looked upon Lenox as being perfectly well. "

"It is not safe to count anyone well, Kate, who carries such a lurking serpent in his bosom. Only forty-three! Just in his prime. Poor Len! " The Judge leaned his head upon his hand, while his thoughts were busy with memories of the gay young brother who had filled the old homestead with his merry nonsense.

"And what will become of Evadne? " Again Mrs. Hildreth's voice broke the silence.

"Evadne? " the Judge looked full in his wife's face. "Why, my dear, there is only one thing to be done. I shall cable immediately to have her come to us. " He rose from the table, his dinner all untasted, and left the room.

Louis was the first to speak. "A Barbadoes cousin. How will you like having such a novelty as that, Sis, to introduce among your acquaintance? " He bowed lazily to Mrs. Hildreth. "Let me congratulate you, lady mother. You will have the pleasure of floating another bud into blossom upon the bosom of society. "

"I do not see any room for congratulation, Louis, " Mrs. Hildreth said discontentedly. "It is a dreadful responsibility. One does not know what the child may be like. "

"Hardly a child, mamma, " pouted Marion. "Evadne must be as old as I. "

"If that is so, Sis, she must have the wisdom of Methusaleh! " and Louis looked at his sister with one of his mocking smiles. "At any rate she will afford scope for your powers of training, Isabelle. It must be depressing to have to waste your eloquence upon an audience of one. "

Isabelle tossed her head. "I am not anxious for the opportunity, " she said coldly. "Likely the child will be a perfect heathen after running wild among savages all her life. "

Louis whistled. "A little less Grundy and a little more geography would be to your advantage, Isabelle! Barbadoes happens to be the crème de la crème of the British Indies. I would not advise you to display your ignorance before Evadne, or your future lecturettes on the conventionalities may prove lacking in vital force. "

"Why, Isabelle, my dear, you must be dreaming! " and her mother looked annoyed. "Don't let your father hear you say such a thing, I beg of you! When he visited Barbadoes he was delighted, and he thought Evadne's mother one of the most charming women he had ever met. If she had lived of course Evadne would be all right, but she has been left entirely to her father's guidance, and he had such peculiar ideas. "

"When, did she die, mamma? " asked Marion.

"I am sure I cannot remember. Six or seven years ago it must have been. But we rarely heard from them. Your Uncle Lenox was always a wretched correspondent, and since his wife's death he has hardly written at all. "

"The house of Hildreth cannot claim to be well posted in the matter of blood relations, " said Louis carelessly, as he helped himself to olives.

\* \* \* \* \*

Upon the deck of one of the Ocean Greyhounds a promiscuous crowd was gathered. Returning tourists in all the glory of field glasses and tweed suits; British officers going home on furlough from the different outposts where they were stationed; merchants from the rich markets of the far East; picturesque foreigners in national costume; and a bishop who paced the deck with a dignity becoming his ecclesiastical rank. There was a continuous hum of conversation, mingled with intermittent ripples of laughter from the different groups which were scattered about the deck. Among the exceptions to the general sociability were the bishop, still pacing up and down with his hands clasped behind him, and a young girl who sat looking far out over the waves, utterly heedless of the noise and confusion around her.

She was absolutely alone. The gentleman under whose care she was traveling made a point of escorting her to meals, after which he invariably secured her a comfortable deck chair, supplied her liberally with rugs and books, and then retired to the smoking-room, with the serene consciousness of duty well performed; and Evadne Hildreth was thankful to be left in peace. She was no longer the buoyant, merry girl. Her vitality seemed crushed. Hour after hour she sat motionless, her hands folded listlessly in her lap, looking out over the dancing waves. She had caught the last glimpse of her beloved island in a grey stupor. Everything was gone, —father and home and friends, —nothing that happened could matter now, — but, oh, the dreary, dreary years! Did the sun shine in far-away New England, and could the water be as blue as her dear Atlantic, with the gay ripple on its bosom and the music of its waves? She looked at the tender sky, as on the far horizon it bent low to kiss the face of the mysterious mighty ocean which stretched "a sea without a shore. " That was like her life now. All the beauty ended, yet stretching on and on and on. And she must keep pace with it, against her will. And there was no one to care. She was all alone! No, there was Jesus Christ!

She started to find that the Bishop's lady was speaking to her. Evadne recognized her, for she sat at the next table, and several times she had stood aside to let her pass to her seat. Something about the solitary, pathetic little figure, the hopeless face and mournful grey eyes, had won the compassion of the good lady, for she was a kindly soul.

"My dear, you have a great sorrow? " she said gently. "I hope you have the consolations of our holy religion to help you bear it. "

Evadne turned towards her eagerly. Her husband was the head of the church. Surely *she* would know.

"Can you help me to find him? " she asked abruptly.

"Find whom, my dear? Have you a friend among the passengers? "

"Jesus Christ. "

"Oh! " The Bishop's lady sat back with the suddenness of the shock, "Are you in earnest, my dear? " she asked with a tinge of severity in her tone. "This is a very serious question, but, if you really mean it, I will lend you my Prayer Book. "

Evadne smiled drearily. "Oh, yes, I am terribly in earnest. My father said I was to make it the business of my life. "

"Oh, ah, yes, to be sure, " said the lady a trifle absently. "That is very proper. Christianity should be the great purpose of our life. "

"I do not want Christianity, " said Evadne impatiently, "I want Christ. "

"My dear, you shock me! The eternal verities of our holy religion must ever be—"

"Do you believe in him? " asked Evadne, interrupting her.

"Believe in him? whom do you mean? "

"Jesus Christ. "

Aghast, the Bishop's lady crossed herself and began repeating the Apostles' Creed.

"That makes him seem so far away, " said Evadne sadly. "I do not want him in heaven if I have to live upon earth. Have *you* found him? " she asked eagerly. "Are you on intimate terms with him? Is he your friend? "

The Bishop's lady gasped for breath. That she, a member of the Church of the Holy Communion of All Saints should be interrogated in such a fashion as this! "I think you do not quite understand, " she said coldly. "I will lend you a treatise on Church Doctrine. You had better study that. "

"Charlotte, " said her husband when she reached her stateroom, "I have arrived at an important decision this afternoon. I have finally concluded to take the Socinian Heresy as my theme for the noon lectures. The subject will admit of elaborate treatment and afford ample scope for scholarship. "

"Heresy! " echoed his wife, who had not yet recovered her equanimity; "why, Bertram, I have just been talking to a young person who asked me if I was on intimate terms with Jesus Christ! "

"Ah, yes, " said the Bishop absently, "the radical tendencies of the present day are to be deplored. Have you seen that my vestments are in order, Charlotte? I shall hold Divine service on board to-morrow. "

In a neighboring stateroom a lonely soul, bewildered and despairing, struggled through the darkness towards the light.

\* \* \* \* \*

The last snow of the winter lay in soft beauty upon the streets of Marlborough as Evadne's train drew into the railway station. Instantly all was bustle and confusion throughout the cars. Evadne shrank back in her seat and waited. Instinctively she felt that for her there would be no joyous welcome. Inexpressibly dreary as the journey had been she was sorry it was at an end. An overwhelming embarrassment of shyness seized upon her, and the chill desolation of loneliness seemed to shut down about her like a cloud.

A young man sauntered past her with his hands in his pockets. When he reached the end of the car he turned and surveyed the passengers leisurely, then he came back to her seat. He lifted his hat with lazy politeness.

"Miss Hildreth, I believe? "

Evadne bowed. He shook hands coolly.

"I have the honor of introducing myself as your cousin Louis. "

He made no attempt to give her a warmer greeting, and Evadne was glad, but how dreary it was!

Louis led the way out of the station to where a pair of magnificent horses stood, tossing their regal heads impatiently. A colored coachman stood beside them, clad in fur.

"Pompey, " he said, "this is Miss Evadne Hildreth from Barbadoes. "

The man bent his head low over the little hand which was instantly stretched out to him. "I'se very glad to see Miss 'Vadney, " he said with simple fervor. "I was powerful fond of Mass Lennux; " and Evadne felt she had received her warmest welcome.

She nestled down among the soft robes of the sleigh while the silver bells rang merrily through the frosty air. It was all so new and strange. A leaden weight seemed to be settling down upon her heart and she felt as if she were choking, but she threw it off. She dared not let herself think. She began to talk rapidly.

"What splendid horses you have! Surely they must be thoroughbreds? No ordinary horses could ever hold their heads like that. "

Louis nodded. "You have a quick eye, " he said approvingly. "Most girls would not know a thoroughbred from a draught horse. You have hit upon the surest way to get into my father's good graces. His horses are his hobby. "

"What are their names? "

"Brutus and Caesar. The Judge is nothing if not classical. "

As they mounted the front steps the faint notes of a guitar sounded from the front room.

"Confound Isabelle and her eternal twanging! " muttered Louis, as he fumbled for his latch-key. "It would be a more orthodox welcome if you found your relations waiting for you with open arms, but the Hildreth family is not given to gush. Isabelle will tell you it is not good form. So we keep our emotions hermetically sealed and stowed away under decorous lock and key, polite society having found them inconvenient things to handle, partaking of the nature of nitroglycerine, you know, and liable to spontaneous combustion. "

He opened the door as he spoke and Evadne followed him into the hall. She shivered, although a warm breath of heated air fanned her cheek. The atmosphere was chilly.

Marion, hurried forward to greet her, followed more leisurely by Isabelle and her mother, who touched her lips lightly to her forehead.

"I hope you have had a pleasant journey, my dear, although you must find our climate rather stormy. I think you might as well let the girls take you at once to your room and then we will have dinner. "

"Where is the Judge? " inquired Louis.

"Detained again at the office. He has just telephoned not to wait for him. He is killing himself with overwork. "

18

To Evadne the dinner seemed interminable and she found herself contrasting the stiff formality with the genial hospitality of her father's table. She saw again the softly lighted room with its open windows through which the flowers peeped, and heard his gay badinage and his low, sweet laugh. Could she be the same Evadne, or was it all a dream?

Isabelle stood beside her as she began to prepare for the night. She wished she would go away. The burden of loneliness grew every moment more intolerable. Suddenly she turned towards her cousin and cried in desperation, —

"Can *you* tell me where I shall find Jesus Christ? "

Isabelle started. "My goodness, Evadne, what a strange question! You took my breath away. "

"Is it a strange question? " she asked wistfully. "Everyone seems to think so, and yet—my father said I was to make it the business of my life to find him. "

"Your father! " cried Isabelle. "Why Uncle Lenox was an——"

Instantly a pair of small hands were held like a vice against her lips. Isabelle threw them off angrily.

"You are polite, I must say! Is this a specimen of West Indian manners? "

"You were going to say something I could not hear, " said Evadne quietly, "there was nothing else to do. "

Isabelle left the room, and, returning, threw a book carelessly upon the table. "You had better study that, " she said. "It will answer your questions better than I can. "

"I told you she was a heathen! " she exclaimed, as she rejoined her mother in the sitting-room; "but I did not know that I should have to turn missionary the first night and give her a Bible! "

Upstairs Evadne buried her face among the pillows and the aching heart burst its bonds in one long quivering cry of pain.

"Dearest! "

## CHAPTER IV.

A day full of light—warm and brilliant. The sun flooding the wide fields of timothy and clover and fresh young grain with glory; falling with a soft radiance upon the comfortable mansion of the master of Hollywood Farm, with its spacious barns and long stretches of stabling, and throwing loving glances among the leaves of its deep belt of woodland where the river sparkled and soft rugs of moss spread their rich luxuriance over an aesthetic carpet of resinous pine needles.

Near the limits of Hollywood the forest made a sudden curve to the right, and the river, turned from its course, rushed, laughing and eager, over a ridge of rocks which tossed it in the air in sheets of silver spray.

Standing there, leaning upon a gun, a boy of about seventeen looked long at a squirrel whose mangled body was staining the emerald beauty of the moss with crimson. His face was earnest and troubled, while the expression of sorrowful contempt which swept over it, made him seem older than he was. It was a strong face, with deep-set, thoughtful eyes which lit up wondrously when he was interested or pleased. His mouth was sensitive but his chin was firm and his brown hair fell in soft waves over a broad, full brow. People always took it for granted that John Randolph would be as good as his word. They never reasoned about it. They simply expected it of him.

He began to speak, and his voice fell clear and distinct through the silence.

"And you call this sport? " There was no answer save the soft gurgle of the river as it splashed merrily over the stones.

"You are a brute, John Randolph! " And the wind sighed a plaintive echo among the trees.

He was silent while the words which he had read six weeks before and which had been ringing a ceaseless refrain in his heart ever since, obtruded themselves upon his memory.

"It is the privilege of everyone to become an exact copy of Jesus Christ. "

"Well, John Randolph, can you picture to yourself Jesus Christ shooting a squirrel for sport? " He tossed aside the weapon he had been leaning upon with a gesture of disgust, and, folding his arms, looked up at the cloud-flecked sky.

"Are you there, Jesus Christ? " he asked wistfully. "Are you looking down on this poor old world, and what do you think of it all? Men made in God's image finding their highest enjoyment in slaughtering his creatures. Game Preserves where they can do it in luxurious leisure; fox hunts with their pack of hunters and hounds in full cry after one poor defenceless fox, and battle-fields where they tear each other limb from limb with Gatling gun and shells; and yet we call ourselves honorable gentlemen, and talk of the delights of the chase and the glories of war! Pshaw! what a mockery it is. "

Stooping suddenly he laid the squirrel upon his open palm and gently stroked the long, silky fur. He lifted the tiny paws with their perfect equipment for service and looked remorsefully at the eyes whose light was dimmed, and the mouth which had forever ceased its merry chatter. A great tenderness sprang up in his heart toward all living things and, lifting his right hand to heaven, he exclaimed, "Poor little squirrel, I cannot give you back your happy life, but, I will never take another! "

Then he knelt, and scooping out a grave, laid the little creature to rest at the foot of a tree in whose trunk the remnant of its winter store of nuts was carefully garnered. When at length he turned to leave the spot the tiny grave was marked by a pine slab, on which was pencilled,

"Here lies the germ of a resolve. July 17th, 18 — "

He walked slowly along the fragrant wood-path, looking thoughtfully at the shadows as they played hide and seek upon the moss, while through the trees he caught glimpses of the sparkling river which sang as it rolled along.

When he reached the border of the woodland he stood still and his eyes swept over the landscape. Hollywood was the finest stock farm in the country. After his father's death he had come, a little lad, to live with Mr. Hawthorne, and every year which had elapsed since then made it grow more dear. He loved its rolling meadows, its breezy pastures and its fragrant orchards. Its beautifully kept grounds and outbuildings appealed to his innate sense of the fitness of things, while its air of abundant comfort made it difficult to realize that the world was full of hunger and woe. He loved the green road where the wild roses blushed and the honeysuckle drooped its fragrant petals, but most of all he loved the graceful horses and sleek cows which just now were grazing in the fields on either side; and the shy creatures, with the subtle instinct by which all animals test the quality of human friendship, took him into their confidence and came gladly at his call and did his bidding.

When he reached the end of the road he stopped again, and, leaning against the fence adjoining the broad gate which led to the house, gave a low whistle. A thoroughbred Jersey, feeding some distance away, lifted her head and listened. Again he whistled, and with soft, slow tread the cow came towards him and rubbed her nose against his arm. He took her head between his hands, her clover-laden breath fanning his cheeks, and looked at the dark muzzle and the large eyes, almost human in their tenderness.

"Well, Primrose, old lady, you're as dainty as your namesake, and as sweet. Ah, Sylph, you beauty! " he continued, as a calf like a young fawn approached the gate, "you can't rest away from your mammy, can you? Primrose, have you any aspirations, or are you content simply to eat and drink? You have a good time of it now, but what if you were kicked and cuffed and starved? You are sensitive, for I saw you shrink and shiver when Bill Wright, —the scoundrel! —dared to strike you. He'll never do it again, Prim! Have you the taste of an epicure for the juicy grass blades and the clover when it is young, — do you love to hear the birds sing and the brook murmur, and do you enjoy living under the trees and watching the clouds chase the sunbeams as you chew your cud? Do you wonder why the cold winter comes and you have to be shut up in a stall with a different kind of fodder? Do you ever wonder who gave you life and what you are meant to do with it? How I wish you could talk, old lady! "

He vaulted over the gate, and whistling to a fine collie who came bounding to meet him, walked slowly on towards the stables.

"Hulloa, John! " and a boy about two years his junior threw himself off a horse reeking with foam. "Rub Sultan down a bit like a good fellow. There'll be the worst kind of a row if the governor sees him in this pickle. "

John Randolph looked indignantly at the handsome horse, as he stood with drooping head and wide distended nostrils, while the white foam dripped over his delicate legs.

"Serve you right if there were! " and his voice was full of scorn. "You're about as fit to handle horseflesh as an Esquimaux. "

"Oh, pish! You're a regular old grandmother, John. There's nothing to make such a row about. " And Reginald Hawthorne turned upon his heel.

John threw off coat and vest, and, rolling up his sleeves, led the exhausted horse to the currying ground. Reginald followed slowly, his hands in his pockets.

"How did you get him into such a mess? " he asked shortly.

"I don't know, I didn't do anything to him, " and Reginald kicked the gravel discontentedly. "I believe he's getting lazy. "

"Sultan lazy! " and John laughed incredulously. "That's a good joke! Why, he is the freest horse on the place! "

"Well, I don't know how else to explain it. He's been on the go pretty steadily, but what's a horse good for? Thursday afternoon we had our cross-country run and the ground was horribly stiff. I thought he had sprained his off foreleg for he limped a good deal on the home stretch, but he seemed to limber up all right the last few miles. I was sorry not to let him rest yesterday; would have put him in better trim I suppose for to-day's twenty mile pull, —but Cartwright and Peterson wanted to make up a tandem, and when they asked for Sultan I didn't like to refuse. They are heavy swells, and you know father wants me to get in with that lot. But that shouldn't have hurt him. They only went as far as Brighton. What's fifteen miles to a horse! "

"Fifteen miles means thirty to a horse when he has to travel back the same road, " said John drily; "and your heavy swells take the toll out of horseflesh quicker than a London cabby. "

"Why, John, what has come to you? You're the last fellow in the world to want me to be churlish. "

"That's true, Rege, —but I don't want them to cripple you as they have poor Sultan. What kind of fellows are they? "

"Oh, not a bad sort, " said Reginald carelessly. "Lots of the needful, you know, and free with it. Not very fond of the grind, but always up to date when there are any good times going. What do you suppose put Sultan in such a lather, John? I was so afraid father would catch me that I came across the fields, and it was just as much as he could do to take the last fence. I made sure he was going to tumble. "

"Well for you he didn't, " and John smoothed the delicate limbs with his firm hand, "these knees are too pretty for a scar. Go into the vet room, Rege, and bring me out a roll of bandage. "

"Hulloa! That will give me away to the governor with a vengeance! What are you going to bandage him for? "

"He is badly strained, and if I don't his legs will be all puffed by the morning. It will be lucky if it is nothing worse. He looks to me as if he was in for a touch of distemper, but I'll give him a powder and perhaps we can stave it off. "

Reginald brought the bandage and then stood moodily striking at a beetle with his riding whip. He was turning away when a hand with a grip of steel was laid on his shoulder and he was forced back to where the beetle lay, a shapeless mass of quivering agony, while a low stern voice exclaimed, —

"Finish your work! Even the cannibals do that. "

Reginald wrenched himself free. "Pshaw! " he said contemptuously, "it's only a beetle. " But he did as he was told.

Then he stood silently watching as with swift skilfulness John swathed the horse's limbs in flannel. "I guess Sultan misses you, John. Over at the college livery their fingers are all thumbs. "

"Poor Sultan! " was all John's answer, as he led the horse into a large paddock thickly strewn with fresh straw.

A night full of stars—silent and sweet. John Randolph leaned on the broad gate which opened into the green road where he had lingered in the afternoon. The thoughts which surged through his brain made sleep impossible, and so, lighting his bull's-eye, he had gone to the stables to see how Sultan was faring, and then wandered on under the mystery of the stars.

The night was warm. A breeze heavy with perfume lifted the hair from his brow. He heard the low breathing of the cattle as they dozed in the fields on either side, and the soft whirr of downy plumage as the great owl which had built its nest among the eaves of the new barn flew past him. Suddenly a warm nose was thrust against his shoulder and, with the assurance of a spoilt beauty, the cow laid her head upon his arm. He lifted his other hand and stroked it gently.

"Hah, Primrose! Are you awake, old lady? What are your views of life now, Prim? Do the shadows make it seem more weird and grand, or does midnight lose its awesomeness when one is upon four legs? "

He looked away to where the stars were throbbing with tender light, crimson and green and gold, and the words of the book which he had been studying every leisure moment for the past six weeks swept across his mental vision.

"'I am the light of the world: he that followeth me shall not walk in darkness, but shall have the light of life. '

"'The light of life, '" he repeated slowly. "Why, to most people life seems all darkness! What is 'the light of life'? "

Still other words came stealing to his memory. 'I am the way, the truth, and the life, no one cometh unto the Father, but by me. ' 'Except ye turn, and become as little children, ye shall in no wise enter into the kingdom of heaven. ' 'This is life eternal, that they should know thee the only true God, and him whom thou didst send, even Jesus. '

A great light flooded John Randolph's soul.

"'I' and 'me, '" he whispered. "Why, it is a personality. It is Jesus himself! He is the way to the kingdom, the truth of the kingdom and the life of it. The kingdom of heaven, not far away in space, but set up here and now in the hearts of men who live the life hid with Christ in God. I see it all! Jesus Christ is the light of the life which God gives us through his Son. "

He stretched his hands up towards the glistening sky.

"Jesus Christ, " he cried eagerly, "come into my life and make it light. I take thee for my Master, my Friend. I give myself away to thee. I will follow wherever thou dost lead. Jesus Christ, help me to grow like thee! "

The hush of a great peace fell upon his soul, while through the listening night an angel stooped and traced upon his brow the kingly motto, 'Ich Dien. '

## CHAPTER V.

"Don, Don, me's tumin', " and the baby of the farm, a little child with sunny curls and laughing eyes, ran past the great barns of Hollywood.

John Randolph was swinging along the green road with a bridle over his arm, whistling softly. He turned as the childish voice was borne to him on the breeze. "All right, Nansie, wait for me at the gate. " Then he sprang over the fence and crossed the field to where a group of horses were feeding.

The child climbed up on the gate beside a saddle which John had placed there and waited patiently. He soon came back, leading a magnificent bay horse, and began to adjust the saddle.

"Now, Nan, I'll give you a ride to the house. Can't go any further to-day, for I have to cross the river. "

The child shook her head confidently. "Me 'll go too, Don. "

"I'm afraid not, Nan. The river is so deep, we'll have to swim for it. That is why I chose Neptune, you see. "

"Me's not 'fraid, wiv 'oo, Don. "

"Better wait, Baby, till the river is low. Well, come along then, " as the wily schemer drew down her pretty lips into the aggrieved curve which always conquered his big, soft heart. She clapped her hands with glee, as he lifted her in front of him and started Neptune into a brisk trot, and made a bridle for herself out of the horse's silky mane.

"Gee, gee, Nepshun. Nan loves you, dear. "

When they reached the fording place John's face grew grave. The river had risen during the night and was rushing along with turbulent strength. There was no house within five miles. His business was imperative. He dared not leave the child until he came back. Crouching upon the saddle, he clasped one arm about her while he twisted his other hand firmly in and out of the horse's mane.

"Are you afraid, Nansie? "

She twined her arms more tightly about his neck until the sunny curls brushed his cheek.

"Me'll do anywhere, wiv 'oo, Don. "

Just as the gallant horse reached the opposite bank Reginald galloped down to the ford on his way home for Sunday.

"Upon my word, John, you're a perfect slave to that youngster! What mad thing will you be doing next, I wonder? "

"The next thing will be to go back again, " said John with a smile, while Nan clung fast to his neck and peeped shyly through her curls at her brother.

"Where are you off to? "

"Henderson's. "

Reginald turned his horse's head. "I might as well go along. A man's a fool to ride alone when he can have company. "

John gave him a swift, comprehensive glance.

"How are things going, Rege? You're not looking very fit. "

Reginald yawned and drew his hand across his heavy eyes. "Oh, all right. Oyster suppers and that sort of thing are apt to make a fellow drowsy. "

"Don't go too fast, Rege. "

"Why not? " said Reginald carelessly. "It suits the governor, and that book you're so fond of says children should obey their parents. "

\* \* \* \* \*

"I declare, John, you're a regular algebraic puzzle! " he exclaimed later in the day, as he stood beside John in the carpenter's shop, watching the curling strips of wood which his plane was tossing off with sweeping strokes. "You put all there is of you into everything you do. You take as much pains over a plough handle as you would over a buggy! "

"Why not? God takes as much pains with a humming-bird as an elephant. Mere size doesn't count. "

"Nan loves you, Reggie, " and a tiny hand was slipped shyly into her brother's.

"All right, Magpie, " he said carelessly. "You had better run home now to mother. Your chatter makes my head ache. "

The laughing lips quivered and the child turned away from him to John and hid her face against his knee. He lifted her up on the bench beside him and gave her a handful of shavings to play with.

"I don't see how you accomplish anything with that child everlastingly under your feet! " Reginald continued, "yet you do two men's work and seem to love it into the bargain. I'm sure if I had to cooper up all the things on the farm as you do, I should loathe the very sight of tools. "

"I *do* love it, Rege. Jesus Christ was a carpenter, you know. I get very near to him out here. "

"Jesus Christ! " echoed Reginald with a puzzled stare. "What is coming to you, John? "

"It has come, Rege, " John said with a great light in his face. "I have found my Master. "

"Upon my word, John, you are the queerest fellow! What next, I wonder? "

"The next thing, Rege, " and John laid his hand affectionately upon his friend's shoulder, "is for you to find him too. "

"So, you're going to turn preacher, John? You'll find me a hard subject. A short life and a merry one is what I am going in for. I've no turn for Christianity. "

"It pays, Rege. "

"Don't believe it. How can life be worth living when you're drivelling psalm tunes all day long? "

John laughed, and there was a new note of gladness in his voice which Reginald was quick to notice. "I haven't begun to drivel yet, Rege; and life counts for a good deal more when a man has an object than when he is living just to please himself. "

"And who should a man please but himself, I should like to know? "

"Jesus Christ. "

\* \* \* \* \*

"Upon my word! " said Reginald some weeks later, as he came upon John sitting astride a cobbler's bench busily mending a pair of shoes, while Nan looked on admiringly. "Do you learn a new trade every month? "

John laughed quietly. "I took up this one because there are so many repairs always needed on the harness, and your father thinks all talent should be utilized. "

There was a quizzical look about his mouth as he spoke. Reginald caught the look and answered hotly.

"The governor ought to be ashamed of himself! Why don't you strike, John? "

"Why should I? Knowledge is power, Rege. "

"Knowledge of shoemaking! " said Reginald contemptuously. "It won't add to your strength much, John. "

"Never can tell, " said John sententiously. "You remember that lame fellow saved a battle for us by knowing how to shoe the general's horse. "

"Next thing you'll be going in for a blacksmith's diploma! "

"I'm thinking of it, " said John coolly. "That fellow at the Forks has no more sense than a hen. He pared so much off Neptune's hoof last week that he has been limping ever since. I had to take him this morning and have the shoes removed. "

"I wish you'd do some shirking, John, like the rest of us. "

"Jesus Christ never shirked, Rege. "

"Pshaw! You're so ridiculous! " and Reginald walked discontentedly away.

"Here, John, John, I say, " he called, when the time came for him to return to College, "go catch and saddle Sultan for me. You're so fond of work, you might as well have two masters. Be quick now, for I'm in the mischief of a hurry. "

John's face flushed. This boy was younger than himself, and his father had been Mr. Hawthorne's friend.

"Do you hear what I say, John? " demanded Reginald. "You're only here as a servant any way, and I'll be master some day, so you might as well learn to obey me now. "

John's brow cleared, while the words echoed in his heart with a glad refrain, —

"A servant of Jesus Christ, " and "The Lord's servant must not strive, but be gentle towards all... forbearing. " After all, life was a matter between himself and the Lord Jesus. What could Reginald's taunts affect him now?

"All right, " he said quietly, and started for the field.

"I declare! " muttered Reginald, as he watched the tall, lithe form cross the field with springing step, "you might as well try to make the fellow mad now, as to storm Gibraltar! What has come to him? "

"Here you are, Sir Reginald, " said John good-humoredly, as he led the freshly groomed horse to the riding-block.

Reginald's voice choked. "Shake hands, John, " he said huskily. "I am a brute! There must be something in this new fad of yours after all. If you had spoken to me as I did to you just now, I should have knocked you down. "

He rode on for a mile or two in moody silence, then he gave his shoulders an impatient shrug.

"I'd like to know what it is about John Randolph that makes me feel so small! I have good times and he is always on the grind. I have all the money I can spend and he has nothing but the pittance the governor gives him, and yet he is three times the better fellow of the two. I envy him his spunk and go. He comes to everything as fresh as a two-year old, and he works everything for all there is in it. To see him climbing that hill yesterday, with the youngster on his shoulder, actually made me feel as if climbing hills was the jolliest thing in life. And it's so with everything he does. Confound it! I don't see why I can't get the same comfort out of things. I don't see where the fellow gets his vim. If I worked as hard as he does, I'd be ready to tumble into bed instead of pegging away at Latin and Mathematics. I'll have to put on a spurt in self-defence or he'll be tripping me up with his questions. He's got the longest head of anyone I know. The idea of the governor daring to set such a fellow as that to cobble shoes! "

"It's queer about the governor, " he continued after a pause. "He's always ready to shell out when I ask him for money, but he keeps poor John with his nose to the grindstone all the year round. I suppose he expects me to pay him in glory. He's set his heart on my being a judge, —Judge Hawthorne of Hollywood. Sounds euphonious, and I verily believe the old gentleman has begun to roll it like a sweet morsel under his tongue. Can't say I have a special aptitude for the profession, and certainly the brains are not in evidence, but I suppose the governor thinks money will take their place. He has found it takes the place of most things.

"Sultan, old boy, we seem down on our luck this morning. We had better take a speeder to raise our spirits. It is hardly the thing for Judge Hawthorne of Hollywood to envy John Randolph his humdrum life of mending rakes and shoes, " and he urged his horse into a mad gallop.

* * * * *

"I believe I'd like to be poor and work, John, " he exclaimed one day. "It gets tiresome having everything laid ready to your hand, with nothing to do but take it. Life must be full of snap when you have to dash your will up against old Dame Fortune and wrest what you want out of her miserly clutches. "

"Yes, " said John simply, "Jesus Christ was poor. "

"Look here, John. If you don't stop that nonsense, people will be dubbing you a crank. "

"I am ready! " he cried, and there was a strange, exulting ring in his voice. "They called him mad, you know. "

## CHAPTER VI.

Evadne found herself one morning in Judge Hildreth's roomy coach-house, watching Pompey, as he skilfully groomed her uncle's pets.

It had been decided that after the summer holidays, she should become a member of the fashionable school which Isabelle and Marion attended. In the meantime she was left almost entirely to her own devices. Her uncle was away all day, Louis at College, and her aunt busy with social duties. Her cousins had their own particular friends, who were not slow to vote the silent girl with the mournful grey eyes, full of dumb questioning, a bore; while Evadne, accustomed to being her father's companion in all his scientific researches, found their vapid chatter wearisome in the extreme.

Horses were a passion with her, and she noted with pleased interest Pompey's deft manipulations. She stood for a long time in silence. Pompey had saluted her respectfully then kept on steadily with his work. Dexterously he swept the curry-comb over the shining coats and then drew it through the brush in his left hand with a curious vocal accompaniment, something between a long-drawn whistle and a sigh, and the horses laid their heads against his shoulder affectionately and looked wonderingly at the stranger out of their large, bright eyes.

"Did you really know my father? " she asked at length.

"Laws, yes, Missy! " and Pompey's honest black face grew tender with sympathy. "Mass Lennux stayed with the Jedge 'fore he went ter Barbadoes, an' he spen' powerful sight of his time out here wid me an' de horses. He wuz allers del'cut, —warn't able ter do nothin' in this yere climate, —but he bed sech a sperit! He wouldn't ever let folks know when he wuz a sufferin'. He use ter call me 'Pompous, '" and Pompey chuckled softly. "He say when I git inter my fur coat I look as gran' on de box as de Jedge do inside; an' one day he braided de horses' manes inter a hunderd tails an' tied 'em wid yaller ribbun, 'cause he said de crimps wuz in de fashun an' yaller wuz de Jedge's 'lecshun color. De Jedge wuz powerful angry. He don't like no sech tricks wid his horses. But, laws, he couldn't keep angry wid Mass Lennux! He jes' stood wid his hans on his sides an' larf an' larf, till de Jedge he hev ter larf too, an' he call him a graceless scamp, an' say he send him ter Coventry, an' Mass Lennux he say 'all right ef de Jedge go 'long too, an' take de horses, he couldn't do widout dem nohow. '"

"Were these the horses my father used to ride? "

"Laws, no, Missy. Dey wuz ez black ez night. Mass Lennux use ter call 'em Egyp an' Erybus. "

Pompey's face softened.

"When my leetle gal died he jes' put his han' on my shoulder an' sez he, —'Pompous, you jes' go home an' cheer up de Missis, yer don't hev no call to worry 'bout de horses. ' An' he tuk care of dem jes' as ef he'd ben a coachman. We'll never fergit it, Dyce an' me. "

Evadne's eyes shone. That was just like her father!

"'Specs little Miss is powerful lonesum 'thout Mass Lennux? "

The soft voice was full of a genuine regret. Evadne sank down on a bench which stood near by and burst into tears.

"Oh, Pompey, I wish I could die! "

"'Specs little Miss hez no call ter wish dat, " said Pompey gently. "'Specs de Lord Jesus wants her to live fer him. "

Evadne opened her eyes in wonder.

"'The Lord Jesus, '" she repeated. "Why, Pompey, do you know him?"

A great joy transfigured the black face.

"He is my Frien', " he said simply.

Evadne leaned forward eagerly. "Oh, Pompey, if that is true, then you can help me find him. "

Pompey smiled joyously. "Miss 'Vadney don't need ter go far away fer dat. He is right here. "

"Here! " echoed Evadne faintly.

"Lo, I am wid you all de days'" Pompey repeated softly. "De Lord Jesus don't leave no gaps in his promises, Miss 'Vadney. He's allers wid me wherever I is workin', an' when I is up on my box a drivin' troo de streets, he's dere. He's wid me continuous. Dere's nuthin can seprate Pompey from de Lord, " he added with a sweet reverence.

"How can you be so sure? " she asked wistfully.

"I hez his word, Missy. You allers b'lieved your father? 'I will not leave you orphuns, I will cum ter you. ' I 'specs dat verse is meant speshully fer you, Miss 'Vadney. "

"But we can't see him, " said Evadne.

"Only wid de eye of faith, Missy. We trusts our friens in de dark. You didn't need ter see your father ter know he wuz in de house? "

"Oh, no! " Evadne's voice trembled.

"It's jes' de same wid my Father, Miss 'Vadney. "

"How can you call God so, Pompey? "

A great sweetness came over the homely face.

"'Cause he hez sent his Sperit inter my heart, an' poor black Pompey can look up inter de shinin of his face an' say 'my Father, ' 'cause I'se hidden away in his Son. I'se a little branch abidin' in de great Vine. I'se one wid de Lord Jesus. "

"I don't know where to look for him! " Evadne cried disconsolately.

Pompey laid aside his curry-comb and brush and folded his toil-worn hands.

"Lord Jesus, " he said quietly, "here is thy little lamb. She's out in de dark mountain, an' she's lonesum an' hungry, an' de col' rain of sorrow is beatin' on her head. Lord, thou is de good Shepherd. Let her hear thy voice a callin' her. Carry this little lamb in thy bosom an' giv her de joy of thy love. "

\* \* \* \* \*

Judge Hildreth sat in his library far into the night. He was reading for the twentieth time the letter which Evadne had placed in his hands the morning after her arrival, and as he read, he frowned.

"It is ridiculous, absurd! " he exclaimed impatiently. "Just of a piece with all of Len's quixotic theories. By what possible chance could a child of that age know how to manage money? She would make ducks and drakes of the whole business in less than a year! "

A letter addressed to Evadne lay upon the pile of age-worn papers in an open drawer at his side.

"I enclose herewith a letter to Evadne, " his brother had written, "giving full and minute explanations as to her best course in the matter. These she will follow implicitly, under your supervision, and I feel confident the result will be a well-developed character along the lines on which women, through no fault of their own, are so lamentably deficient, namely, the proper conduct of business and management of money. "

Judge Hildreth looked again at the envelope with its clear, bold address. "That is not the handwriting of a fool, " he muttered. "I wish I could make up my mind what to do. "

Through the solemn hush of midnight his good and evil angels contended for his soul. In a strange silence he listened to their voices, the one insidious, tempting, the other urging him to take the upright course. Had his eyes not been holden he would have seen them, the one dark-browed, malignant, clothed in shadows, the other robed in light; while other angels hovered near and looked on pityingly. The white-robed angel spoke first.

"It is not a question to be decided by your judgment. There is no other course left open to you. "

Mockingly the other answered. "It is a most unprecedented proceeding. You should have been appointed her guardian, with sole control. "

"It is your brother's last will and testament. "

"Some wills are made to be broken. This one is against sound reason."

"It is the only honorable thing to do. "

"It is unnecessary. The child need not know, and, if she did, would thank you for saving her from care. "

"It is your brother's money. He had a right to do as he will with his own. "

"If he had known to what straits this year's speculations have brought you, he would be glad to give you a lift. If you do not have money now what are you going to do? This has come just in time, for you know your credit is already strained to its utmost. " "Your niece will be anxious to have your advice as to profitable investments. You can borrow the money from her. "

"That would be awkward, in case the bottom fell out of the mine. A little capital in hand would give you a chance to water the Panhattan stock and develop a new lead in the Silverwing. "

"If you use money that does not belong to you, you will be a thief! "

"If you do not use it, you will be a pauper. You have paper out now to five times the amount of your income. This is an interposition of Providence to save you from ruin. "

"What right had you to put yourself in the way of ruin? "

"You did it to advance the interests of your family. The Bible says, 'If any provide not for his own, especially his own kindred, he... is worse than an infidel. '[Footnote: Marginal rendering A. V.]"

"If you do this thing you will be dishonored in the sight of God. "

"If you do not save yourself from this temporary embarrassment, you will be disgraced in the eyes of the world. You owe it to your position in society, and the church, to keep above the waves. " The listening spirits heard a low, malicious laugh of triumph and the white-robed angel turned sadly away.

Judge Hildreth had thrust Evadne's letter, with his own, far under the pile of papers, and double-locked the drawer!

\* \* \* \* \*

Above the coach-house was a large room where Pompey kept a store of hay and grain, and there Evadne often found herself ensconced with Isabelle's Bible, during the long mornings when she was left to amuse herself as best she might. The atmosphere of the house stifled her, and Pompey had loved her father! It was scrupulously clean. Under Pompey's régime spiders and moths found no tolerance, and a magnificent black cat effectually frightened away the audacious rodents which were tempted to depredations by the toothsome cereals in the great bins. In one corner Pompey had improvised for her a luxurious couch of hay and rugs, and in this fragrant retreat Evadne studied her strange new book. She brought to it a mind absolutely untrammeled by creed or circumstance, and in this virgin soil God's truth took root. Slowly the light dawned. Hers was no shallow nature to leap to a hasty conclusion and then forsake it for a later thought. Gradually through the darkness, as God's flowers grow, this human flower lifted itself towards the light.

Sometimes she would sit for hours with the stately cat upon her knee, thinking, thinking, thinking, while Pompey sang his favorite hymns about his work and the mellow strains floated up the stairway and soothed her lonely heart. His childlike faith became to her a tower of refuge, and often, when bewildered by life's inconsistencies, she felt as if the eternal realities were vanishing into mist, she was calmed and comforted by his happy trust.

"I cannot imagine, Evadne, " said Isabelle one evening at dinner, "what pleasure you can find in sitting in a stable in company with a negro! It certainly shows a most depraved taste. "

"Christ was born in a stable, Isabelle. "

"What in the world has that to do with you? "

"I am beginning to think he has everything to do with me, " answered her cousin quietly.

"Well, " said Isabelle with a toss of her head, "we are known by the company we keep. I should imagine Pompey's curriculum of manners was not on a very elevated plane. "

"Pompey! Isabelle, " said Judge Hildreth suddenly. "Why, my dear, Pompey is a modern Socrates, bound in ebony. There is no danger to be apprehended from him. "

"Well, it is a peculiar companionship for Judge Hildreth's niece, that is all I have to say, " said Isabelle coldly, "but *chacun à son goût*. "

"I read this morning in your Bible that God had chosen the base things of the world, and things which are despised, and things which are not, to bring to nought things that are. What does that mean, Isabelle? "

"Really, Evadne, we shall have to send you to live with Doctor Jerome! " said her aunt, with a careless laugh. "You are getting to be a regular interrogation point. We are not Bible commentators, child, you cannot expect us to explain all the difficult passages.

"The Embroidery Club meets here tomorrow, Evadne, " exclaimed Marion, "and I don't believe you have touched your table scarf since they were here before. What will Celeste Follingsby think? She works so rapidly, and her drawn work is a perfect poem. "

"No, I have not, " confessed Evadne. "It seems such silly work, to draw threads apart and then sew them together again. "

Isabelle elevated her eyebrows with a look of horror.

Louis laughed. "She's a hopeless case, Isabelle. You'll never convert her into an elegant trifler. You might as well throw up the contract. "

"It seems to me, Evadne, " said his sister icily, "that you might have a little regard for the decorums of society. Don't, I beg of you, give utterance to such heresies before the girls. And I wish you would not call it *my* Bible. I did not make it. "

"That is quite true, Evadne, " said Louis gravely. "If she had, there would have been a good deal left out. "

Isabella shot an angry glance at him but made no remark. Her brother's sarcasms were always received in silence.

"Eva, " she said after a pause, "I intend to call you by that name in future, —your full one is too troublesome. "

Evadne shivered. Her father was the only one who had ever abbreviated her name. "I shall not answer to it, " she said quietly.

"Why, pray? "

"Because, I suppose, in common with the rest of the lower animals, I have a natural repugnance to being cut in two. "

"How tiresome you are! " exclaimed Isabelle with a pout. "I do not object to my first syllable. All the girls at school call me Isa. Mamma, did you remember to order the tulle for our wings? Claude Rivers has finished hers and they are perfectly sweet. She showed them to me this afternoon. "

"Wings, Isabelle! What in the world are you up to now? "

"A Butterfly Social, Papa. We must raise money in some way. The church is frightfully in debt. "

"That is a deplorable fact, but I did not know butterflies were famed as financiers. "

"Oh, of course it is just for the novelty of the thing. The last social we had was a Mother Goose, and we have had Brownie suppers and Pink teas and everything else we could think of. We must have something to attract, you know. "

"I wonder if it really pays? " ventured Marion. "It never seems to me there is much left, after you deduct the cost of the preparation.

People might as well give the money outright. It would save them a world of trouble. "

"Why, you silly child, it is to promote sociability in the church. As to the trouble, of course we do not count that. We must expect to make sacrifices. "

"But they do not make the church any more sociable, " said Marion boldly, who, having struck for freedom of thought, was following up her advantage. "The same people take part every time and the others are left outside. "

"Nonsense! " said Isabelle hotly. "It is only those who cannot afford to take part, and think what a treat it is for them to look on! "

"A sort of half-price theatre, " said Louis with a sneer.

"I don't believe they find the looking on such fun as you think, " said Marion, who was astonished at herself. "Suppose you try if they wouldn't like to take part and offer your place in the Cantata to Jemima Dobbs. "

"Well done, Sis! " and Louis applauded softly.

Isabelle's lip curled. "Upon my word, Marion, you bid fair to become as hot an anarchist as Louise Michel. It is a mystery to me where you find out the Christian names of all the ungainly people in the congregation. The other sopranos would feel complimented to have a prima-donna with a face like a full moon and hands like a blacksmith's foisted upon them! One must have a little regard for appearances, " and Isabelle drew her graceful figure up to its full height.

"Jemima Dobbs isn't dynamite, and I have no anarchical tendencies, " persisted Marion stoutly, —"but beauty is only skin deep, Isabelle. She supports a sick mother and five children and that is more than any of the rest of us could do, " and Marion, frightened at her momentary temerity, shrank back into her shell.

"It is a most unaccountable thing, Lawrence, " said Mrs. Hildreth, "why the church should be so heavily encumbered. I am sure you contribute handsomely and the pew rents are high. There is always a large congregation. I cannot understand. "

"It is largely composed of transients though, my dear, and they never carry more than a nickel in their pockets, so the weight of the burden falls upon a few. The expenses are very heavy. Jerome wants to make it the most popular church in the city, and the new quartette proves an extravagant luxury. "

"Oh, well, " said Mrs. Hildreth, "of course one cannot grudge the money for that. Professional singing is such an attraction! The way Madame Rialto took that high C last Sunday was superb. "

"Well, " said Isabelle, "I don't think there is any doubt that Doctor Jerome is the most popular preacher in the city. He is going to preach next Sunday on the moral progress of social sciences, and next month he commences his series of sermons on the social problems of the day. He does take such an interest in sociology. "

"But why doesn't he preach Jesus Christ? " asked Evadne wonderingly.

"You will get to be a regular fanatic, Evadne, if you ring the changes on that subject so often. Doctor Jerome says he wants his people to have an intelligent idea of the progress of events. Of course everyone understands the Bible.

"I do think he is the loveliest man! " she continued rapturously, "he is so sympathetic; and Celeste Follingsby says he is 'perfectly heavenly in affliction. ' Her little sister died last week, you know. It is so awkward that it should have happened just now. She will not be able to take any part in the Cantata, and she had the sweetest dress! "

"Very ill-timed of Providence! " said Louis gravely. "What a pity it is, Isabelle, that you couldn't have the regulation of affairs. " He yawned and strolled lazily towards the fireplace. When he looked round again, Evadne was the only other occupant of the room.

"Well, coz, what do you think of the situation? I belong to the worldlings, of course, but I confess the idea of Jesus Christ at a Butterfly Social is tremendously incongruous. We have the best of it,

Evadne, for we live up to our theories. Give it up, coz. You'll find it a hopeless task to make the Bible and modern Christianity agree. "

He looked at his watch.

"I say, Evadne, Jefferson is playing at the Metropolitan in Richard III. to-night. Let us go and hear him. "

And Evadne went, and enjoyed it immensely.

## CHAPTER VII.

"I am going for a long ride into the country, Evadne, " said her uncle one morning, "would you like to come with me? "

Evadne gave a glad assent. After her beautiful tropical life, it seemed to her as if she should choke, shut away from the wide expanse of sky which she loved, among monotonous rows of houses and dingy streets.

As they left the city behind them and the road swept out into the open, she gave a long sigh of delight. Her uncle laughed.

"Well, Evadne, does it please you? "

"It is the first time I have felt as if I could breathe, " she said.

"So you don't take kindly to Marlborough? Well, I suppose it is a rude awakening from your sunny land, but you will get used to it. We grow accustomed to all life's disagreeable surprises as time rolls on. "

Evadne shivered. "I do not think I shall ever grow accustomed to it, Uncle Lawrence. "

"Ah, you are young. We grow wiser as our hair turns grey. "

"If that is wisdom, I do not care to grow wise. "

"Not grow wise, Evadne! " said her uncle quizzically. "In this age, when women claim a surplusage of all the brain power bestowed upon the race! What will you do when you have to attend to business? "

"Business, " echoed Evadne, "I have never thought about it, Uncle Lawrence. "

"No turn for dollars and cents, eh? Did your father never consult you about his affairs? "

Evadne's lip quivered. "Oh, yes, " she said, and her words were a cry of pain, "he consulted me about everything, but I do not think there was ever any mention of money. Does money constitute business, Uncle Lawrence? "

"Wealth gives power, Evadne. Money is one of the greatest things in the world. While we are on the subject I may as well tell you that your father wrote me concerning the disposition of his property. I shall look after your interests carefully, together with my own, and give you the same quarterly allowance that my own girls have. When you are older I will go more into detail, but it is not worth while now to worry your head over columns of uninteresting figures. I shall open an account for you at the National Bank and you can draw on that for your expenses. Your aunt will initiate you into the mysteries of shopping. By the way, you must have gone through that experience in Barbadoes. How did you manage there? "

Evadne turned her head away and clenched her hands tightly as the flood of bitter-sweet memories threatened to engulf her.

"Papa always went with me, " she said slowly, "whatever he liked I chose. "

Judge Hildreth gave a sigh of relief. He had extricated himself from a difficult position with diplomatic skill. It did not occur to him that a lie which is half the truth is the meanest kind of a lie. He had acquainted his niece with all that was necessary for her to know at present, and at the same time left himself a loophole of escape from the imputation of disregarding his brother's wishes. When she became old enough to assume the responsibility, and he got his affairs straightened out sufficiently to admit of transferring to her care the funds which were so absolutely essential to his present success, he would put Evadne in full possession of her inheritance. Results had proved the wisdom of his decision. By her own acknowledgment his niece had never given a thought to the subject. His brother's plan would be a height of imprudence from which he was bound to shield her.

In Evadne's mind also thought was busy. "Money is one of the greatest things in the world, " her uncle had said, and she had read that morning, "tongues shall cease, and knowledge shall be done away, but love never faileth. Now abideth faith, hope, and love; the greatest of these is love. " Was Louis right? Did Christians and the Bible not agree? And the business of *her* life was to find Jesus Christ. Was there any money in that?

When they reached Hollywood, where Judge Hildreth had business with Mr. Hawthorne, Evadne was in an ecstasy of silent rapture. She had never dreamed what a New England farm might be. Its varied beauty, clad in the dazzling robes of early summer, came upon her with the suddenness of a revelation. She begged to be allowed to wait for her uncle out of doors, and wandered slowly on past the great barns to where the wide gate stretched across the green road. When she reached it she stopped and looked with keen delight at the beautiful creatures in the fields on either side. The sunshine fell upon her with loving warmth; in the distance she could hear the whirr of a mowing machine and the shouts of the men at work. A magnificent young horse thrust his head familiarly over the fence near by, and under the shade of a great tree Primrose, with her graceful calf beside her, was lazily chewing her cud.

Everything spoke of contentment and comfort and peace. An unutterable longing seized upon the lonely girl. Here at least she would have God's creatures to love, and his woods and the sky! She laid her head down upon the gate with a smothered cry.

"If I only belonged, —like the cows! "

"Pitty lady! "

Startled by the sweet, baby voice, Evadne looked up to find a pair of laughing blue eyes peeping sympathetically at her. The sun-bonnet had fallen back and the golden curls were tossed in luxurious confusion over the little head.

Evadne caught the child in her arms.

"You little darling! "

"Yes, me is, " said the child, resting contentedly within Evadne's embrace, as if, with the mysterious telepathy of childhood, she recognized a spiritual affinity which she was bound to help. "Me's very nice. Don says so. "

"And who is Don? " asked Evadne.

"Don's my bootiful man. Me's doin' to marry Don when me gets big. Oh, dere he is! " and breaking from Evadne, she rolled herself between the bars of the gate and ran at the top of her speed towards John Randolph, who just then appeared around a bend in the road, one arm thrown lightly over the neck of the horse he had been training.

"Halloo, Nansie! " Evadne heard his cheery greeting, saw him stoop and lift the child on to the horse's back, and was so interested in the pretty scene that she forgot she was a stranger. When she came to herself with a start the little cavalcade had reached the gate and John Randolph stood before her with his hat in his hand.

Evadne bowed. "It is so beautiful! " she said. "I have been waiting for my uncle and lost myself among the harmonies of Nature. "

John Randolph's eyes lightened. "It is God's world, " he answered with a sweet reverence.

Evadne looked full into the shining face. "Do you know Jesus Christ? " she asked impulsively.

The face softened into a great tenderness. "He is my King. "

"And do you love him? "

"With all there is of me. "

A servant came just then to say the Judge was waiting.

"I will come at once, " Evadne said courteously. Then she turned once more to John. "And what do *you* think of life? " she cried softly.

"Life! " he said, and there was a strange, exultant ring in his voice. "Life is a beautiful possibility. "

There was no time for more, but in the spirit realm of kinship no multitude of words is needed. Only a few moments had passed, yet in that little space two souls had met. What did it matter if the devious turnings of life should lead them far apart, or the barring gate of circumstance forever separate them? They had found each other!

"Pitty lady! —Nan loves oo, dear, " and the child whom John held seated on the broad top rail of the gate, held up her rosy lips for a kiss.

Instinctively Evadne held out her hand to John. Spiritual ethics laugh at the conventionalities of time. "Good-bye, " she said, "and thank you. "

She looked back once to wave her hand to little Nan. John was standing as she had left him, one arm encircling the child who nestled close to him, while over his right shoulder the horse had thrust his handsome head. Always afterward she saw him so. It was a parable of what God had meant man to be.

\* \* \* \* \*

Long after the sound of the carriage wheels had died away John stood motionless, beholding again as in a vision the earnest face and wonderful grey eyes. Then he stooped for his hat which had fallen to the ground when he had taken her hand in his. As he did so, he saw a dainty bit of lawn lying on the other side of the gate. He put his hand between the bars and caught it just as the breeze was about to blow it away. He looked at the name which was delicately traced in one corner with a strange sense of pleasure: Evadne.

"It fits her, " he said to himself. "There's a sweet elusiveness about her. She makes me think of a bird. She'll let you come just so far, until she gets to trust you, and then you'll have all her sweetness. "

He drew a long breath which was strangely like a sigh, and, folding the handkerchief carefully, put it in his pocket.

"Pitty lady, " murmured little Nan drowsily, and John caught her up and kissed her, —he could not have told why.

\* \* \* \* \*

"I do think Dorothy Bruce is the kindest creature! " exclaimed Marion one Saturday morning as they lingered with a pleasant sense of leisure over the breakfast table. "She offered to give up the whole of to-day to me. I thought it was lovely when she works so hard all the week. "

"Give it up to you. Why, what do you mean, Marion? We never have anything to do with her in school. What could you possibly want of her here? "

"Oh, it is that doleful algebra, " sighed Marion. "It is utterly impossible for me to get it into my head, and Dorothy takes to it like a duck to water, and she is a born teacher. Madame Castle says her aptitude for imparting knowledge amounts to genius. You must allow it was kind of her, Isabelle. "

Isabelle shrugged her shoulders. "Self-interested, most likely. That sort of people would do anything to obtain a foothold. "

"Oh, Isabelle! " cried Evadne. "Do have a little faith in your fellow-man! Why should you set yourself up on a pinnacle and despise everyone who is poor, when the father of us all hoed for a living? "

Louis looked up from the paper he was reading. "There are two things Isabelle has no faith in, Evadne. The Declaration of Independence and the book she loaned you. One says all men are free and equal, —the other that God has made of one blood all the nations of the earth. Her Serene Highness objects to this. She will have the blue blood come in somewhere, though where she gets it from heaven only knows! "

"Louis, I do wish you would not be so radical! " Isabelle said, peevishly. "You must admit there is such a thing as culture and refinement. "

"Certainly I admit it. The only thing I object to is that you talk as if you possessed a monopoly of the article, whereas I hold that it is just a question of environment. It is no thanks to you that you were not born a Hottentot or a Choctaw. Give yourself the same ancestors and surroundings as your chimney-sweep and wherein would you be superior to him? And when it comes to ancestry, by the way, probably Miss Bruce can trace back to some of the grand old

Highland chiefs who covered themselves with glory long before the lineage of Hildreth had emerged from obscurity. "

"I don't know anyone who likes to choose his company better than you! " observed Isabelle sarcastically.

"Certainly I do. Similarity of environment presupposes similarity of tastes. Probably my idea of enjoyment would not accord with the chimney-sweep's, but at the same time I don't look down on the poor beggar because he hasn't been as fortunate as I in getting his bread well buttered. There is a law of cultivation for humanity as well as plants. Surround a succession of generations with all the advantages of wealth, education and travel, and you produce the aristocrat; just as you get the delicate Solanum Wendlandi from the humble potato blossom. Set your aristocrat in the wilderness to earn his living by the sweat of his brow, —let the rain and wind beat upon his delicate skin, —shut him away from all the elevating influences to which he has been accustomed, and, in course of time, what have you? His descendants have retrograded. The Solanum has become a potato again. "

"That is all very well, " said Isabelle, "but I believe the instinct of culture will be dormant somewhere. "

"Then why do you not recognize it in your chimney-sweep? For all you know he may be the descendant of some impecunious sire of a lordly house. Probably plenty of them are. "

Louis rose and tossed the paper carelessly to his mother, who had been an amused listener to the discussion. It never occurred to him to do so before. What did women want to know about politics or the turf?

"Jesus Christ never seemed to care about externals, " said Evadne softly. "He chose his friends among the common people. "

"For pity's sake, Evadne! " cried Isabelle. "When will you learn that the Bible is not to be taken literally? "

"Not to be taken literally! " echoed Evadne in wonderment. "How is it to be taken then? "

"Isabelle means that we have to make allowances, " said her aunt. "Christ could do a great many things that you cannot. "

Evadne was silent, while the words of Jesus kept ringing in her ears: "For I have given you an example, that ye also should do as I have done to you. " If only she could understand!

"By the way, Evadne, " said Mrs. Hildreth, "I beg you will not repeat your mistake of yesterday. "

"What do you mean, Aunt Kate? "

"Bringing such a disreputable character into the house. When I came in and found her sitting in the hall and you talking to her I was perfectly paralyzed. Horrible! Why her rags were abominable, and her feet were bare! "

"But she had no shoes, Aunt Kate, and she was just my height. I was so glad that my clothes would fit her. "

"A pretty thing to have your clothes paraded through the streets by such a creature! Most likely she would pawn them for gin. I am sure she was an improper character. "

"But, Aunt Kate, " pleaded Evadne, "Jesus Christ says we must clothe the naked and feed the hungry if we would be his followers. I must do as he tells me for I am going to follow him. "

"Your uncle does enough of that for the family, " said her aunt coldly. "I do not wish you to try any such experiments again. "

Puzzled and chilled, Evadne left the room. Was obeying the commands of Christ only an "experiment" after all?

She crept up to her favorite retreat and threw herself upon her gayly covered couch. "Oh, Jesus Christ! " she cried passionately, "I am *glad* I did not live in Galilee when you were there! Aunt Kate and Isabelle would have thought it bad form for me to follow you in the crowd where the sinners were. But they can't keep me from doing so now!

"Oh, I wish I were dead! No one would care. Yes, Pompey would be sorry. Louis would call it 'a sable attachment, ' but Pompey loved my father. Oh, dearest! dearest! "

She buried her head in her hands while wave after wave of desolation broke over the lonely soul. "A beautiful possibility" her knight of the gate had said. Could life become that to her?

Downstairs Pompey began to sing, —

> "Shall we meet beyond the river,
> Where the surges cease to roll,
> Where in all the bright forever
> Sorrow ne'er shall press the soul?"

The rich vibrations rolled up and trembled about her. She held out her arms and her voice broke in a cry of triumphant faith, "Yes, we *shall* meet, Lord Jesus, face to face! "

## CHAPTER VIII.

"Pompey, " said Evadne one morning, "I am going to see your wife."

The black face beamed with satisfaction. "Dyee'll be mighty uplifted, Miss 'Vadney. She think a powerful sight o' Mass Lennux. "

Evadne stood watching him as he gave finishing touches to the silver mountings of the handsome harness. "I don't believe there is another harness in Marlborough that shines like yours, Pompey, " she said with a laugh. "You are as particular with it as though every day was a special occasion. "

"So 'tis, Miss 'Vadney, " said Pompey simply. "Can't slight nuthin' when de Lord's lookin' on. Whoa, Brutis! Dere's goin' ter be Holiness to de Lord written on de bells ob de horses bimeby, Missy. I'se got it writ dere now. "

"I believe you have, Pompey, " said Evadne soberly, "for you do your work just as perfectly whether Uncle Lawrence is going to see it or not. It almost seems as if you were trying to please someone out of sight. "

Pompey drew himself up to his full height. "I'se a frien' ob de Lord Jesus, Miss 'Vadney. I'se got ter do everything perfect 'cause ob dat. Couldn't bring no disgrace on my Lord. "

"But would that disgrace him? " asked Evadne in wonderment.

"Why, yes, Missy. Ef I wuz a poor, shifles' crittur, only workin' fer de praise o' men, folks would say, —'he's no differen' frum de rest; you've got to keep yer eye on him ef yer want tings done properly. De King's chillen ain't no better dan de worl's chillen be. '

"De Lord Jesus, he say to me, —'Pompey, you must be faithful in de little things as well as in de big. I never slurred nuthin when I wuz a walkin' up and down troo Palestine. I sees you, Pompey; don't make no difference whether de earthly master does or not. ' So I does all de little tings to de Lord, Miss 'Vadney, an' de Jedge knows he can depen' on Pompey. Whenever he wants me, I'se here. "

"That is lovely! " said Evadne softly. "But don't you get dreadfully tired doing the same work over and over? Every day you have to do exactly the same things. It is as bad as a tread-mill. You just keep on going round and round. "

Pompey gave one of his low chuckles. "'Specs dat's de way in dis worl', Miss 'Vadney. We'se got ter keep on eatin', an' we can't sleep enuff one night ter last fer a week, —but I 'low it's jes' one o' de beautiful laws ob de Lord, —de sun an' de moon an' de stars keeps a'goin over de same ground most continuous. So long as we'se doin' his will, Missy, it don't matter much whether we'se goin' roun' an' roun' or straight ahead. Stan' over, Ceesah! " and Pompey gave a final polish to the horse's already immaculate legs.

"Why don't you blacken their hoofs, Pompey? They used to do it in Barbadoes. "

Pompey's eyes twinkled. "Dat's a no 'count livery notion, Miss 'Vadney, a coverin' up de cracks an' makin' de horse's hufs look better dan dey is. De King's chillens can't stoop ter any sech decepshuns. De Lord Jesus says, 'Pompey, I is de truff. You's got ter speak de truff an' live de truff ef you belongs ter me. ' We ain't got no call ter cover up anything, Miss 'Vadney, ef we'se livin' ez de Lord wants us to. 'Sides, der ain't no 'cashun fer it. Ef we keeps de stable pure an' de food good an' gives de horse de right kind of exercise an' plenty of 'tention, de hufs will take care ob demselves, " and he held Caesar's foot up for her inspection.

"Halloo, Evadne, are you taking lessons in farriery? What's the matter, Pompey? Has Caesar got a sand crack? " and Louis sauntered up, the inevitable cigar between his lips.

"I don't 'low my horses ever hez sech things, Mass Louis, " said Pompey grandly.

"Ha, ha! what a conceited old beggar you are. But I'll give the devil his due and acknowledge the horses are a credit to you. " He held a dollar towards him balanced on his forefinger. "Here, take this and fill your pipe with it. "

"Don't want no pay fer doin' my dooty, Mass Louis. "

"Pshaw, man! Take a tip, can't you? "

Pompey shook his head. "I don't smoke, Mass Louis. "

"Don't smoke! " ejaculated Louis. "You don't here, I know, because the Judge is afraid of fire, but you'll never make me believe that you don't spend your evenings over the fire with your pipe. You darkeys are as fond of one as the other. "

"You's mistaken, Mass Louis, " said Pompey quietly.

"'Pon my word! And why don't you smoke, Pomp? You don't know what you're missing. It is the greatest comfort on earth. "

"'Specs I don't need sech poor comfort, Mass Louis. I takes my comfort wid de Lord. "

Pompey's voice was low and sweet. Evadne felt her heart glow.

"But come now, Pomp, " persisted Louis, "that's all nonsense. You must have some reason for not smoking. Everybody does. Come, I insist on your telling me. "

Pompey was silent for a moment. "'The pure in heart shall see God, '" he said slowly. "I 'low, Mass Louis, de King's chillen's got ter be pure in body too. "'

"You insolent scoundrel! How dare you? " and Louis dashed the glowing end of his cigar in the negro's face.

For a moment Pompey stood absolutely still, —the cigar which had left its mark upon his cheek lying smouldering at his feet, —then he turned quietly and walked away.

Louis strode out of the coach-house. Evadne followed him, her eyes blazing. "You are a coward! " she cried passionately. "You would not have dared to do that to a man who could hit you back. You forced him to tell you and then struck him for doing it! If this is your culture and refinement, I despise it! I am going to be a Christian, like Pompey. That is grand! "

"Well done, coz! " and Louis affected a laugh. "There's not much of the 'meek and lowly' in evidence just now at any rate. "

He looked after her as she walked away, her indignant tones still lingered in his ears. "By Jove! there's something to her though she is so quiet! I must cultivate the child. "

Seen through Evadne's clear eyes his action looked despicable and his better nature suggested an apology, but he swept the suggestion aside with a muttered "Pshaw! he's only a nigger, " and turned carelessly on his heel.

"You are Dyce! " cried Evadne impulsively when she reached the cottage in whose open doorway a pleasant-faced colored woman was standing. "Pompey has told me about you. I think your husband is one of the grandest men I know. "

"Thank you, Missy. Walk right in, I'se proper glad ter see Mass Lennux's chile. "

"Why, how did you know me? " asked Evadne wonderingly.

The woman laughed softly. "Laws, honey, you'se de livin' image of yer Pa. "

She excused herself after a few moments and Evadne laid her head against the cushions of a comfortable old rocking chair and rested. She wondered sometimes where her old strength had gone. She had never felt tired in Barbadoes. The tiny room was full of a homely comfort which did her heart good. There were books lying on the table and flowers in the window, a handsome cat purred in front of the fireplace, and on a bracket in one corner an asthmatic clock ticked off the hours with wheezy vigor. In an adjoining room Evadne could see a bed with its gay patchwork quilt of Dyce's making, and in the little kitchen beyond she heard her singing as she trod to and fro. A couple of dainty muslin dresses were draped over chairs, for Dyce was the finest clear starcher in Marlborough, and her kitchen was all too small to hold the products of her skill. She entered the room again bearing a tray covered with a snowy napkin on which were quaint blue plates of delicious bread and butter, pumpkin pie, golden browned as only Dyce could bake it, and a cup of fragrant coffee.

"I did not know anything could taste quite so good! " Evadne said when she had finished, "you must be a wonderful cook. "

Dyce laughed, well pleased. "When de Lord gives us everything in perfecshun, 'specs it would be terrible shifles' of me ter spoil it in de cookin', Miss 'Vadney. "

"The Lord, " repeated Evadne. "You know him too, then? You must, if you live with Pompey. "

Dyce's face grew luminous. "He is my joy! " she said softly.

"And does he make you happy all the time? " asked the girl wistfully. "You seem to have to work as hard as Pompey. What is it makes you so glad? "

"Laws, honey, how kin I help bein' glad? De chile o' de King, on de way ter my Father's palace. Ain't dat enuff 'cashun ter keep a poor cullered woman rejoicin' all de day long? I'se so happy I'se a singin' all de time over my work, an' in de street; it don't matter where I be."

"But you can't sing in the streets, Dyce! "

"Laws, chile, don't yer know de heart kin sing when de lips is silent? It's de heart songs dat de King tinks de most of, but when de heart gits too full, den de lips hez ter do deir share. "

"But suppose you were to lose your eyesight, or Pompey got sick, or— —"

Dyce gave one of her soft laughs. "Laws, honey, I never supposes. De Lord's got no use fer a lot o' supposin' chillen who's allers frettin' demselves sick fer fear Satan'll git de upper han'. De Lord's reignin', dat's enuff fer me. I 'low he'll take care o' me in de best way. "

Evadne looked again at the exquisitely laundered dresses. "Why do you work so hard? " she asked. "Doesn't Pompey get enough to live on? "

"Oh, yes, honey; de Jedge gives good wages; but yer see, we wants to do so much fer Jesus dat de wages don't hold out. "

"So much for Jesus! "

"Why, yes, Missy. He says ef we loves him we'll do what he tells us, an' he's tol' us ter feed de hungry, an' clothe de naked, an' go preach de gospel. So, when we cum ter talk it ober, it seem dreffulshifles' in me ter be doin' nothin' when de Lord worked night an' day, so I begun ter take in laundry work an' now we hev more money ter spen' on de Lord. But we never hez enuff. De worl's so full o' perishin' souls an' starvin' bodies. I tells Pompey I never wanted ter be rich till I began ter do de King's bizniss. It's dreffulcomfortin' work, Miss 'Vadney. "

\* \* \* \* \*

The chill March wind blew fiercely along the streets of Marlborough one afternoon and Evadne shivered. She had been standing for an hour wedged tightly against the doors of the Opera House by an impatient crowd which swayed hither and thither in a fruitless effort to force an entrance. It was Signor Ferice's farewell to America and it was his whim to make his last concert a popular one, with no seats reserved. Every nerve in her body seemed strained to its utmost tension and her head was in a whirl. She turned and faced the crowd. A sea of faces; some eager, some sullen, some frowning, all impatient. The scraps of merry talk which had floated to her at intervals during the earlier stages of the waiting were no longer heard. A gloomy silence seemed to have settled down upon every one. Suddenly a laugh rang out upon the keen air, —so full of a clear joyousness that people involuntarily straightened their drooping shoulders, as if inspired with a new sense of vigor and smiled in sympathy.

Evadne started. Surely she had heard that voice before! It must be, — yes, it was, —her knight of the gate! Their eyes met. A great light swept over his face and he lifted his hat. Then the surging crowd carried him out of her range of vision.

"I don't see what you find to look so pleased about, Evadne, " grumbled Isabelle, as they drove homeward. "For my part I think the whole thing was a fizzle. "

"I was thinking, " said Evadne slowly, "of the power of a laugh. "

"The power of a laugh! What in the World do you mean? "

"I mean that it is a great deal better for ourselves to laugh than to cry, and vastly more comfortable for our neighbors. "

"Evadne will not be down, " announced Marion the next morning as she entered the breakfast room. "She caught a dreadful cold at the concert yesterday and she can't lift her head from the pillow. Celestine thinks she is sickening for a fever. "

"Dear me, how tiresome! " exclaimed Mrs. Hildreth. "I have such a horror of having sickness in the house, —one never knows where it will end. Ring the bell for Sarah, Marion, to take up her breakfast. "

"It is no use, Mamma. She says she does not want anything. "

"But that is nonsense. The child must eat. If it is fever, she will need a nurse, and nurses always make such an upheaval in a house. "

"You had better go up, my dear, and see for yourself, " said Judge Hildreth. "Celestine may be mistaken. "

"Mercy! " cried Isabelle, "it is to be hoped she is! I have the most abject horror of fevers and that is enough to make me catch it. Fancy having one's head shorn like a convict! The very idea is appalling. "

"Oh, of course if there is the slightest danger, you and Marion will have to go to Madame Castle's to board, " said her mother. "It is very provoking that Evadne should have chosen to be sick just now."

"Not likely the poor girl had much choice in the matter, " laughed Louis. "There are a few things, lady mother, over which the best of us have no control. "

"I wish you would go up and see the child, Kate, " said Judge Hildreth impatiently. "If there is the least fear of anything serious I will send the carriage at once for Doctor Russe. It is a risky business transplanting tropical flowers into our cold climate. "

The kind-hearted French maid was bending over Evadne's pillow when Mrs. Hildreth entered the room. She had grown to love the quiet stranger whose courtesy made her work seem light, and it was with genuine regret that she whispered to her mistress, —"It is the feevar. I know it well. My seestar had it and died. "

Evadne's eyes were closed and she took no notice of her aunt's entrance. Mrs. Hildreth spoke to her and then left the room hurriedly to summon her husband. Even her unpractised eyes showed her that her niece was very ill.

Doctor Russe shook his head gravely. "It is a serious case, " he said, "and I do not know Where you will find a nurse. I never remember a spring when there was so much sickness in the city. I sent my last nurse to a patient yesterday and since then have had two applications for one. It is most unfortunate. The young lady will need constant care. She requires a person of experience. "

Pompey, waiting to drive the doctor home, caught the words, spoken as he descended the steps to enter the carriage, and came forward eagerly. "If you please, Missus, " he said, touching his hat, "Dyce would come. She's hed a powerful sight of 'sperience nussin' fevers in New Orleans. She'd be proper glad ter tend Miss 'Vadney."

"How is that? " questioned the busy doctor. "Oh, your wife, my good fellow? The very thing. Let her come at once. "

So Dyce came, and into her sympathetic ears were poured the delirious ravings of the lonely heart which had been so suddenly torn from its genial surroundings of love and happiness and thrust into the chilling atmosphere of misunderstanding and neglect.

Every day the patient grew weaker and after each visit the doctor looked graver. Mrs. Hildreth began to feel the gnawings of remorse, as she thought of the lonely girl to whom she had so coldly refused a daughter's place; and the Judge's thoughts grew unbearable as he remembered his broken trust; even Louis missed the earnest face which he had grown to watch with a curious sense of pleasure; while the girls at school felt their hearts grow warm as they thought of the young cousin so soon to pass through the valley of the shadow.

But Evadne did not die. The fever spent itself at last and there followed long days of utter prostration both of mind and body. Dyce's cheery patience never failed. Her sunny nature diffused a bright hopefulness throughout the sick chamber, until Evadne would lie in a dreamy content, almost fancying herself back in the old home as she listened to the musical tones and watched the dusky hands which so deftly ministered to her comfort. One day after she had lain for a long time in silence, she looked up at her faithful nurse and the grey eyes shone like stars.

"Dyce! " she cried softly. "I have found Jesus Christ! "

## CHAPTER IX.

Reginald Hawthorne lay upon a couch on the wide veranda of his lovely home. The birds held high carnival around him, —nesting in the large cherry tree, playing hide and seek among the fragrant apple blossoms and making the air melodious with their merry songs. Brilliant orioles flashed to and fro like gleams of gold in the sunlight, as they built their airy hammocks high among the swaying branches of the great willow, and one inquisitive robin swept boldly through the clustering vines which screened the front of the veranda and perched upon his shoulder. He heard the merry hum of the bees at work and the strident call of the locusts, mingled with the distant neighing of horses and the soft lowing of the cows, but all the sweetness of nature was powerless to lift the gloom which seemed to envelop him as in a shroud. His face was white and drawn with pain and there were heavy rings beneath his eyes. Reginald Hawthorne would be a cripple for life.

The College Football Club had met a New York team in the yearly contest, which was looked forward to as one of the events in the athletic world, and Reginald had been foremost among the leaders of the play. Fierce and long had been the fight and the enthusiastic spectators had shouted themselves hoarse with applause or groaned in despair when the honor of Marlborough seemed likely to be lost. Then had come a mighty onward rush and the opposing forces concentrated into one seething mass of struggling humanity. When they drew apart at last the College boys had made the welkin ring with shouts of victory, but their bravest champion lay white and still upon the field.

Long days and nights of pain had followed, when John and Mrs. Hawthorne were at their wits' end to alleviate the sufferings of the unfortunate boy. Now the pain had resolved itself into a dull aching but Reginald would never walk without a crutch again.

The mortification to his father was extreme. A passionate man, he had centred all his hopes upon his son, whose position in life he fondly expected to repay him for his years of unremitting toil, and this was the end of it all! He grew daily more overbearing and hard to please, and his ebullitions of disappointment and rage were terrible to witness. He vented his anger most frequently upon John, the sight of whose superb strength goaded the unhappy man into a frenzy, and John's forbearance was tried to the utmost, but there was a sweet patience growing in his soul which made it possible to endure in silence, however capricious or unreasonable the commands of his master might be, and Reginald, watching him critically, marvelled at the mysterious inner strength of his friend.

He came along now with his quick, light step and drew a chair up beside Reginald's couch. He planned his work so as to be with the invalid as much as possible, and his constant sympathy and cheer were all that made the days bearable to him.

"Well, Rege, how goes it? " he asked in tones as tender as a woman's.

Reginald looked up at him with envious eyes. There was such a freshness about this strong young life, as if every moment were a separate joy.

"I wish I was dead! " he answered moodily.

"Don't dare to wish that! " said John quickly, "until you have made the most of your life. "

"The most of my life! " echoed Reginald contemptuously. "That's well put, John, I must say! What is my life worth to me now? You see what my father thinks of it. A useless log, as valuable as a piece of waste paper. I believe it would have pleased him better if I had been killed outright. He wouldn't have had the humiliation of it always before his eyes. If it had been any sort of a decent accident, I believe I could bear it better, but to be knocked over in a football match, like the precious duffer that I am—bah! "

The concentrated bitterness of the last words made John's heart ache. "Looking backward, Rege, " he said quietly, "will never make a man of you. It is only a waste of time and vital tissue. But there are lots of noble lives in spite of limitations. Paul had his thorn in the flesh, you know, and Milton his blindness. Difficulties are a spur to the best that is in us. "

"Difficulties, John. You never look at them, do you? "

John laughed. "It is not worth while except to see how to surmount them. "

"I wish you could be idle just for an hour, " said Reginald peevishly, "you make me nervous. "

John took another stitch in the halter he was mending. "Old Father Time's spoiling tooth is never still, Rege. I have to work to keep pace with it. "

"I should think you would need a month of loafing to made up for the sleep you have lost. You're ahead of Napoleon, John, for he only kept one eye open, but I've never been able to catch you napping once. How have you stood it, man? "

"Forty winks is a fair allowance sometimes, Rege. "

Reginald groaned. "Your pluck is worth a king's ransom, John. I wish I had it. "

John began to whistle softly as he drew his waxed ends in and out.

"I declare, John, I can't fathom you! " and Reginald moved impatiently upon his couch. "You are invulnerable as Achilles. I never saw a fellow get so much comfort out of everything as you do, and yet your life is a steady grind. What does it all mean? "

"It means, " said John softly, "that I am a Christ's man, and he has lifted me above the power of circumstances. Jesus is centre and circumference with me now, Rege.

"You were talking yesterday about some men wanting the earth. I *own* the earth, because it belongs to my Father, —the best part of it, you know, —there is a truer giving than by title deeds to material acres—and the world has grown very beautiful since my Father made me heir of all things through his Son. The birds' songs have a new note in them, and the sunlight is brighter, and there is a different blue in the sky. I'm monarch of all I survey because I get the good out of everything, —mere earthly possession doesn't amount to much, a man has to leave the finest estates behind him, —but I get the concentrated sweetness of it all wherever I am. It is God's world, you know, and he is my Father. "

John was called away just then to attend to some gentlemen who had come to look at the horses, and Reginald waited for his return in vain. He heard his father's voice once, raised high in stormy wrath, then all was still again. Some time afterwards, through the leafy curtain of his veranda, he saw Mr. Hawthorne drive past with a face so distorted with passion that he shivered.

"There's been no end of a row this time, " he soliloquized. "It is a mystery to me why John puts up with it. He's free to go when he chooses. I'm sure I'd clear out if I wasn't such a good-for-nothing. The governor is getting to be more like a bear than a human being, it's a dog's life for everybody unlucky enough to be under the same roof with him. "

\* \* \* \* \*

Down at the bend of the river a tall figure lay stretched upon the moss. The river laughed and the birds sang, but John Randolph's face was buried in his arms.

To leave Hollywood—that very night! The place whose very stones were dear to him, where he had learned all he knew of home. To be turned off like a beggar, without a moment's warning, after all his years of toil! To say good-bye forever to the human friends who loved him, and the dear, dumb friends whom he had fondled and tended with such constant care. Never again to swing along through the sweet freshness of the morning before the sun was up to find the earliest snowdrops for Mrs. Hawthorne, or take a spin in the moonlight with every nerve a-tingle across the frozen bosom of the lake, or wander in delight along the wood roads when every tree was clad in the witching beauty of a silver thaw, or sweep across the wide stretching country in the very poetry of motion, or hear the soft swish of the tall grass as it fell in fragrant rows before the mower, or the creak of the vans as they bore its ripened sweetness towards the great barns, while bird and bee and locust joined in the harmony of the Harvest Home, until the sun sank to rest amidst cloud draperies of royal purple and crimson and gold and the sweet-voiced twilight soothed the world into peace.

On and on the hours swept while John fought his battle. At length he rose, and with long, lingering glances of good-bye to every tree and rock and flower, began his homeward way. He would think of it so while he could. In a few short hours he would be a wanderer upon the face of the earth. A sudden joy crept into the weary eyes. So was Jesus Christ!

"Why, John, what has happened! " cried Reginald, as his faithful nurse came to make him comfortable for the night. "You look like a ghost, and you have had no dinner! What the mischief is to pay? You must have been precious busy to leave me alone the whole afternoon. "

"I have been, Rege, " said John quietly, "very busy. "

"I declare, John, I'd make tracks for freedom if I were in your shoes. You're a regular convict, and, since you've had me on your hands, a galley slave is a gentleman of leisure in comparison! Why don't you go, John? You've had nothing but injustice at Hollywood. "

John fell on his knees beside the bed. "I am going, Rege. Your father has ordered me away. "

When the thought which has floated—nebulous—across our mental vision, suddenly resolves itself into tangible form and becomes a solid fact to be confronted and battled with, the shock is greater than if no shadowy premonition had ever haunted the dreamland of our fancy. Reginald gave a low cry, then he lay looking at John with eyes full of a blank horror. His mind utterly refused to grasp the situation.

"You see, Rege, it is this way, " said John gently. "Your father seems to have taken a dislike to me and lately I have fancied he was only waiting for an excuse to turn me off. As soon as those fellows began to talk to him about the horses I saw there was trouble brewing. Everything I did was wrong, and once he swore at me. He would order me to bring one horse and then change his mind before I got half across the field, and then he would rail at me for not having brought the first one.

"They pitched on Neptune at last, and asked if he had been registered. I said 'No, ' so then they refused to pay the price your father asked, and he had to come down on him. He was furious, and, as soon as the men's backs were turned, he ordered me out of his sight forever. He says I have ruined the reputation of Hollywood, " John's voice broke.

"But, John, you mustn't go! " cried Reginald. "You cannot! My father is out of his mind. People don't pay any attention to the ravings of a lunatic. "

John shook his head sadly. "He is master here, Rege. There is nothing else for me to do. "

"But, John, it is impossible—preposterous! Why, everything will go to ruin without you, and I will take the lead. "

"No, no! " said John quickly. "You will be a rich man some day, Rege. Wealth is a wonderful opportunity. Prepare yourself to use it well. "

"I tell you I can't do anything without you, John. I am like a ship without a rudder. It is no use talking. I cannot spare you. You must not go! "

"If you take the great Pilot aboard, Rege, you will be in no danger of drifting. It is only when we choose Self for our Captain that the ship runs on the rocks. "

\* \* \* \* \*

"Don, Don! " The child heard his step in the hall long before he reached the door. He was coming, as he did every night, to give her a ride in his arms before she went to by-by. She held out her little arms from which the loose sleeves had fallen back. John lifted her up, for the last time.

He laid his strong, set face against the rosy cheek, and looked into the laughing eyes which the sand man had already sprinkled with his magic powder. "Nansie, baby, I have come to say good-bye. "

"Not dood-bye, Don, oo always say dood-night. "

"But it is good-bye this time, little one, there will be no more good-nights for you and me. I am going away. "

A bewildered look swept over the child's face. "Away! " she echoed, "to leave Nan an' Pwimwose an' the horsies? Me'll do too, Don. He'll do anywhere wid oo, Don. "

"I wish I could take you! " and John strained her to his breast. "But there is no Neptune to carry us now, little one. Your father sold him this afternoon. "

"My nice Nepshun! " The child's lip quivered, but something in the suffering face above her made her say quickly, "Me'll be dood, Don, an' when oo turn back, me'll be waitin' at de gate. "

She patted his cheek confidingly. "Nice Don! Nan loves oo, dear, an' Desus. Nan loves Desus 'cause oo do, Don. "

John's voice choked. "Keep on loving, Nansie. "

"Yes, me will. Does Desus carry de little chil'en in his arms like oo do, Don? Me's so comf'able. Me loves Desus. "

The little arm, soft and warm, crept closer around his neck, while the golden curls swept his cheek. "Oo's my bootiful man, Don. Me'll marry oo when me gets big, " and then, all unconscious of the sorrow which should greet her in the morning, the baby slept.

To and fro across the floor John trod lightly with his precious burden. His arms never felt the weight. They would be such empty arms bye-and-bye! Then at last he laid her down, and, taking a pair of scissors from his pocket, he carefully severed one of the golden rings of hair, and laid it within the folds of the handkerchief which he still carried in his vest pocket. The fair girl and the little child. These should be his memory of womanhood.

\* \* \* \* \*

In Reginald's room kind-hearted Mrs. Hawthorne was weeping bitterly. She loved John as her own son, but no one ever dreamed of disputing the tyrannical dictates of the master of Hollywood, however unjust they might be.

Reginald lay as John had left him with his face buried in the pillows and utterly refused to be comforted. What comfort could there be if

John was going away? It never occurred to him that his mother needed cheer as much as he. Like all selfish souls his own pain completely filled his horizon.

## CHAPTER X.

"I don't see what we are to do about Evadne! " and Mrs. Hildreth sighed disconsolately. "She looks like a walking shadow. I should not be surprised if she had inherited her father's disease, and they say now that consumption is as contagious as diphtheria. "

"Horrors! " cried Isabelle. "Do quarantine her somewhere, Mamma, until you are quite sure there is no danger. I haven't the faintest aspirations to martyrdom. "

"It is a great care, " sighed Mrs. Hildreth. "All of you children have always been so healthy. I don't believe Doctor Russe will listen to her going to the seaside, and the mountains are so monotonous! Other people's children are a great responsibility. "

Suddenly Isabelle clapped her hands. "I have it! " she cried. "Send her up to Aunt Marthe, and then we can tease Papa to let us go to Newport. Marion is going to spend the summer with Christine Drayton, you know, and Papa does not intend to leave the city, so we can persuade him that it is our duty to seize such a golden opportunity of doing things economically. I am sure I don't know what people must think of us, never going to any of the fashionable places. For my part I think we owe it to Papa's position to keep up with the world. "

"I believe it might be managed, " said Mrs. Hildreth after some consideration. "It was very clever of you to think of it, Isabelle. You ought to be a diplomat, my dear, " and she smiled approvingly on her daughter.

\* \* \* \* \*

The train swept along through the picturesque Vermont scenery and Evadne looked out of her window with never ending delight.

"I am like a poor, lonely bird, " she said to herself, "who flits from shore to shore, seeking rest and finding none. Another journey in the dark! I wonder what will be at the end of this one? Well, I'll hope for the best. Aunt Marthe's letter was kind, and her name sounds as cheery as Aunt Kate's sounds cold. "

Mr. Everidge came to meet her as the train steamed into the little station, and Evadne soon found herself seated in a comfortable carriage behind a handsome chestnut mare, bowling along a fragrant country road, catching glimpses at every turn of the verdure-clad hills.

She found her new uncle very pleasant. There was a silver-tongued suavity about him in striking contrast to the growing preoccupation of Judge Hildreth, and a sort of airy self complaisance which took it for granted that he should be well treated by the world.

"I am very glad you have come, my dear niece, " he said, "to relieve the tedium of our uneventful existence. You must let our Vermont air kiss the roses into bloom again in your pale cheeks. It has a world-wide reputation as a tonic. I hope you left our Marlborough relatives in a pleasant attitude of mind? It is one of the evidences of this progressive age that you should woo 'tired Nature's sweet restorer' one night under the roof of my respected brother-in-law, the next under my own. The ancients, with their primitive modes of laborious transit, were only half alive. We of to-day, thanks to the melodious tea-kettle and inventive cerebral tissue of the youthful Watt, live in a perpetual hand-clasp, so to speak, and, by means of the flashing chain of light which girdles the globe are kept in touch with the world. It is food for reflection that the thought which is evolved from the shadowy recesses of our brain to-day, should be, by the mysterious camera of electricity, photographed upon the retina of the Australian public to-morrow, and we need to have the archives of our memory enlarged to hold the voluminous correspondence of the century.

"Ah, Squire Higgins, good-evening. My niece by marriage, Miss Hildreth of Barbadoes. "

The Squire lifted his hat, there was a little desultory conversation, then the carriages went on their separate ways, and soon Evadne found herself at her destination.

She looked eagerly at the pretty house with its *entourage* of flowers and lawns, grand old trees and distance-purpled hills, then Aunt Marthe appeared in the doorway and she saw nothing else.

She was of medium height with a crown of soft, brown hair, and eyes whose first glance of welcome caught Evadne's heart and held her captive. There was a wonderful sweetness about the smiling mouth, and the face, although not classically beautiful, possessed a subtle spiritual charm more fascinating than mere physical perfection of color and form. She moved lightly with a buoyant youthfulness strangely at variance with the stately dignity of Mrs. Hildreth and the studied repose of Isabelle.

"You dear child! " The soft arms held her close, the sweet lips caught hers in a kiss, and Evadne felt with a great throb of joy that the weary bird had found a resting-place at last.

She led her into a cool, tastefully furnished room, drew her down beside her on the couch and took off her hat and gloves, then she handed her a fan and went to make her a lemon soda.

Evadne looked round the room with its soft curtains swaying in the breeze, the cool matting on the floor with a rug or two, the light bookcases with their wealth of thought, the comfortable wicker rockers, the bamboo tables holding several half cut magazines, an open work-basket, a vase with a single rose, while on the low mantel a cluster of graceful lilies were reflected in the mirror. "Why, this is home! " she cried and she laid her head against the cushions with a delightful sense of freedom.

The early supper was soon announced and Evadne found herself in a cozy dining-room seated near a window which opened into a bewildering vista of summer beauty. There were flowers beside each plate as well as in the quaintly carved bowl in the centre of the table. Evadne caught herself smiling. That had always been a conceit of hers in Barbadoes.

Everything was simple but delicious. The tender, juicy chicken, the delicate pink ham, the muffins browned to a turn, the Jersey butter moulded into a sheaf of wheat, and moist brown bread of Aunt Marthe's own making, the blocks of golden sponge cake, the crisp lettuce, the fragrant strawberries, the cool jelly frosted with snow. Evadne drank her tea out of a chocolate tinted cup, fluted like the bell of a flower, and felt as if she were feasting on the nectar of the gods, while Mr. Everidge's silvery tones kept up a constant stream of talk and Aunt Marthe's beautiful hospitality made her feel perfectly at home.

"Tea, my dear Evadne, " he said, as he passed her cup to be refilled, "is an infusion of poison which is slowly but surely destroying the coatings of the gastronomical organ of the female portion of society. I tremble to think of the amount of tannin which analysis would show deposited in the systems of the votaries of the deadly Five o'clock, and the unhealthy nervous tension of the age is largely traceable to the excessive consumption of the pernicious liquid. Chocolate, on the contrary, taken as I always drink it, is simple and nutritive, with no unpleasant after effects to be apprehended, but this decoction of bitter herbs, steeped to death in water far past its proper temperature, is concentrated lye, my dear Evadne, nothing but concentrated lye. By the way, Marthe, I wish you would give your personal supervision to the preparation of my hot water in the future. Nothing comparable to hot water, Evadne, just before retiring. It aids digestion and induces sleep, and sleep you know is a gift of the gods. The Chinese mode of punishing criminals has always seemed to me exquisite in its barbarity. They simply make it impossible for the unhappy wretches to obtain a wink of sleep, until at length the torture grows unbearable and they find refuge in the long sleep which no mortal has power to prevent. So, my dear Marthe, see to it if you please in future that my slumber tonic is served just on the boil. The worthy Joanna does not understand the mysteries of the boiling process. Water, after it has passed the initiatory stage becomes flat, absolutely flat and tasteless. What I had to drink last night was so repugnant to my palate that I found it impossible to sink into repose with that calm attitude of mind which is so essential to perfect slumber.

"See to it also, my dear, that I am not disturbed at such an unearthly hour again as I was this morning. Tesla, the great electrician, has put himself on record as intimating that the want of sleep is a potent factor in the deplorably heavy death rate of the present day. He thinks sleep and longevity are synonymous, therefore it becomes us to bend every effort to attain that desirable consummation. "

Involuntarily Evadne looked at Mrs. Everidge. Her face was slightly turned towards the open window and there was a half smile upon her lips, as if, like Joan of Arc, she was listening to voices of sweeter tone than those of earth. She came back to the present again on the instant and met her niece's eyes with a smile, but in the subtle realm of intuition we learn by lightning flashes, and Evadne needed no further telling to know that the saddest loneliness which can fall to the lot of a woman was the fate of her aunt.

Immediately after supper Mrs. Everidge persuaded Evadne to go to her room. The long journey had been a great strain upon her strength and she was very tired.

"I wish you a good night, Uncle Horace, " she said as she passed him in the doorway.

"And you a pleasant one, " he rejoined with a gallant bow. "'We are such stuff as dreams are made of — and our little life is rounded with a sleep. '"

She lay for a long time wakeful, revelling in the strange sense of peace which seemed to enfold her, while the evening breeze blew through the room and the twilight threw weird shadows among the dainty draperies. At length there came a low knock and Mrs. Everidge opened the door.

Evadne stretched out her hands impulsively. "Oh, this beautiful stillness! " she exclaimed. "In Marlborough there is the clang of the car gongs and the rumble of cabs and the tramp of feet upon the pavement until it seems as if the weary world were never to be at rest, but this house is so quiet I could almost hear a pin drop. "

Mrs. Everidge smiled. "You have quick ears, little one. But we are quieter than usual to-night; Joanna is sitting up with a sick neighbor, your uncle went to his room early, and I have been reading in mine."

She drew a low chair up beside the bed. "Now we must begin to get acquainted, " she said.

"Dear Aunt Marthe! " cried Evadne, "I feel as if I had known you all my life. "

She gave her a swift caress. "You dear child! Then tell me about your father. "

Evadne looked at her gratefully. No one had ever cared to know about her father before. Forgetting her weariness in the absorbing interest of her subject, she talked on and on, and Mrs. Everidge with the wisdom of true sympathy, made no attempt to check her, knowing full well that the relief of the tried heart was helping her more than any physical rest could do.

"And now, oh, Aunt Marthe, life is so desperately lonely! " she said at last with a sobbing sigh.

Mrs. Everidge leaned over and kissed the trembling lips. "I think sometimes the earthly fatherhood is taken from us, dear child, that we may learn to know the beautiful Fatherliness of God. We can never find true happiness until our restless hearts are folded close in the hush of his love. Human love—however lovely—does not satisfy us. Nothing can, —but God! "

"The Fatherliness of God, " repeated Evadne. "That sounds lovely, but people do not think of him so. God is someone very terrible and far away. "

"'And God shall wipe away all tears from their eyes. ' Does that sound as if he were far away, little one? 'As one whom his mother comforteth, so will I comfort you. ' Why, God is father and mother both to us, dear child. Can you think of anyone nearer than that? "

Evadne caught her breath in a great gladness. "I believe you are his angel of consolation, " she said in a hushed voice.

"'Even unto them will I give... a place and a name better than of sons and daughters, '" quoted Aunt Marthe softly. "That means a location and an identity. Here, sometimes, it seems as if we had neither the one nor the other. Christ follows out the same idea in his picture of the abiding place which is being prepared for you and me. Everything on earth is so transitory, and the human heart has such a hunger for something that will last. "

"Have you felt this too? " cried Evadne. "I thought I was the only one. "

Mrs. Everidge laughed. "The only one in all the world to puzzle over its problems! Oh, yes, the older we grow, the more we find that the great majority have the same feelings and perplexities as ourselves, although some may not understand their thought clearly enough to put it into words. "

"What is your favorite verse in all the Bible? " asked Evadne after a pause.

Mrs. Everidge laughed again, and Evadne thought she had never heard a laugh at once so merry and so sweet.

"You send me into a rose garden, dear child, and tell me to select the choicest bloom out of its wilderness of beauty. How can I when every one has a different coloring and a fragrance all its own? Two of my special favorites are in the Revelation, —'To him that overcometh, to him will I give of the hidden manna, and I will give him a white stone, and upon the stone a new name written, which no one knoweth but he that receiveth it. ' 'And they shall see his face, and his name shall be on their foreheads. '

"That means a possession and a belonging. It is the spiritual symbol which binds us to our heavenly lover for eternity just as the wedding ring is a pledge of fidelity for our earth time. It is only as we see it so, that we get the full beauty of the religion of Jesus. His church—the inner circle of his chosen 'hidden ones'—is his bride, and what can be more glorious than to be the bride of the King of kings? The dear souls who only serve him with fear do not get the sweetness out of it at all. How can they, when their lives are all duty? 'Perfect love casteth out fear' and there is no duty about it, for when we love, it is a joy to serve and give. It hurts the Christ to have us content to be simply servants when he would lift us up to the higher plane of friendship, when he has put upon us the high honor of the dearest friend of all! Earthly brides spend a vast deal of time and thought over their trousseau, so I think Christ's bride should walk among men with a sweet aloofness while the spiritual garments are being fashioned in which she is to dwell with him. The Bible says a great deal about dressing. 'Let thy garments be always white'—the sunshine color, the joy color—for bye and bye we are to walk with him in white, you know. Our spiritual wardrobe must be fitted and worn down here. It is a terrible mistake to put off donning the wedding robes until we come to the feast. And the wardrobe is very ample. Christ would have his bride luxuriously appareled. 'Be clothed with humility. ' That is a fine, close-fitting suit for every day, but over it we are to wear the garment of praise and the warm, shining robe of charity. Can you fancy anything more beautiful than a life clothed in such garments as these? And to me the loveliest of all is charity. The highest praise I ever heard given to a woman was that 'she had such a tender way of making excuses for everybody. '

"Very fair must be the bride in the eyes of her royal lover, clothed in the garments which he has selected, —all light and joy and tenderness, for, the King's daughter is all glorious within. "

"Aunt Marthe, " said Evadne, after a long silence, in which they had been tasting the sweetness of it, "I do not need to ask if you know Jesus Christ? "

The lovely face took on an added beauty. "He is my life, " she said.

## CHAPTER XI.

Evadne was swinging in the hammock one golden summer afternoon, humming soft snatches of her old songs while she played with her aunt's pet black and tan. The sweet freshness of her new existence was rapidly restoring tone to her mental system, and life no longer seemed a hopeless task. The days were full of dreamy contentment. She spent long mornings under the murmuring pines in the deep belt of forest which stretched for miles behind the house, or helped Mrs. Everidge keep the rooms in dainty order; drove with her along the grass-bordered roads, while ears and eyes feasted on the symphonies of Nature and the ever changing beauty of the hills; or stood beside Joanna in a trance of delight out in the fragrant dairy, whose windows opened into a wild sweetness of fluttering leaves, and whose cool stone floor made a channel for a purling brook, watching her as with dexterous hands she shaped and moulded the bubbley dough or tossed up an omelet or made one of her delicious cherry pies, conscious through it all of the sweet influence which seemed to pervade every corner of the house and grounds.

"I wonder what it is about you, you dear Aunt Marthe? " she soliloquized, as she pulled Noisette's silky ears. "When you are away I cannot bear to go into the house, —everything seems so different, so cold and dark, —but the moment you come home again it is as lovely as ever. Concentrated light. Yes, that name would suit you, for light is sweet and pure and stimulating and precious. If all the people in the world were like you, *what* a world it would be! "

She looked up as she heard footsteps approaching, and then rose to welcome her visitor. A woman twenty years her senior, bright, capable, energetic, with a shrewd face and kindly eyes whose keen glance was quick to pierce the flimsy veil of humbug, and a tongue whose good-natured sarcasm had made more than one pretender feel ashamed.

"How do? " she said briskly, as she took the chair Evadne offered. "I hope you're feelin' better sence you've cum? "

"Much better, thank you. I am very sorry my aunt is not at home. "

"I'm sorry likewise, though it don't make as much difference as it might have done, as I'm callin' a purpose to see you. "

"That is very good of you, " said Evadne with a laugh. There was a spicy flavor about this child of the mountains which she found refreshing.

"It's a bit awkward, " continued her visitor with a twinkle in her eye, "as we'll have to do our own introducin'. My name's Penelope Riggs, Penel for brevity. What's yours? "

"Evadne Hildreth. "

"Evadne. That's uncommon and pretty. I'm goin' to call you so if you're not objectionable to it. Life's too short for handles. "

Evadne laughed merrily. "I'm not in the least objectionable, " she said.

"No, that's a fact, " said her visitor after a moment's kindly scrutiny. "You're true and thorough. I knew I was goin' to like you when I saw you in meetin'. "

Evadne flushed with pleasure. "Why, that is a beautiful character! I only wish I deserved it. But I fear you are very much mistaken in me, though it is very kind in you to think such nice things. "

"Nonsense, child! I don't waste my time thinkin'. Let me have a good look at your face for half an hour and I'll know as much about you as you could tell me in a week. Malviny Higgins has just come back from Bosting with her head full of sykick forces an' mental affinities an' the dear knows what else, but I think it's just a cultivation of our common senses—number, five. You can feel a person without touching them; it's in the air all round you; and you don't need much discrimination to know whether what you will say will hurt them or be a blessin'. The main thing is to put yourself in their shoes before you begin to talk. "

"Their shoes, Miss Riggs, " laughed Evadne, "why they might not fit."

"Penelope, " corrected her visitor, "Penel for brevity. Yes, they will too, that kind of shoe leather is elastic. It's the old Bible doctrine, 'never do anything to others that you wouldn't like others to do to you. ' If people got the shoes well fitted before they let their tongues loose, there would be a deal less sorrow and heartburn in the world."

"'Love thy neighbor as thyself, '" said Evadne. "I never thought of it in that way before. "

"Well, " said Miss Riggs briskly, "I'm dredful glad you've cum, Evadne. It'll do Mis' Everidge a sight of good to have you, though Marthe Everidge is raised above the need of humans as far as any mortal can be on this earth. With all their inventions there ain't nobody discovered how to make spiritual photographs yet, or I would have the picture of *her* character in all the windows of the land. 'Twould do more good than miles of tracts. I agree with Paul that livin' epistles make the best readin' an' it don't seem fittin' that she should be shut up in this little place where only a few of us have the right kind of spectacles to see her through. Most of the folks just allow it's Mis' Everidge's way, and would as soon think of tryin' to imitate her as a tadpole would a star. "

"But we are to imitate Christ, " said Evadne.

"'Course, child! But it's dredful comfortin' to have a human life in front of us to show us that is possible. Lots of times when life looks like a long seam an' the sewin' pricks my fingers, a new light falls on this picture, and I sez to myself, 'Penel, ' says I, 'look at Marthe Everidge. The Lord has made you both out of the same material. There ain't no reason why she should be always gettin' nearer heaven and you goin' back to earth. She has difficulties and worriments, same as you have, but if she can make every trial into a new rung for the ladder on which she is mountin' up to God, there ain't no reason why you should make a gravestone out of yours to bury yourself under; and so I start on with a new courage, an' when we get to the end of the journey, I'll not be the only one who'll have to thank Marthe Everidge for showin' the way. "

Evadne's eyes shone. "You make me feel, " she cried, "as if I would rather live a beautiful life than do the most magnificent thing in the world! "

"That's a safe feelin' to tie to, " said Penelope with an approving smile; "for character is the only thing we've got to carry with us when we go. "

"Well, " she continued, "I must be goin'. I did think I'd be forehanded in callin', but mother's been dredful wakeful lately, and when daylight comes, it don't seem as if I had the ambition of a snail. She don't like to be left alone for a minit, mother don't, so it's a bit of a puzzle to keep up with society. "

She laughed cheerily as she held out her hand. "Well, I'm dredful pleased to have met you. I'll be more than glad to have you come in whenever you're down our way. "

Evadne watched her as she walked briskly along the road. "She is not Aunt Marthe, " she said slowly; "I suppose Louis would call it a case of the solanum and the potato blossom, but she is one of the Lord's plants all the same. "

"Aunt Marthe, what *is* culture? " she asked suddenly, as later in the afternoon Mrs. Everidge sat beside her hammock. "Is Louis right? Is it just the veneer of education and travel and environment? "

"You can hardly call that a veneer, little one. Real education goes very deep. Emerson says 'nothing is so indicative of deepest culture as a tender consideration of the ignorant. ' I think that culture, to be perfect, must have its root in love. It is impossible that anyone filled with the love of Christ should ever be discourteous or lack in thoughtfulness for the feelings of others. "

"Why that must be what Penelope Riggs meant by her 'elastic shoe leather, '" said Evadne with a laugh, and then she repeated the conversation.

"Oh, she has been here! I am glad. It will do you good to know her. She is the cheeriest soul, and the busiest. She always acts upon me as a tonic, for I know just how much she has had to give up and how hard her life has been. "

"Why, Aunt Marthe, she says when she gets to heaven she will have to thank you for showing her the way. She thinks you are perfection."

"'Not I, but Christ, '" said Aunt Marthe with a happy smile. She went into the house and returned with a book in her hand. "You asked what culture really was. This writer says 'Drudgery. ' Listen while I give you a few snatches, then you shall have the book for your own.

"'Culture takes leisure, elegance, wide margins of time, a pocket-book; drudgery means limitations, coarseness, crowded hours, chronic worry, old clothes, black hands, headaches. Our real and our ideal are not twins. Never were! I want the books, but the clothes basket wants me. I love nature and figures are my fate. My taste is books and I farm it. My taste is art and I correct exercises. My taste is science and I measure tape. Can it be that this drudgery, not to be escaped, gives 'culture? ' Yes, culture of the prime elements of life, of the very fundamentals of all fine manhood and fine womanhood, the fundamentals that underlie all fulness and without which no other culture worth the winning is even possible. Power of attention, power of industry, promptitude in beginning work, method and accuracy and despatch in doing it, perseverance, courage before difficulties, cheer, self-control and self-denial, they are worth more than Latin and Greek and French and German and music and art and painting and waxflowers and travels in Europe added together. These last are the decorations of a man's life, those other things are the indispensables. They make one's sit-fast strength and one's active momentum, —they are the solid substance of one's self.

"'How do we get them? High school and college can give much, but these are never on their programmes. All the book processes that we go to the schools for and commonly call our 'education' give no more than opportunity to win the indispensables of education. We must get them somewhat as the fields and valleys get their grace. Whence is it that the lines of river and meadow and hill and lake and shore conspire to-day to make the landscape beautiful? Only by long chiselings and steady pressures. Only by ages of glacier crush and grind, by scour of floods, by centuries of storm and sun. These rounded the hills and scooped the valley-curves and mellowed the soil for meadow-grace. It was 'drudgery' all over the land. Mother Nature was down on her knees doing her early scrubbing work! That was yesterday, to-day—result of scrubbing work—we have the laughing landscape.

"'Father and mother and the ancestors before them have done much to bequeath those mental qualities to us, but that which scrubs them into us, the clinch which makes them actually ours and keeps them ours, and adds to them as the years go by, —that depends on our own plod in the rut, our drill of habit, in a word our 'drudgery. ' It is because we have to go and go morning after morning, through rain, through shine, through toothache, headache, heartache to the appointed spot and do the appointed work, no matter what our work may be, because of the rut, plod, grind, humdrum in the work, that we get our foundations.

"'Drudgery is the gray angel of success, for drudgery is the doing of one thing long after it ceases to be amusing, and it is 'this one thing I do' that gathers me together from my chaos, that concentrates me from possibilities to powers and turns powers into achievements. The aim in life is what the backbone is in the body, if we have no aim we have no meaning. Lose us and the earth has lost nothing, no niche is empty, no force has ceased to play, for we have no aim and therefore we are still—nobody. Our bodies are known and answer in this world to such or such a name, but, as to our inner selves, with real and awful meaning our walking bodies might be labelled 'An unknown man sleeps here! '

"'But we can be artists also in our daily task, —artists not artisans. The artist is he who strives to perfect his work, the artisan strives to get through it. If I cannot realize my ideal I can at least idealize my real—How? By trying to be perfect in it. If I am but a raindrop in a shower, I will be at least a perfect drop. If but a leaf in a whole June, I will be a perfect leaf. This is the beginning of all Gospels, that the kingdom of heaven is at hand just where we are. '"

"Oh! " cried Evadne, drawing a long breath, "that is beautiful! I feel as if I had been lifted up until I touched the sky. "

"Marthe, " exclaimed Mr. Everidge reproachfully, suddenly appearing in the doorway with a sock drawn over each arm, "it is incomprehensible to me you do not remember that my physical organism and darns have absolutely no affinity. "

Mrs. Everidge laughed brightly. "If you will make holes, Horace, I must make darns, " she said.

"Not a natural sequence at all! " he retorted testily. "When the wear and tear of time becomes visible in my underwear it must be relegated to Reuben. "

"But Reuben's affinity for patches may be no stronger than your own, Uncle Horace, " said Evadne mischievously.

Mr. Everidge waved his sock-capped hands with a gesture of disdain. "The lower orders, my dear Evadne, are incapable of those delicate perceptions which constitute the mental atmosphere of those of finer mould. The delft does not feel the blow which would shiver the porcelain into atoms, and Reuben's epidermis is, I imagine, of such a horny consistency that he would walk in oblivious unconcern upon these elevations of needlework which are as a ploughshare to my sensitive nerves. It is the penalty one has to pay for being of finer clay than the common herd of men. "

Evadne looked at Mrs. Everidge. A deep flush of shame had dyed her cheeks and her lips were quivering.

"Oh, Horace, " she cried, "Reuben is such a faithful boy! "

"My dear, " said her husband airily, "I make no aspersions against his moral character, but he certainly cannot be classed among the velvet-skinned aristocracy. By the way, I wish you would see in future that my undergarments are of a silken texture. My flesh rebels at anything approaching to harshness, " and then he went complacently back to his library to weave and fashion the graceful phrases which flowed from his facile pen.

"Why should he go clothed in silk and you in cotton! " cried Evadne, jealous for the rights of her friend.

Mrs. Everidge's eyes came back from one of their long journeys, "Oh, I have learned the luxury of doing without, " she said lightly.

Evadne threw her arms around her impulsively. "But why, oh, Aunt Marthe, why should not Uncle Horace learn it too? "

"We do not see things through the same window, " she answered with a smile and a sigh.

## CHAPTER XII.

John Randolph walked slowly through the soft dawning. It had been a brilliant night. The late moon had risen as he was bidding good-bye to the graceful creatures he should never see again, and Hollywood had been clad in a bewitching beauty which made it all the harder to say farewell. Far into the night he had lingered, visiting every corner of the dearly loved home, then at last he had turned away and walked steadily along the road which led to Marlborough.

The sun rose in a blaze of splendor and the birds began to twitter. The gripsack which he carried grew strangely heavy, and he felt faint and weary. The long strain of the day before was beginning to tell upon him, and it was many hours since he had tasted food.

A sudden turn of the road brought him in sight of a trig little farm, against whose red gate a man was leaning, leisurely enjoying the beauty of the morning before he began work. He had a pleasant face, strong and peaceful. No one had ever known Joseph Makepeace to be out of temper or in a hurry. He would have said it was because he commenced every day listening to the inner voice among the silences of Nature. Joseph Makepeace was a Quaker.

"Why, John, lad! " he cried, "thou art a welcome sight on this fair morning. Come in, come in. Breakfast will soon be ready and thou art in sore need of it by the look of thy face. " He gave John's hand a mighty grasp and took his gripsack from him.

"Why, John, hast thou walked far with this load? Where were all the horses of Hollywood? Is anything wrong, John? I don't like thy looks, lad. "

John's voice trembled. "I have left Hollywood" he said. "Mr. Hawthorne has turned me off. "

"Left Hollywood! You don't mean it, John? Well, well, folks say Robert Hawthorne has not been right in his mind since his boy got hurt. I believe it now. It's a comfort that the great Master will never turn us off, lad. Thee'd better lie down on the lounge and rest thee a bit, John, while I go and tell mother. "

He entered the spotless kitchen where his wife was moving blithely to and fro. "Thee has another 'unawares angel' to breakfast, Ruth. It's a grand thing being on the public road! "

Ruth Makepeace laughed merrily. "An angel, Joseph? I hope he's not like thy last one, who stole three of my best silver spoons! "

"So, so, thee didst promise to forget that, Ruth, if I replace them next time I go to Marlborough. "

"Well, so I do, except when thee does remind me. Is this a very hungry angel, Joseph? Does thee think I'd better cook another chicken? "

"He ought to be hungry, poor lad, but I doubt if he eats much. Does thee remember friend Randolph, Ruth? "

"Of course I do. But he's been dead these ten years. Thee doesn't mean he's come back to breakfast with us? "

Her husband put his hand on her shoulder and shook her gently. Then he kissed her. "Thee is fractious this morning, Ruth. Friend Randolph had a son, thee dost mind, whom Robert Hawthorne took to live at Hollywood. It is he whom the good Lord has sent to us to care for, Ruth. He's just been turned adrift. "

"If thee wasn't so big I would shake thee, Joseph! The idea of John Randolph being in this house and thee beating round the bush with thine angels! " and with all her motherhood shining in her eyes, Ruth Makepeace started for the parlor.

In spite of the overflowing kindness with which he was surrounded John found the meal a hard one. He had been used to breakfast with little Nan upon his knee.

"When thee is rested we'll have a talk, lad, " said his host, as they rose from the table; "but thee'd better bide with us for the summer and not fret about the future: thee dost need a holiday. "

"Of course thee dost, John! " said blithe little Mrs. Makepeace. "I wish thee would bide for good. "

Her husband laid his hand upon his shoulder. "Thou knowest, lad, there is the little grave out yonder. Thee should'st have his place in our hearts and home. Would'st thee be content to bide, John? "

John Randolph looked at his friends with shining eyes. "You have done me good for life! " he said, "but the world calls me, I must go. I mean to work my way through college, and be a physician, Mr. Makepeace. "

"So! so! Well, we mustn't stand in the way, Ruth. Thee'll make a good one, John. But how art thee going to manage it, lad? "

"The Steel Works in Marlborough pay good wages. I mean to get a place there if I can, and study in the evenings. "

"Why, John, lad, the Steel Works shut down yesterday afternoon. "

For an instant the brave spirit quailed, only for an instant. "Then I must find something else, " he said quietly.

"It's a bad season, John, and the times are hard. " Joseph Makepeace thought for a moment. "There's friend Harris up the river. What dost thee think, Ruth? "

"Why, he wants men to pile wood, " exclaimed his wife. "Thee would'st not set John at that! "

"Lincoln split rails, " said John with a smile, "why should not I pile them? It's clean work, and honest, Mrs. Makepeace. "

"He has a logging camp in the winter. Thee would'st have good pay then, John. "

"But thee would'st be so lonely, John, amongst all those rough men! And thee did'st say once it was dangerous, Joseph. It's not fit work for John. "

"I am not afraid of work, Mrs. Makepeace, and I can never be lonely with Jesus Christ. "

\* \* \* \* \*

# A Beautiful Possibility

In far Vermont Evadne was reading aloud from a paper she had brought from the post-office. "The whole sum of Christian living is just loving. " "Do you believe that, Aunt Marthe? "

"Surely, dear child. Love is the fulfilling of the law, you know. When we love God with our whole heart, and our neighbor as ourselves, there is no danger of our breaking the Decalogue. 'He who loveth knoweth God, ' and 'to know him is life eternal. '"

"Just love, " said Evadne musingly. "It seems so simple. "

"Do you think so? " said Aunt Marthe with a smile. "Yet people find it the hardest thing to do, as it is surely the noblest. Drummond calls it 'the greatest thing in the world' and you have Paul's definition of it in Corinthians. Did you ever study that to see how perfect love would make us?

"'Love suffereth long, ' that does away with impatience; 'and is kind, ' that makes us neighborly; 'love envieth not, ' that saves from covetousness; 'vaunteth not itself, ' that does away with self-conceit; 'seeketh not its own, ' that kills selfishness; 'is not provoked, ' that shows we are forgiving; 'rejoiceth not in unrighteousness, ' makes us love only what is pure; 'covereth [Footnote: Marginal rendering. ] all things, ' that leaves no room for scandal; 'believeth all things, ' that does away with doubt; 'hopeth all things, ' that is the antithesis of distrust; 'endureth all things, ' proves that we are strong; and then the beautiful summing up of the whole matter, 'love never faileth. ' If that is true of us, it can only be as we are filled with the spirit of the Christ of God, 'whose nature and whose name is love. '"

"You see such beautiful things in the Bible! " said Evadne despairingly, "why cannot I get below the surface? "

"You will, dearie. You forget I have been digging nuggets from this precious mine for years and you have just begun to search for them. Would you like another drive, or do you feel too tired? "

"Not in the least. What can I do for you? "

"I would like to send some of that currant jelly I made yesterday to old Mrs. Riggs, if you are sure you would like to take it? "

"As sure as sure can be, dear, " said Evadne with a kiss, "Where shall I find it? "

"In the King's corner. "

"'The King's corner? '" echoed Evadne with a puzzled look.

"Oh, I forgot you did not know. I always give the Lord the first fruits of my cooking, and keep them in a special place set apart for his use, then, when I go to see the sick, there is always something ready to tempt their fancy. It is wonderful what a saving of time it is. I rarely have to make anything on purpose, —there is always something prepared. "

She followed her niece out to the carriage, helped her pack the jelly safely, with one of her crisp loaves of fresh brown bread, bade her a merry farewell and went back to the house again singing.

"Oh, Aunt Marthe! " cried Evadne, as she drove slowly under the trees, "shall I ever, ever learn to be like you? "

She found the old lady sitting by the fire wrapped up in a shawl, although the day was sultry.

"Good-morning, " said Evadne, as she deposited her parcels on the table. "I come from Mrs. Everidge. She thought you would fancy some of her fresh brown bread and currant jelly. "

"Hum! " said the old lady ungraciously, "I hope it's better than the last wuz. Guess Mis' Everidge ain't ez pertickler ez she used ter be. "

"Aunt Marthe! " cried Evadne indignantly. "Why, everything she does is perfection! "

"Land, child! There ain't no perfecshun in this world. It's all a wale, a wale o' tears. We'se poor, miserable critters, —wurms o' the dust, — that's what we be. "

"There isn't any worm about Aunt Marthe, " cried Evadne with a laugh. "I think you must be looking through a wrong pair of spectacles, Mrs. Riggs. "

"Land, child! I ain't got but the one pair, an' they got broke this morning. But it's jest my luck. Everything goes agin me. "

"But you can get them mended, " said Evadne.

"Sakes alive! There ain't much hope o' gettin' them mended, with Penel behindhand on the rent, an' the firin' an' the land knows what else. I don't see why Penel ain't more forehanded. I tell her ef I wuz ez young an' ez spry ez she be, I guess I'd hev things different, but, la! that's Penel's way. She's terrible sot in her own way, Penel is. She's not willin' ter take my advice. Children now-a-days allers duz know more than their mothers. "

"Where is Penelope? " asked Evadne.

"Oh, skykin' round. She's gone over to Miss Johnsing's ter help with the quiltin'. That's the way she duz, an' here I am all alone with the fire ter tend ter, an' not a livin' soul ter do a hand's turn fer me! She sez she hez ter do it ter keep the pot bilin'—'pears ter me Penel's pots take a sight uv bilin'. "

"But she has left a nice pile of wood close beside you, Mrs. Riggs. "

"La, yes, " grumbled the old lady, "but it's dretful thoughtless in her ter stay away so long, when she knows the stoopin' cums so hard on my rheumatiz. An' it's terrible lonesome. I get that narvous some days I'm all of a shake. 'Tain't ez ef she kep within' call, but t'other day she went clean over ter Hancocks, —a hull mile an' a half! She sez she hez ter go where folks wants things done, but that's nonsense, folks oughter want things done near at hand, —they know how lonesome I be. Why, a bear might cum in an' eat me up for all Penel would know. She gits so taken up a' larfin' an' singin', she ain't got no sympathy. Oh, it's a wale o' tears! "

"But there are no bears in Vernon, Mrs. Riggs, " laughed Evadne.

"Land, child! you never know what there might be! " said the old lady testily. "Be you a' stayin' at Mis' Everidge's? "

"Yes, " said Evadne, "she is my aunt. "

"Hum! I never knew she hed any nieces, 'cept them two gals uv Jedge Hildreth's down ter Marlborough. "

"I am their cousin, Mrs. Riggs. I used to live in Barbadoes. "

"Well, I declar! Why, Barbaderz is t' other side of nowhere! Used ter be when I went ter school. Well, well, some folks hez a lion's share uv soarin' an' here I've ben all my life jest a' pinin' my heart out ter git down ter Bosting, an' I ain't never got there! But that's allers the way. I never git nuthin'. I'm sixty-nine years old cum Christmas an' I ain't never ben further away frum hum than twenty miles hand runnin', an' here's a chit like you done travelin' enuff ter last a lifetime. "

"But I didn't want to travel, Mrs. Riggs, " said Evadne gently. "I would so much rather have stayed at home. "

"There you go! " grumbled the old lady. "Folks ain't never satisfied with their mercies. Allers a' flyin' in the face uv Providence. I tell you we'se wurms, child; miserable, shiftless wurms, a' crawlin' down in this walley of humiliation, with our faces ter the dust. "

"But you've got a great deal to be thankful for, Mrs. Riggs, " ventured Evadne, "in having such a daughter. Aunt Marthe thinks she is a splendid character. "

"So she oughter be! " retorted the old lady, "with sech a bringin' up ez she's hed. But land! childern's dretful disappointin' ter a pusson. There ain't a selfish bone in *my* body, but Penel's ez full uv 'em. She'll let me lie awake by the hour at a time while she's a' snoozin' on the sofy beside me. She don't sleep in her own bed any more because I hev ter hev her handy ter rub me when the rheumatiz gits ter jumpin'. She sez she can't help bein' drowsy when she's workin' through the day, but land! she'd manage ter keep awake ef she hed any sympathy! She ain't got no sympathy, Penel ain't; an' she ain't a bit forehanded. "

"But I don't 'spect nuthin' else in this world. It's a wale o' tears an' we ain't got nuthin' else ter look fer but triberlation an' woe. Man ez born ter trouble ez the sparks fly upward, an' a woman allers hez the lion's share. "

Evadne burst into the sitting-room with flashing eyes. "Aunt Marthe, if I were Penelope Riggs, I would shoot her mother! She's just a crooked old bundle of unreasonableness and ingratitude! "

Mrs. Everidge laughed. "No, you wouldn't dear, not if you *were* Penelope. "

"But, Aunt Marthe, how does she stand it? Why, it would drive me crazy in a week! To think of that poor soul, working like a slave all day, and then grudged the few winks of sleep she gets on a hard old sofa. I declare, it makes me feel hopeless! "

"The day I climbed Mont Blanc, " said Mrs. Everidge softly, "we had a wonderful experience. Down below us a sudden storm swept the valley. The rain fell in torrents, and the thunder roared, but up where we stood the sun was shining and all was still. When we walk with Christ, little one, we find it possible to live above the clouds. "

"An Alpine Christian! " cried Evadne. "Oh, Aunt Marthe, that is beautiful! "

## CHAPTER XIII.

"The ancient Egyptians, Evadne, " remarked Mr. Everidge the next day at dinner, as he selected the choicest portions of a fine roast duck for his own consumption, "during the period of their nation's highest civilization, subsisted almost exclusively upon millet, dates and other fruits and cereals; and athletic Greece rose to her greatest culture upon two meals a day, consisting principally of maize and vegetables steeped in oil. Don't you think you ladies would find it of advantage to copy them in this laudable abstemiousness? There is something repugnant to a refined taste in the idea of eating flesh whose constituent particles partake largely of the nature of our own."

"Why, certainly, Uncle Horace, " said Evadne merrily. "I am quite ready to become a vegetarian, if you will set me the example. The feminine mind, you know, is popularly supposed to be only fitted to follow a masculine lead. "

"Ah, I wish it were possible, my dear Evadne, but the peculiar susceptibility of my internal organism precludes all thought of my making such a radical change in the matter of diet. Even now, in spite of all my care, indigestion, like a grim Argus, stares me out of countenance. I wish you would bear this fact more constantly in mind, my dear Marthe. This duck, for instance, has not arrived at that stage of absolute fitness which is so essential to the appreciation of a delicate stomach. A duck, Evadne, is a bird which requires very careful treatment in its preparation for the table. It should be suspended in the air for a certain length of time, and then, after being carefully trussed, laid upon its breast in the pan, in order that all the juices of the body may concentrate in that titbit of the epicure, —then let the knife touch its richly browned skin, and, presto, you have a dish fit for the gods! The skin of this duck on the contrary presents a degree of resistance to the carver which proves that it has been placed in the oven before it had arrived at that stage of perfection. "

"Why, Horace, " laughed Mrs. Everidge, "I thought this one was just right! You remember you told me the last one we had, had hung five hours too long. "

"Exactly so. My friend, Trenton, will tell you that five hours is all the length of time required to seal the fate of nations. It is a pet theory of his that the finale of the material world will be rapid. He bases his conclusions upon the fact of the steady decrease in the volume of the surrounding atmosphere and the almost instantaneous action of all of Nature's destructive forces, fire and flood, storm and sunstroke, lightning and hail, earthquake and cyclone. Oh, *apropos* of my erudite friend, Marthe, he has promised to spend August with us, so you will have to look to your culinary laurels, for he is accustomed to dine at Delmonico's. "

"Professor Trenton coming here in August! " cried Mrs. Everidge in dismay. "Why, Horace, you never told me you had invited him! "

"My dear, I am telling you now. "

"But I meant to take Evadne up to our mountain camp in August. I am sure the resinous air would make her strong. I had my plans all laid. "

"'The best laid plans of mice and men gang aft agley, '" said her husband suavely. "Evadne's mental strength cannot fail to be developed by intercourse with such a clever man. We must not allow the culture of the body to occupy so prominent a place in our thoughts that we forget the mind, you know. "

"A fusty old Professor! " pouted Evadne. "Oh, Uncle Horace, why didn't you leave him among his tomes and his theories and let us be free to enjoy? "

"Mere sensual gratification, Evadne, " said Mr. Everidge, as he replenished his plate with some dainty pickings, "is not the true aim of life. I consider it a high honor that the Professor should consent to devote a month of his valuable time to my edification, for he is getting to be quite a lion in the literary world. You had better have your chamber prepared for his occupancy, Marthe. As I remember him at college he had a fondness amounting almost to a craze for rooms with a western aspect. "

Joanna came in to announce the arrival of a visitor whom Evadne had already learned to dread on account of her continual depression.

"Oh, Aunt Marthe! " she exclaimed, "must you waste this beautiful afternoon listening to her dolorosities. I wanted you to go for a drive!"

"You go, dearie, and take Penelope Riggs. It will be a treat to her and you ought to be out in the open air as much as possible. "

Evadne went out on the veranda. Through the open window she could hear the visitor's ceaseless monotone of complaint mingled with the soft notes of Mrs. Everidge's cheery sympathy. "Oh, dearest, " she murmured, "if you had seen this beautiful life, you would have known that there is no sham in the religion of Jesus! "

She waited long, in the hope that Mrs. Everidge would be able to accompany her, then she started for the Eggs cottage. She found the old lady alone. "Where is Penelope, Mrs. Riggs? "

"Oh, skykin' round ez usual, " was the peevish response. "It's church work this time. When I wuz young, folks got along 'thout sech an everlastin' sight uv meetins, but nowadays there's Convenshuns, an' Auxils an' Committees, an' the land knows what, till a body's clean distracted. Fer my part I hate ter see wimmen a' wallerin' round in the mud till it takes 'em the best part uv the next day ter git their skirts clean. "

"But there is no mud now, Mrs. Riggs, " laughed Evadne.

"Land alive, child! There will be sometime. In my day folks used ter stay ter hum an' mind their childern, but now they've all took ter soarin' an' it don't matter how many ends they leave flyin' loose behind 'era. "

"But Penelope has no children to mind, Mrs. Riggs. "

"Land alive! She hez me, an' I oughter be more ter her than a duzzen childern, —but she ain't got no proper feelin's, Penel ain't. When I'm a' lyin' in my coffin she'll give her eyes ter hev the chance ter rub my rheumatiz, an' run for hot bottles an' flannels an' ginger tea. It's an ongrateful world but I allcrs sez there ain't no use complainin'; it's what we've got ter expec', —triberlation an' anguish an' mournin' an' woe. It's good enuff fer us too. Sech wurms ez we be! "

"Well, Evadne, how do you do, child? I'm dretful glad to see you, " and Penelope, breezy and keen as a March wind, came bustling into the room. "Why, yes, I'm well, child, if it wasn't for bein' so tumbled about in my mind. "

"What has tumbled you, Penelope? " asked Evadne with a merry laugh.

"The Scribes and Pharisees, " was the terse rejoinder. "I've just cum from a Committee meeting of the Missionary Society an' I'm free to confess my feelin's is roused tremendous. Seems to me nowadays the church is built at a different angle from the Sermon on the Mount an' things is measured by the world's yardsticks till there ain't much sense in callin' it a church at all. Ef you'd seen the way Squire Higgins' girls sot down on poor little Matildy Jones this afternoon, just because her father sells fish! Their father sells it too, but he's got forehanded an' can do it by the gross, an' so they toss their heads an' set a whole garden full o' flowers a' shakin' upan' down. They're allers more peacocky in their minds after they git their spring bunnets. The Lord said we was to consider the lilies, but I guess he meant us to leave 'em in the fields, for I notice the more folks carries on the tops of their heads the less their apt to be like 'em underneath."

"But what did they say to her? " asked Evadne.

"You're young, child, or you'd know there's more ways of insultin' than with the tongue, an' poor little Matildy is jest the one to be hurt that way. Some folks is like clams, the minute you touch 'em, they shut themselves up in their shells an' then they don't feel what you do to 'em any more'n the Rocky mountains, but Matildy isn't made that way. She just sot there with the flushes comin' in her cheeks an' the tears shinin' in her pretty eyes till my heart ached. I leaned over to her an' whispered, 'Don't fret, Matildy, they ain't wuth mindin'. She gave me a little wintry smile but the tears kep a' comin' an' by an' bye she got up and went out, an' ef she don't imitate the Prophet Jeremi an' water her piller with her tears this night, then I've changed my name sence mornin'.

"I was so uplifted in my mind with righteous indignation that I felt called upon to let it loose, so I begun in a musin' tone, as ef I was havin' a solil. "

"'A solil?'" said Evadne in a mystified tone.

"Why, yes; talkin' to myself, child. I did think, ef there was any place folks was free an' eqal 'twould be in the Lord's service, ' sez I. 'The Bible teaches it's a pretty dangerous bizness to offend one uv these little ones. I'm not much of a hand at quotations, but there's an unpleasant connection between it an' a millstun, ' sez I.

"Malviny Higgins tossed her head an' giv me one uv her witherinest looks, but I'm not one uv the perishin' kind, so I kep on a' musin'.

"'It's wonderful what a difference there is between sellin' by the poun' an' the barrel, ' sez I. 'It's unfortunet that there's only one way to the heavenly country, an' it's a limited express with no Pullman attached. The Lord hedn't time to put on a parlor car fer the wholesale trade; seems like as if it was kind uv neglectful in him. It would hev been more convenient an' private. '

"Malviny's cheeks got as red as beets an' the flowers on her bonnet danced a Highland Fling as she leaned over to whisper somethin' to her sister, but I hed relieved my feelin's an' could join in quite peaceful like when Mrs. Songster said we'd close the meetin' by singin' 'Blest be the tie that binds. ' Well, there'll be no clicks in heaven, that's one blessin'. "

"'Clicks, ' Penelope? "

"Why, yes, child, the folks that gets off by themselves in a corner an' thinks nobody outside the circle is fit to tie their shoe. I expect to hev edifyin' conversations with Moses an' Elija, an' the first thing I mean to ask him is what kind of ravens they really were. "

"'Ravens, '" echoed Evadne bewildered, "what *do* you mean, Penelope? "

"Sakes alive, child! Haven't you read your Bible? and don't you know the ravens fed the old gentleman in the desert, an' that folks now say they were Arabs, because the ravens are dirty birds an' live on carrion, an' it stands to reason Elija couldn't touch that if he hed an ordinary stumach. As if the Lord couldn't hev made 'em bring food from the king's table if he hed chosen to do it! It's all of a piece with the way folks hev now of twistin' the Bible inside out till nobody knows what it means. For my part I believe if the Lord hed meant Arabs he would hev said Arabs an' not hev deceived us by callin' 'em birds uv prey. Folks is so set against allowin' anything that looks like a meracle that they'll go all the way round the barn an' creep through a snake fence if they can prove it's jest an ordinary piece of business. They do say there are some things the Lord can't do, but I'm free to confess I've never found them out. "

* * * * *

"Aunt Marthe, " said Evadne, when they had settled down for their evening talk, "what does it all mean? 'The victory of our faith, ' you know, and the 'Overcometh' in Revelation? I thought Christ got the victory for us? "

"So he does, dear child, and we through him. I came across a lovely explanation of it some time ago which I will copy for you; it has been such an inspiration. Listen, —

"'When you are forgotten or neglected or purposely set at naught and you smile inwardly, glorying in the insult or the oversight, — that is victory.

"'When your good is evil spoken of, when your wishes are crossed, your tastes offended, your advice disregarded, your opinions ridiculed, and you take it all in patient and loving silence, —that is victory.

"'When you are content with any food, any raiment, any climate, any society, any position in life, any solitude, any interruption, —that is victory.

"'When you can bear with any discord, any annoyance, any irregularity or unpunctuality (of which you are not the cause), —that is victory.

"'When you can stand face to face with folly, extravagance, spiritual insensibility, contradiction of sinners, persecution, and endure it all as Jesus endured it, —that is victory.

"'When you never care to refer to yourself in conversation, nor to record your works, nor to seek after commendation; when you can truly love to be unknown, —that is victory. '"

"Now I see! " exclaimed Evadne. "It means the beautiful patience with which you bear aggravating things and the gentle courtesy with which you treat all sorts of troublesome people. Oh, my Princess, I envy you your altitude! "

## CHAPTER XIV.

Professor Trenton had come and gone and the glory of the autumn was over the land. The early supper was ended and Evadne had ensconced herself in her favorite window to catch the sun's last smile before he fell asleep. In the room across the hall Mr. Everidge reclined in his luxurious arm-chair and leisurely turned the pages of the last "North American Review. " It was Saturday evening.

"Why, Horace, can this be possible? " Mrs. Everidge entered the room quickly and stood before her husband. Neither of them noticed Evadne.

"My dear, many things are possible in this terrestrial sphere. What particular possibility do you refer to? "

"That you have discharged Reuben? " The sweet voice trembled. Mr. Everidge's tones kept their usual complacent calm.

"That possibility, my dear, has taken definite form in fact. "

"But, Horace, the boy is heart-broken. "

"Time is a mighty healer, my love. He will recover his mental equipoise in due course. "

"But you might have given him a month's warning. Where is the poor boy to find another place? It is cruel to turn him off like this! "

"Really, my dear Marthe, I do not feel myself competent to solve all the problems of the labor question, " said Mr. Everidge carelessly. "Reuben must take his chances in common with the rest of his class."

"But, Horace, I cannot imagine what your reason for this can be! Where will you find so good a boy? "

"I am not aware that Socrates thought it necessary to acquaint the worthy Xantippe with the reasons for his conduct, " remarked Mr. Everidge suavely. "The feminine mind is too much disposed to jump to hasty conclusions to prove of any assistance in deciding matters of importance. The masculine brain, on the contrary, takes time for calm deliberation and weighs the pros and cons in the scale of a well balanced judgment before arriving at any definite decision. But my reason in this case will soon become apparent to you. I do not intend to keep a boy at all. "

"But who will take care of Atalanta? Are you going to forsake your cherished books for a curry-comb? "

"Really, Marthe! " exclaimed her husband in an aggrieved tone, "it is incomprehensible that you should have such a total disregard for the delicacy of my constitution, —especially when you know that the very odor of the stable is abhorrent to my olfactory senses. Atalanta has quarters provided for her at the Vernon Livery, and one of the grooms has orders to bring the carriage to the door at two o'clock every afternoon. "

"But that will make it very awkward, Horace. I so often have to use the carriage in the morning. "

"'Have, ' my dear Marthe, is a word which admits of many substitutions, —'cannot' in this case will be a suitable one. I find it is necessary to resume possession of the reins. Atalanta is retrograding and is rapidly losing that characteristic of speed which made her name a fitting one. There is a lack of mastery about a woman's handling of the ribbons which is quickly detected by horses, especially when they are of more than average intelligence. "

"But, Horace, if Reuben goes, Joanna will go too. You know she promised her mother she would never leave him. "

"In that event, my dear, you will have an opportunity to become more intimately acquainted with the mysteries of the culinary art, " observed Mr. Everidge cheerfully. "It will be a splendid chance to evolve that finest of character combinations, Spartan endurance coupled with American progressiveness. "

Mrs. Everidge smiled. "But what if I do not have the Spartan strength, Horace? "

"That is merely a matter of imagination, my love. It proves the truth of my theory that necessity develops capacity. A woman of leisure, for want of suitable mental pabulum, grows to fancy she has every ill that flesh is heir to, whereas, when she is obliged by compelling circumstances to put her muscles into practice, her mind acquires a more healthy tone. Self-contemplation is a most enervating exercise and involves a tremendous drain on the moral forces. "

"Do you think I waste much time in that way, Horace? " Mrs. Everidge spoke wistfully, and Evadne, forced to be an unwilling listener to the conversation, felt her cheeks grow hot with indignation.

"My dear, I merely refer to the deplorable tendency of your sex. All you require is moral stamina to tear yourself away from the arms of Morpheus at an earlier hour in the It is a popular illusion, you know, that work performed before sunrise takes less time to accomplish and is better done than later in the day. My mother used to affirm that she accomplished the work of two days in one when she arose at three a. m., but then my mother was a most exceptional woman, " with which parting thrust Mr. Everidge retired behind the pages of his magazine.

Upstairs in her own room Evadne paced the floor with tightly clenched hands. "Oh! " she cried, "what shall I do? I hate him! I hate him! How dare he! He ought to be glad to go down on his knees to serve her, she is so sweet, so dear! Oh, I cannot bear it! That she should be compelled to endure such servitude, and I can do nothing to help, nothing! nothing! " She threw herself across the bed and burst into a passion of tears. Was this the silent girl whom Isabelle had voted tiresome and slow?

A little later than usual she heard the low knock which always preceded the visit which she looked forward to as the sweetest part of the day. Could it be possible she would come to-night? Was no thought of self ever permitted to enter that brave, suffering heart?

She rose and opened the door. The dear face was paler than usual but there was no shadow upon the smooth brow. Marthe Everidge had crossed the tempest-tossed ocean of human passion into the sun-kissed calm of Christ's perfect peace.

Evadne threw her arms around her neck and laid her storm-swept face upon her shoulder. "Forgive me! " she cried, "I heard it all. I could not help it. I think my heart is breaking. Do not be angry, you see I love you so! How can I bear to have you subjected to this? You are so tender, so true. There is such a charm about you! You are so beautifully unselfish! Oh, my dear, my dear, how can you, do you bear it? "

Mrs. Everidge lifted her face tenderly and kissed the quivering lips. "It is 'not I but Christ, ' dear child. That makes it possible. " Then she drew her over to the lounge and began to undress her as if she had been a baby. "My dear little sister. You are utterly exhausted. You are not strong enough to suffer so. "

"Oh, will you let me be your sister and help you bear your burdens? " cried Evadne, unconscious that all the time the skilful hands were keeping up their sweet ministry and that her burden was being lifted for her by the one who had the greater burden to bear.

When she was comfortably settled for the night Mrs. Everidge drew her low chair up beside the bed. Evadne caught her hand in hers and kissed it reverently. "I wish I could make you understand how I honor you! " she said.

"You must not do it, dear! " said Aunt Marthe quickly. "Honor the King. "

After a pause she began to speak slowly and her voice was sweet and low. "When, the first night you came, you asked me if I knew Jesus Christ, I told you he was my life. That explains it all. It is very sweet of you to say the kind things that you have about me but they are not true. In and of herself, Marthe Everidge is nothing. The moment she tries to live her own life she utterly fails. If there is anything good about her life, it is only as she lets Christ live it for her. "

"I do not understand, " said Evadne with a puzzled look. "How is it possible for any one else to live our lives for us? "

"No one can but Jesus, " said Aunt Marthe with a smile. "He does the impossible. Take that exquisite fifteenth chapter of St. John and study it verse by verse. 'Abide in me, and I in you. ' There you have the two abidings. We are *in* Christ when we believe in him and are accepted through the merit of his blood and brought by adoption into the family of God, but not until he abides in our hearts shall our lives become as beautiful as God means them to be. Fruitfulness, — that is the cry everywhere. Men are calling for intellectual fruitfulness and mechanical fruitfulness, and are bending their energies to find the soil which will develop at once the best quality and greatest amount of fruit. Take a tree, to make my meaning clearer. The tree may abide in the soil and be just alive, but it is not until the essence of the soil enters into and abides in the tree, that it really grows and bears fruit. Growers of the finest varieties will show you plums that look as if they had been frosted with silver, and peaches with cheeks like the first blush of dawn. The 'fruits of the Spirit, ' have a wondrous bloom and an exquisite fragrance. "

"'Love, joy, peace, '" Evadne repeated slowly, "'long-suffering, gentleness, goodness, faith. ' But those belong to the Spirit, Aunt Marthe. "

"Yes, dear child, the Spirit of Jesus. The Spirit whom he sent to comfort his people when he took his bodily presence from the earth. The holy, indwelling presence which is to reveal the Christ to us and prepare us for the abiding of the Father and the Son. It is the beautiful mystery of the Trinity. "

"But we cannot have the Trinity abiding in our hearts! " said Evadne in an awestruck voice.

"The Bible teaches us so. "

"Not God, Aunt Marthe! "

"Jesus is God, little one. He said to the Jews, 'I and my Father are one. ' He says plainly, 'If any man love me, he will keep my word and my Father will love him, and we will come unto him and make our abode with him, ' and in another place we are told to be filled with the Spirit. It is three persons but three in one. "

"I do not understand, Aunt Marthe. "

"No, dear, we never shall, down here. Thomas wanted to do that and Christ said 'Blessed are they that have not seen and yet have believed. ' The Spirit is continually giving us deeper insight into the love of the Son, just as the Son came to make known to the world the wonderful love of the Father. "

"But 'be filled, '" said Evadne. "That looks as if we had something to do with it. "

"So we have, dear child. Suppose a man owned one hundred acres of land and gave you the right of way through it from one public road to another, —that would leave him many acres for his own use on which you have no right to trespass. I think we treat Jesus so. We are willing that he should have the right of way through our hearts, but we forget that every acre must be the King's property. There must be no rights reserved, no fenced corners. Jesus must be an absolute monarch. "

Mrs. Everidge spoke the last words softly and Evadne, looking at her uplifted face, shining now with the radiance which always filled it when she spoke of her Lord, saw again that glowing face which she had watched across the gate at Hollywood and heard the strange, exultant tones, 'He is my King! ' Ah, that was beautiful! That was what Aunt Marthe meant, and Pompey and Dyce.

"Jesus must come to abide, not merely as a transient guest, " Aunt Marthe continued in her low tones. "We must give him full control of our thought and will. We must hand him the keys of the citadel. We must give the all for the all, —that is only fair dealing. You see, dear child, Christ cannot fill us until we are willing to be emptied of self. He must have undivided possession. There is a vast amount of heartache, little one, in this old world, and self is at the bottom of it all, when we stop to analyze it. We want to be first, to be thought much of, to be loved best. No wonder that the selfless life seems impossible to most people. Think what a continuous self-sacrifice Christ's life was! So utterly alone and lonely among such uncongenial surroundings with people uncouth and totally foreign to his tastes. Ah! we don't realize it. We look at him doing the splendid things amidst the plaudits of the multitude, but think of the monotonous, weary days, going up and down the sun-baked streets surrounded by a crowd of noisy beggars full of all sorts of loathsome disease, and the humdrum life in Nazareth; and all the time the great heart aching with that ceaseless sorrow, —'His own received him not! ' Oh, what a waste of love! We do not realize that it is in these footsteps of his that we are called to follow. We are willing to do the great things, with the world looking on, but not for the loneliness and the pain! It seems a strange antithesis that Paul should count that as his highest glory, and yet how comparatively few seem counted worthy to enter with Christ into the shadow of that mysterious Gethsemane which lasted all his life. 'The fellowship of his sufferings. ' It must surely mean the privilege of getting very near his heart, just as human hearts grow closer in a common sorrow, — knit by pain. Yes, dear child, self must die: and it is a cruel death, — the death of the cross. But then comes the newness of life with its strange, sweet joy which the world's children do not know the taste of. How can they when it is 'the joy of the Lord, ' and they reject him? "

"You talk of the cross, Aunt Marthe, and other people talk of crosses. Aunt Kate and Isabelle are always talking about the sacrifices they have to make, and Mrs. Rivers carries a perfect bundle of crosses on her back. She is wealthy and has everything she wants, and yet she is always wailing, while Dyce is as happy as the day is long. Do the poor Christians always do the singing while the rich ones sigh? "

Mrs. Everidge smiled. "We make our crosses, dear child, when we put our wishes at right angles to God's will. When we only care to please him everything that he chooses for us seems just right. I have heard people speak as if it were a cross to mention the name of Christ. How could it be if they loved him? Do you find it a cross to talk to me about your father? People make a terrible mistake about this. The only cross we are commanded to carry is the cross of Christ."

"And what is that, Aunt Marthe? "

"Self renunciation, " said Aunt Marthe softly, "the secret of peace.

"Among all the pictures of the Madonna, " she continued after a pause, "the one I like best is where Mary is sitting, holding in her hands the crown of thorns; everything else had been wrenched from her grasp, but this they had no use for. What a legacy it was! As I look at it I see how he has gathered all the thorns of life and woven them into that kingly garland which is his glory. All the wealth of the Indies could not shed as dazzling a light as that thorny crown. Like the brave soldier who gathered into his own breast the spears of the enemy, Christ has taken the sting from our sorrows and made us more than conquerors over the wounds of earth. Surely he has tasted it all for us, —the baseness and coldness and ingratitude and treachery which have wrung human hearts all through the ages, — when Judas betrayed him, Peter denied him and they all forsook him and fled, do you suppose any other pain was comparable to that? Only our friends have the power to wound us, you know, and, 'he was wounded in the house of his friends. ' When people talk of the crucifixion they think of the nail-torn hands and pierced side, —I think of his heart! Oh, my Lord, how *could* they treat thee so! "

Evadne looked wistfully at the rapt face, irradiated now by the moonlight which was streaming in through the window. "*How* you love him, Aunt Marthe! "

"He is my all, " she answered simply. The girl stroked the hand which she still held in both her own. She is absolutely satisfied, she thought sorrowfully, she wants nothing that I can give her. And then "I love thee because thou hast first loved me,

> And purchased my pardon on Calvary's tree;
> I love thee for wearing the thorns on thy brow,
> If ever I loved thee, my Jesus, 'tis now."

## CHAPTER XV.

"Dear Aunt Marthe, " cried Evadne one afternoon, "what is love? "

"I will answer you in the words of one who for years has lived the love-life, " said Mrs. Everidge.

"'One must be himself infinite in knowledge to define it, infinite in comprehension to fathom it, infinite in love to appreciate it. Love is God in man, for "God is love, " and "every one that loveth is born of God; " but love is not merely veneration, nor respect, nor justice, nor passion, nor jealousy, nor sympathy, nor pity, nor self-gratification; to love something as our own is but a form of self-love; to love something in order to win it for ourselves is just a perpetration of the same mistake. ' Dr. Karl Gerok wrote, —'Love is the fundamental law of the world. First, as written in heaven, for God is love; second, as written on the cross, for Christ is love; third, as written in our hearts, for Christianity is love, ' And Drummond tells us that 'Love—is the rule for fulfilling all rules, the new commandment for keeping all the old commandments, Christ's one secret of the Christian life. ' And another writer says, —'You are a personality only as your heart lives, and the heart lives only as it loves. Love is all action, therefore the amount of your active love measures the size of your personal heart.'"

"Love has been defined as 'the desire to bless. ' That is like divine love, for there can be no self thought in God. God's love is over all and above all, but when our love responds to his, his love becomes to us a personal experience. Love can reach down when in loving trust we reach up. Love is like the seed. It manifests no life until it begins to grow. Like the seed it must rise out of the dark ground into the light of heaven, —out of self thought into God. God's love to us is like the sunlight. We can make it our own only by being in it, if we try to shut up the sunlight, we shut it out. We forget to do wrong when loving God. As we love God, the love we feel for him goes out to others. "

Evadne sighed. "You make it seem a wonderful thing to be a Christian, " she said.

"To be a Christian, little one, Andrew Murray tells us, 'just means to have Christ's love. ' Real love means giving always, of our best. "

God so loved that he gave his Son, the essence of himself. Jesus gave his life, not only in the final agony of the crucifixion, but all through the beautiful years of ministry in Nazareth and Galilee. There is a truer giving than of our temporal goods. Our friends, if they really love us, want most of all what we can give them of ourselves. It is those who give themselves to the world's need who come nearest to the divine pattern Christ has set for us to copy, and, if we truly love him, we shall want not his gifts but himself.

"People seek after holy living instead of perfect loving, they do not realize that we can be truly holy only as we love, for 'love is the great reality of the spiritual world. '"

Evadne laid her cheek caressingly against Mrs. Everidge's. "If it were only you, dear, how delightfully easy it would be, but do you suppose it is possible for me to love Aunt Kate and Isabelle? "

"Yes, dear child, with the love of God. "

"You can't imagine how I dread the idea of going back! " Evadne said with a sigh. "This summer has been like a lovely dream. How shall I endure the cold reality of my waking? "

"Where is your joy, little one? "

"Joy, Aunt Marthe! " exclaimed Evadne drearily, "why, I haven't got any apart from you. Just the mere thought of the separation makes my heart ache. "

"'The joy of the Lord, '" said Mrs. Everidge softly. "If Jesus Christ is able to fill heaven don't you think he ought to be able to fill earth too? The trouble is we turn away from him and pour our wealth of love at earthly shrines. Mary showed us the better way, —she *broke* the box, that every drop of the precious ointment might fall on his dear head. What is going to be the crowning satisfaction of heaven? Not that we shall meet our friends, as so many seem to think, but that we shall awake in *his* likeness and see *his* face. We shall be 'together, '—we have that comfort given us, but it will be 'together with the Lord. ' He is to be the centre of attraction and delight always. What an unfathomable mystery it must be to the angels that he is not so with us now! "

Evadne took a long, yearning look at the dear face, as if she would imprint it upon her memory forever. "He *is* with you, " she said softly. "*You* will never be a puzzle to the angels. "

\* \* \* \* \*

The time of her stay in Vernon drew near its close, and on the last day but one she went to say good-bye to Penelope Riggs. She found her sitting alone in the house, her mother having taken a fancy to have a sun bath. Her right hand was doubled up and she was rubbing it slowly up and down the palm of her left while she sang softly.

"Why, Penelope, what are you doing? " cried Evadne in amaze.

"Polishin', child. I learnt it long ago. One day I was that wore out I wouldn't have cared if the sky had fallen, —things had been goin' crooked, an' Mother hadn't slept well for a fortnight, an' I was that narvous an' tuckered out I thought I'd fly to pieces. There's an old hymn Mother's dredful fond of, —I don't remember how it goes now, but there's one line she keeps repeatin' over an' over till I feel ready to jump. It's this, —'What dyin' wurms we be. ' So, when she begun her wurm song that mornin' I just let fly. 'Ef I *am* a wurm, ' sez I, 'I ain't goin' ter be allers lookin' to see myself squirm! ' and with that I up and out of the house. My head was that tight inside I felt if I didn't git out that minit somethin' would snap. I went straight up to Mis' Everidge's. She's one of the people you see who always lives on a hill, inside an' out. When I got there I couldn't speak. My heart's weak at the best of times an' the weather in there was pretty stormy. I just dropped into the first chair an' she put her hands on my two shoulders an' sez she, —'You poor child! ' an' then she went away an' made me a syllabub. "

"'Look on the bright side, ' sez she in her cheery way when I had finished drinkin'. "

"'Sakes alive, Mis' Everidge, ' sez I, 'there isn't any bright side! '"

"'Then polish up the dark one, ' sez she, ez quick ez a flash. I've been tryin' to do it ever since. "

"You dear Penelope! " exclaimed Evadne, "I think you have! "

"It's all a wale, child, a wale o' tears, " old Mrs. Riggs complained as she bade her good-bye in the porch, but when she reached the turn in the road she heard Penelope singing, —

> "Thy way, not mine, O Lord,
>     However dark it be!
> Lead me by Thine own hand;
>     Choose out my path for me.
> I dare not choose my lot,
>     I would not if I might;
> Choose Thou for me, My God,
>     So shall I walk aright."

and Evadne knew that in the brave heart the voice of Christ had made the storm a calm.

"You dear Aunt Marthe! How am I ever going to thank you for all you have been to me; and what shall I do without you? " Evadne spoke the words wistfully. They were making the most of their last evening.

"Why, dear child, we can always be together in spirit. 'It is not distance in miles that separates people but distance in feeling. ' Emerson says, —'A man really lives where his thought is, ' so you can be in Vernon and I in Marlborough, —each of us held close in the hush of God's love, which 'in its breadth is a girdle that encompasses the globe and a mantle that enwraps it. '"

Evadne caught Mrs. Everidge's face between her hands and kissed it reverently. "I mean to devote my life to making other people happy, as you do, my saint, " she said.

\* \* \* \* \*

"Board! " The conductor's cry of warning smote the air and the train passengers made a final bustle of preparation for a start. Mrs. Everidge caught Evadne close in a last embrace.

"My precious little sister, I shall miss you every day! " Then she was gone, and Evadne, looking eagerly out of her window, saw the dear face, from which the tears had been swept away, smiling brightly at her from the platform.

"You magnificent Christian! " she cried. "You will give others the sunshine always! "

\* \* \* \* \*

The train steamed into the station at Marlborough and again Louis came forward to greet her with a look of admiration on his unusually animated face.

"Well done, Evadne! If the atmosphere of Vernon can work such transformation as this, it ought to be bottled up and sold at twenty dollars the dozen. You go away looking like a snow-wraith, and you return a blooming Hebe. "

Evadne laughed merrily. "Thank you. The atmosphere of Vernon has a wonderful power, " but it was not of the material ozone she was thinking as she spoke.

"I believe I will try it. My constitution is running down at the rate of an alarm clock. I must take my choice between a tonic and an early grave. Will you vouch for like good results in my case? "

Evadne shook her head. "I do not believe it would have the same effect upon everyone, " she said.

"Ah, then I shall be compelled to go to Europe. "

Evadne looked at him. "Yes, " she said, "I think Europe would suit you better. "

"That is unfortunate, —for the Judge's purse. How is Aunt Marthe? "

"She is well, " she answered with a sudden stillness in her voice. She could not trust herself to talk about this friend of hers to careless questioners. "How is Uncle Lawrence, and all the others? "

"The Judge is in his usual state of health, I fancy. We rarely meet except at the table and then you know personal questions are not considered in good form. The others are well, and Isabelle, having just returned from the metropolis of Fashion, is more than ever *au fait* in the usages of polite society. But none of them have improved like you, little coz. What has changed you so? "

And she answered softly, with a new light shining in her lovely eyes, —"Jesus Christ. "

\* \* \* \* \*

"You poor Evadne! " said Marion that evening, "what a dreary summer you must have had, shut away among those stupid mountains! If you could only have been with me, now. I never had such a lovely vacation in my life. There seemed to be some excitement every day; —picnics and boating parties and tennis matches and five o'clocks— —"

Evadne laughed. "You would better not let Uncle Horace know you are 'a votary of the deadly five o'clock' or he will empty his vials of denunciation upon your unlucky head.

"Oh, Aunt Kate, he sent you a large bundle of fraternal greetings. He says that, 'viewed through the glamour of memory, you impress him like an Alpine landscape, when the sun is rising, and he hopes the soft brilliance of prosperity will ever envelop you in its radiance and serve to enhance the beauty of your stately calm. '"

Mrs. Hildreth smiled, well pleased. "Horace is so poetical, " she said, "but all the Everidges are clever. What a shame it seems that a man of his talent should be forced by ill health to exist in a place where there is not a single soul capable of appreciating his rare qualities. Even his wife does not begin to understand him. It seems like casting pearls before swine. "

Evadne's eyes flashed and her lips pressed themselves tightly together, but Mrs. Hildreth's gaze was fixed intently upon the lace shawl she was knitting and Louis just then gave a sudden turn to the conversation.

She went up to her room with a great homesickness surging at her heart. Only last night all had been lightsome and happy, now the old darkness seemed to have settled down about her again. She knelt before her window and looked at the strip of sky which was all a Marlborough residence allowed her. "Happy stars! " she murmured, "for you are shining on Aunt Marthe! "

Far into the night she knelt there, until a great peace flooded her soul. She raised her hands towards the sparkling sky. "To make the world brighter, to make the world better, to lift the world nearer to God. Blessed Christ, that was thy mission. I will make it mine! "

The next morning Louis drew her aside. "So, little coz, you did not coincide with the lady mother's eulogium of our respected collateral last night? "

"Why, I said nothing! " cried Evadne in astonishment.

Louis laughed. "Have you never heard of eyes that speak and faces that tell tales? " he said. "I will just whisper a word of warning before you play havoc with your web of destiny. Don't let a suspicion of your dislike cross the lady mother's mind, for Uncle Horace is her beau-ideal of a man. I agree with you. I think he is a cad. "

## CHAPTER XVI.

"An invitation to Professor Joliette's, " and Isabelle tossed a gilt-edged card across the table to Marion; "Wednesday evening. It's not a very long invitation. What dress will you wear? "

"But you are engaged, Marion, " said Evadne; "Wednesday evening, you know. "

"Yes, " said Marion with a sigh, "it is awkward. I do wish they would choose some other night for prayer meeting. Wednesday seems such a favorite with everybody. "

"What a little prig you are getting to be, Evadne! " said Isabelle with a sneer. "Your only diversion seems to be prayer meeting and church. You are as bad as Aunt Marthe. "

"Aunt Marthe a prig! Oh, that is too funny! " and Evadne gave one of her low, sweet laughs. "Besides, does keeping one's engagements constitute a prig, Isabelle? You wouldn't think so if you were invited to the President's reception. "

"The President's reception! What does get into the child! I don't see much analogy between the two cases. No one considers prayer meeting a binding engagement, and I'm sure we go as often as we can. "

"Not binding! " echoed Evadne. "So Christ is not of as much importance as the President of the United States! "

"You do have such a way of putting things, Evadne! " said Marion thoughtfully. "I expect we had better refuse, Isabelle. "

"Refuse, —nonsense! " said Isabelle sharply. "You always meet the best people at the Joliettes', —besides, why should we run the risk of offending them? "

"Why should they run the risk of offending you, by choosing a night they know you cannot come? " asked Evadne.

"Ridiculous! What do they care about our church concerns? The Joliettes are foreigners. People in polite society do not give religion such an unpleasant prominence as you delight in, Evadne. For my part, I consider it very bad form. "

"Breakers ahead, Evadne, " said Louis with his cynical laugh. "Good form is Isabelle's fetich. Woe betide the unlucky wight who dares to hold an opinion of his own. "

"But, " said Evadne, the old puzzled look coming into her eyes, "I wish I could understand. Are Christians ashamed of the religion of Jesus? "

"That's about the amount of it, little coz. It is a sort of kedge anchor which they keep on board in case of danger. For my part I think it is better to sail clear. It is only an uncomfortable addition which spoils the trim of the ship. "

"Oh, Louis, don't! " exclaimed Marion with a sigh. "It is so hard to know what is right! Sometimes I wish I were a nun, shut up in a convent, and then I should have nothing else to do. "

"Doubtless the Lord would appreciate that sort of faithfulness, " said Louis gravely, "although I notice Christianity seems to be a sort of Sing-Sing arrangement with the majority. Everything is done under a sense of compulsion, and the air is lurid with trials and lamentations and woe. It is not an alluring life, and, in my opinion, the jolly old world shows its sense in steering clear of it. "

"Your irreverence is shocking, Louis, " said Isabelle severely, "and you are as much of an extremist as Evadne. No one could live such a life as you seem to expect. Religion has its proper place, of course, but I do not think it is wise to speak of the deep things of life on all occasions. "

"'I determined not to know anything among you, save Jesus Christ, and him crucified, '" quoted Evadne. "Was Paul mistaken then? "

"Certainly, my dear coz, " said Louis, as he prepared to leave the room. "The greatest men are subject to that infirmity. The only one who has never been mistaken is Isabelle. "

\* \* \* \* \*

"It is so provoking that we cannot have the carriage, " grumbled Isabelle, as, when Wednesday evening came, they waited for Louis in the dining-room. "At the Joliettes' of all places! I am sure I don't see, Papa, why you cannot insist upon Pompey's taking some other night off when we need him on Wednesdays. It is horribly awkward!"

Her father shook his head as he slowly peeled an orange. "Because I have given him my word, my dear. The only stipulation he made when I engaged him was that he should not be required to drive on Sundays and Wednesday evenings, and, when I hear people complaining about their surly, incapable coachmen, I consider it is a light price to pay. Pompey is as sober as a church and as pleasant-tempered in a rain storm as a water-spaniel, —no matter what hour of the night you keep him waiting; so it is the least we can do to let the poor fellow be sure of one evening to himself; " and the Judge opened his Times and began to study the money market.

"Well, " said Isabelle crossly. "I, for one, don't believe in allowing servants to have such cast-iron rules. It savors too much of socialism."

"Exactly so, " said Louis from the doorway, where he stood leisurely buttoning his gloves. "You will never pose as the goddess of liberty, *ma belle soeur*. It is a good thing that Lincoln got the Emancipation bill signed before you came into power, or dusky millions might still be weeping tears of blood. "

Isabelle swept past him with an indignant toss of her head, and the front door closed after the trio with a metallic clang.

"I don't wonder the poor child is annoyed, " said Mrs. Hildreth as she played with her grapes. "It is very embarrassing when people know that we keep a carriage; and the Joliettes are such sticklers in the matter of etiquette. It is a ridiculous fad of yours, Lawrence, to be so punctilious. "

"But, my dear, I gave him my word of honor! "

"What if you did? There are exceptions to every rule. "

"Not in the Hildreth code of honor, Kate. "

"Nonsense! What does a colored coachman understand about that! Why, Evadne, you cannot go to prayer meeting alone! " she exclaimed, as Evadne came into the room with her hat on. "Your uncle is busy and I am too tired, so there is no way for you to get home. "

"I am going to Dyce's church, Aunt Kate. Pompey will bring me home. "

"Among a lot of shouting negroes! You must be crazy, child! "

"Their souls are white, Aunt Kate, and there is no color line on the Rock of Ages. "

"Oh, well, tastes differ, " said her aunt carelessly, "but it is a strange fancy for Judge Hildreth's niece. Next thing you will suggest going to board with Pompey. "

"I might fare a good deal worse, " said Evadne with her soft laugh. "Dyce keeps her rooms like waxwork and she is a capital cook. "

"Really, Evadne, I am in despair! You have not an iota of proper pride. How are you going to maintain your position in society? "

"I don't believe I care to test the question, Aunt Kate; but I think my position will maintain itself. "

"Well said, Evadne, " said her uncle, looking up from his paper. "You will never forget you are a Hildreth, eh? "

"Higher than that, uncle, " said Evadne softly. "I am a sister of Jesus Christ. "

"I don't know what to make of the child, " said Mrs. Hildreth discontentedly, as the door closed behind her. "I believe she would rather associate with such people than with those of her own class. She has a bowing acquaintance with the most *outré* looking individuals I ever saw. I really don't think Dr. Jerome is wise setting young girls to visit in the German quarter. It doesn't hurt Marion, now. She only does it as a disagreeable duty and is immensely relieved when her round of visits is made for the month, but Evadne takes as much interest in them as if they were her relations. Next thing we know, she will be wanting to take up slum work. I hope she won't come to any harm down among those crazy blacks. They always seem to get possessed the moment they touch religion. "

"I do not think Evadne will ever come to any harm, " the Judge said slowly. "The Lord takes pretty good care of his own. "

His wife looked at him with a puzzled expression. "I fully intended going to prayer meeting myself to-night, " she said, "but it gets to be a great tax, —an evening out of every week, —and I do dread the night air so much. "

Mrs. Judge Hildreth dipped her jeweled fingers into the perfumed water of her finger glass and dried them on her silk-fringed napkin. "Oh, Lawrence, don't forget Judge Tracer's dinner to-morrow night. You will have to come home earlier than usual, for it is such a long drive, and it will never do to keep his mulligatawny waiting. And, by the way, I made a new engagement for you to-day. Mrs. General Leighton has invited us to join the Shakespearean Club which she is getting up. It is to be very select. Will meet at the different houses, you know, with a choice little supper at the close. She says the one she belonged to in Atlanta was a brilliant affair. She comes from one of Georgia's first families, you remember. "

"A Shakespearean Club! " and Judge Hildreth smiled incredulously. "Why, my dear, I never knew you and the immortal Will had much affinity for each other! "

"Oh, of course it is more for the prestige of the thing. Mrs. Leighton said the General assured her you would never find leisure for it, but I said I would promise for you. It is only one evening a week you know. She thinks we Americans retire far too early from the enjoyments of life in favor of our children, and I believe she is right. I certainly do not feel myself in the sere and yellow, " and Mrs. Judge Hildreth regarded herself complacently in the long mirror before which she stood. "You will manage to make the time, Lawrence? "

"What other answer but 'yes' can Petruchio make to 'the prettiest Kate in Christendom'? " replied the Judge, bowing gallantly to the face in the mirror as he came up and stood beside his wife. It was a handsome face but there was a hardness about it, and the lines around the mouth which bespoke an indomitable will, had deepened with the years.

"Only one evening a week, Kate, but you thought that too much of a tax just now. "

"How absurd you are, Lawrence! When shall I make you understand that there are sacrifices that must be made. We owe a duty to society. We cannot afford to let ourselves drop wholly out of the world. "

A little later Judge Hildreth entered his library with a heavy sigh. He had attained the ends he had striven for, he was respected alike in the church and the world, he held a high and lucrative position, he had a well appointed home, over which his handsome wife presided with dignity and grace, and yet, as he took his seat before his desk in the lofty room whose shelves were lined with gems of thought in fragrant, costly bindings, life seemed to have missed its sweetness to Lawrence Hildreth.

Evadne's words haunted him, and, like an accusing angel, the letter which still lay hidden under the mass of papers in the drawer which he never opened, seemed to look at him reproachfully.

"A sister of Jesus Christ. " Sisters and brothers lived together. Was it possible that Jesus Christ could be in this house, —this very room? The idea was appalling. He was familiar with the truism that God was everywhere, but he had never really believed it; and, as the years passed, he had found it convenient to remove him to a shadowy distance in space, less likely to interfere with modern business methods. Jesus Christ, enshrined in a far off glory among his angels, appealed to the decorum of his religious sentiment; but Jesus Christ, face to face, to be reckoned with in the practical details of honesty and fair dealing; that was a different matter. And this was the violation of a dead man's trust, who had put everything in his power because he had faith in him!

He saw again the young brother, handsome, easy-going to a fault, but with a sense of honor so fine as to shrink in indignation from the slightest breath of shame; read again the closing words of the farewell letter which he had read for the first time on the day now so long ago, which he would have given worlds to recall, and which, from out the shadowy recesses of eternity, laughed at his futile wish.

"So, my dear brother, " the letter ran, "I am giving you this responsibility as only a brother can. I have left Evadne absolutely untrammelled. I have no fear that my little girl will abuse the trust. She is wise beyond her years, with a sense of honor as keen as your own. "

The Judge's head sank upon his hands. It was for Evadne's good he had persuaded himself. She was too much of a child, —and now, — the letter could not be delivered. It meant disgrace and shame. It was his duty as a father to shield his family from that. How well he could picture Evadne's look of bewildered, incredulous surprise, and then the pain, tinged with scorn, which would creep into the clear eyes. And Jesus Christ! The Judge's head sank lower as he heard the voice which has rung down through the ages in scathing denunciation of all subterfuge and lies.

"Woe unto you... hypocrites! for ye tithe mint and anise and cummin, and have left undone the weightier matters of the law, justice and mercy and faith. "

"Woe unto you... hypocrites! for ye cleanse the outside of the cup and of the platter, but within they are full from extortion and excess."

"Woe unto you... hypocrites! for ye are like unto whited sepulchres which outwardly appear beautiful, but inwardly are full of dead men's bones. "

Lower and lower sank the Judge's head, until at last it rested upon the desk with a groan.

* * * * *

They were singing when Evadne reached the humble church which Dyce and Pompey called their spiritual home. The walls were white-washed and the seats were hard, for the "Disciples of Jesus" possessed but little of this world's goods. Two prayers followed, full of rich imagery and fervid passion, and then a young girl with a deep contralto voice began to sing, —

"Steal away, steal away,
    Steal away to Jesus!
Steal away, steal away home,
    We ain't got long to stay here."

The soft, deep notes of the weird melody ended in a burst of triumph, and Evadne bent her head while her tired heart thrilled with joy. When she looked up again Dyce was speaking.

"I've ben thinkin', friens, " she said, "that we don't get the sweetness of them words inter our hearts ez we should. We'se too much taken up wid de thought of de heavenly manshuns to 'member dat de King's chillen hez an inheritance on de earth. We'se not poor, lonesome people widout a home! De dear Christ promised, 'I will not leave youse orphans, I will come to youse, ' an' he who hez de Lord Jesus alongside, hez de best of company. 'Pears like we don't let our Father's message go any deeper dan de top of our heads. Ef we believes we'se preshus in his sight, —an' de Bible sez we is, — we'll hev no occashun fer gettin discouraged, fer de dear Lord's boun ter do de best fer his loved ones. Ef we'se keepin' company wid Jesus we'se no call ter want de worl's invitashuns, an ef we'se hidden away in Christ's heart dere's no need fer us ter be frettin' about de little worriments of earth. Satan don't hev no chance where Jesus is. Ef we'se tempted, friens, an' fall inter sin, it's 'cause we'se not livin' close ter de Saviour.

"I knows we allers tinks of a home as a place where dere is good times, an' dere don't seem much good times goin' for some of us in dis worl', but dere ain't no call fer us ter spec' ter be better off dan our Lord, an ef we'se feedin' on de Lord Jesus all de time we won't min' ef de worl's bread is scarce; de soul ain't dependin' on dem tings fer nourishmen' an' de Lord Jesus makes de hard bed easy an' de coarse food taste good.

"'Tain't good management fer us ter be allers groanin' in dis worl' while we 'spect ter be singin' de glory song up yonder. De best singers is dem dat's longes' trainin' an' I'se feared some of us'll find it drefful hard ter git up ter de proper concert pitch in heaven ef we sings nuthin but lamentashuns on earth. De dear Lord don't seem ter hev made any sort of pervishun for fault findin'. He 'low dere'll be trubble, but he tells us ter be of good cheer on account of hevin' him ter git de victry for us, an' ef we keep singin' all de time, dere ain't no time fer sighs. Let us keep a-whisperin' to our Father, my friens. It's

124

a beautiful worl' he's put us in, an' dere ain't no combine ter keep us back from enjoyin' de best tings in it. De sky belong ter us ez much as to de rich folks, an' de grass an' de trees an' de birds an' de flowers; de rollin rivers an' de mighty ocean belongs ter us. De only priviluge de rich folks hez is dat dey kin sail on deir billows while we hez ter stan' alongside, —but dey's powerfu' unhappy sometimes when dey hez so much ter look after, an' we kin enjoy lookin' at deir fine houses widout hevin' any of de care.

"We'se not payin' much complimen' ter Jesus, friens, when we 'low dat de good tings of dis worl' kin make people happier dan he kin, an' 'pears like we ought ter be 'shamed of ourselves. De Bible sez we'se ter 'live an' move an' hev our bein' in God, ' an' it don't 'pear becomin' when we hev such a home pervided fer us, ter be allers grumblin' 'cause we can't live in de brown stone fronts an' keep a kerridge. We don't begin ter understan' how ter live up ter our privilegus, friens, an' I'se bowed in shame as I tink how de dear Lord's heart must ache as he sees how little we'se appresheatin' his lovin' kindness. "

The tender, pleading voice ceased and then Dyce lifted her clasped hands, —"Oh, Lord Jesus, help us ter glorify thee before de worl'. Help us ter understan' an 'preciate de wonderful honor thou hez put upon us. Make us used ter dwellin' wid thee on de earth, so as we won't feel like strangers in heaven. Oh, blessed Jesus, by de remembrance of de thorn marks an' de nail prints an' de woun' in thy side forgive thy ungrateful chillen. We'se ben a' lookin' roun on de perishin' tings of earth fer our comfort, an' a' seekin' our homes in this worl'. Lord, help us ter find our real home in thee! Help us ter steal away ter Jesus, when de storm cloud hangs low and de billows roar about our heads. Dere's no shadows in de home thou makes, fer 'de light of de worl' is Jesus, ' an' ebery room is full of de sunshine of thy love. Dere's no harm kin cum to us ef we'se inside de fold, fer thou art de door, Lord Jesus; dere's no danger kin touch us ef we'se hidden in de cleft of de rock. Lord, make us abide in de secret place of de Almighty an' hoi' us close forever under de shadow of thy wing. "

Then the congregation dispersed to the humble homes, glorified now by the possibility of being made the dwelling-place of the King of kings.

## CHAPTER XVII.

It was intensely warm in the Marlborough Steel Works. Outdoors the sun beat fiercely upon the heads of toiling men and horses while the heat waves danced with a dazzling shimmer along the brick pavements. Indoors there was the steady thud of the engine, and the great hammers clanked and the belts swept through the air with a deafening whirr, while the workmen drew blackened hands across their grimy foreheads and John Randolph gave a sigh of longing for the cool forest chambers of Hollywood, as he leaned over to exchange a cheery word with Richard Trueman, beside whom he had been working for over a year and for whom he had come to entertain a strong feeling of affection.

Varied experiences had come to him since he had said good-by to his kind Quaker friends and started on his search for work. Monotonous days of wood piling in a lumber yard, long weeks of isolation among the giant trees of the forest, where no sound was to be heard except the whistle of the axes, as they cleaved the air, and the coarse jokes of the workmen, —then had come days when even odd jobs had been hailed with delight, and he had sat at the feet of the grim schoolmistress Necessity and learned how little man really needs to have to live. And then the Steel Works had opened again and he had forged his way up through the different departments to the responsible position he now held. His promotion had been rapid. The foreman had been quick to note the keen, intelligent interest and deft-handedness of this strangely alert new employé. He finished his work in the very best way that it was possible to do it, even though it took a little longer in the doing. Such workmen were not common at the Marlborough Steel Works. He put his heart into whatever he did. That was John Randolph's way. There was something about the work which pleased him. It gave him a feeling of triumph to watch the evolution of the crude chaos into the finished perfection, and see how through baptism of fire and flood the diverse particles emerged at length a beautifully tempered whole. He read as in an allegory the discipline which a soul needs to fit it for the kingdom, and so throughout the meshes of his daily toil John Randolph wove his parable.

When evening came he would stride cheerily along the dingy street to the house where he and his fellow-workman lodged, refresh himself with a hot bath, don what he called his dress suit, and after their simple meal and a frolic with little Dick, the motherless boy who was the joy of Richard Trueman's heart, he would settle down for a long evening of study among his cherished books. John Randolph never lost sight of the fact that he was to be a physician by and by.

*****

Somewhere in one of the great centers of the world's industry a workman had blundered. His conscience urged him to confess his mistake, while Satan whispered with a sneer, —"Yes, and get turned adrift for your pains, with a rating into the bargain! "

"Never mind if you do lose a week's wages, " conscience had pleaded, "your hands will be clean, " and the workman shrugged his shoulders with a muttered, "Pshaw! What do I care for that, so long as I don't git found out. I'll fix it so as no one kin tell it was me. "

The work was passed upon by the foreman and the Company's certificate attached. The man chuckled, "Hooray! Now that it's out from under old Daggett's eyes nobody'll ever be able to lay the blame on me! " and he had gone home whistling. He forgot God!

*****

The long, stifling day was drawing near its close. Half an hour more and the workmen would be free to rest. Only half an hour! Suddenly there was a sharp clicking sound, then a cry, and in an instant all was bustle and confusion at the Marlborough Steel Works. The great hammers hung suspended in mid-air, the whirling wheels were still, while the workmen, with faces showing pale beneath the grime, gathered hastily around a fallen comrade. Summoned by telephone the Company's surgeon was driving rapidly towards the Works, but his services would not be required.

An accident. No one knew just how it happened. There must have been a flaw, a defect in some part of the machinery. These things do happen. Somewhere there had been carelessness, dishonesty, and the price of it was—a life!

The dying man opened his eyes suddenly and looked full at John Randolph, who knelt beside him supporting his head on his arm.

"Little Dick, " he murmured.

"All right, Trueman, I will take care of him. "

"God bless you, John! " and with the fervid benediction, the breath ceased and the spirit flew away.

The body was prepared for the inquest, and through the gathering dusk John, strangely white and silent, entered the house he called home, gathered the fatherless boy into his arms and let him sob out his grief upon his shoulder.

\* \* \* \* \*

Some days after the funeral the Manager sent for John to come to his private office. He was a pleasant man and had taken a kindly interest in the capable young workman from the start.

"Well, Randolph, this is a terrible business of poor Trueman, " he said, as he pointed him to a chair. "Terrible! I can't get over it. A fine man and one of our best finishers too. Well, we can't do anything for him now, poor fellow, but he left a boy I think? "

"Yes, sir, " said John simply; "I have taken him to live with me. "

"Shake hands, Randolph! We *talk* about what ought to be done and you *do* it. Is that your usual mode of procedure? "

John laughed. "There was nothing else to do, " he said.

"H'm. Most fellows in your position would have thought it was the last thing possible. Have you any idea what it means to saddle yourself with a child like this? Whatever put such an idea into your head? "

"Jesus Christ, " answered John quietly.

"Well, well, you're a queer fellow, Randolph. But how are you going to make the wages spin out? A boy is 'a growing giant of wants whom the coat of Have is never large enough to cover. '"

"His father managed, so can I. " John's voice shook a little.

"His father! But he *was* his father, you see. That makes a mighty difference. Well, Randolph, I give you up. You are beyond me. "

John rose. "Was that all you wished to say to me, Mr. Branford? "

"Sit down, man! What the mischief are you in such a hurry for? It stands to reason the Company can't let you bear the brunt of this most deplorable occurrence, though I don't believe we could have found a better guardian for the poor little lad. But guardians expect to be paid for their trouble. What price do you set, Randolph? "

"I don't want any pay for obeying my Master, Mr. Branford. "

"Your Master, Randolph? " said the Manager with a puzzled stare.

"Yes, sir, Jesus Christ. "

"Upon my word, Randolph, you're a queer fellow! Well, if you don't want pay, I want some one with a head on his shoulders in this office. Any of the fellows in the outside office would be glad of the chance to get in here, but I want a man who understands what he is doing as well as I do myself. You have practical knowledge, Randolph, you're the man I want. I shall expect you to start in here tomorrow morning. The salary will be double your present wages. And, since you have constituted yourself guardian of the boy, I may as well tell you that the Company has decided to set aside a yearly sum for his maintenance and education.

"Now you can go, if you are in such a tremendous hurry, Randolph: only don't try any more of such toploftiness with me. It won't go down, you see; " and the Manager chuckled softly, as John, with broken thanks, left the room. "I rather think I got the better of him that time! " he said to himself.

## CHAPTER XVIII.

Judge Hildreth sat in his private office, immersed in anxious thought. Every day brought new difficulties to be wrestled with in connection with the multitudinous schemes which were making an old man of him while he was still in his prime. His hair was grey, his hands trembled, his eyes were bloodshot, and his face had the unhealthy pallor which accompanies intense nervous pressure and excitement.

He knew that it was so, and the knowledge did not tend to sweeten his disposition. He told himself again and again that he could not help it, —it was the force of circumstances and the curse of competition. Like the fly in the spider's parlor, he found himself inextricably enveloped in the silken maze of deceit which he had entered so blithely years ago. He had ceased to question bitterly whether the game was worth the candle. He told himself the Fates had decreed it, and the game had to be played out to the end, The principal thing now was to keep the pieces moving and prevent a checkmate, for that would mean ruin!

One of the office boys knocked at the door and presented a card, for into this *sanctum sanctorum* no one was permitted to enter unannounced. The card bore the name of the nominal president of the Consolidated Provident Savings Company, which was one of the numerous schemes that Judge Hildreth had on hand. It was not always wise to have his name appear. He believed in sleeping partnerships. As he explained it to himself, that gave one a free hand.

The Consolidated Provident Savings Company was a popular institution in Marlborough. There were conservative financiers who shook their heads and feared that its methods were not based on sound business principles and savored too much of wild-cat schemes and fraudulent speculations, but they were voted cranks by the majority, and the Consolidated Provident Savings Company grew and flourished. It paid large dividends, and its stockholders were duly impressed with the magnificence of its buildings and the grandiose tone of its officials.

Judge Hildreth frowned heavily as he read the name, and was about to deny himself to the visitor, but on second thought he curtly ordered the boy to show him in.

The man who obeyed the invitation bowed deferentially to his chief and then took a chair in front of him, with the table between. He was elaborately dressed, and the shiny silk hat which he deposited on the table looked aggressively prosperous. His manner betokened a man suddenly inflated with a sense of his own importance. His hair was sandy, and the thin moustache and beard failed to cover the pitifully weak lines of his mouth and chin.

"Good-morning, Peters. " The Judge nodded carelessly as he spoke, but he moved uneasily in his chair. Of late the sight of this man fretted him. It seemed as if he always saw him accompanied by a ghostly form. He tried to shake off the impression, and told himself angrily that he was falling into his dotage; but his memory would not yield. He saw again the pleading, trustful face of the man's mother as, years ago, she had besought him to do what he could for her son.

"Just make a man of him, like yourself, Judge Hildreth, " she had pleaded. "I will be more than satisfied then. I want my boy to be respected and to have a place in the world. Folks needn't know how hard his mother had to work. "

The Judge smiled grimly as he thought of her phrasing, —"a man like yourself. " She did not know how near to it he had come!

The boy had a surface smartness, and he had proved himself an apt scholar. The Judge had found him a willing tool in many of his deep laid schemes to get money for less than money's worth. But within the last few months there had been a change. A spark of manhood had asserted itself, and in the presence of his minion the Judge found himself upon the rack.

He was the first to speak. "I hope there is nothing out of the usual? " he said. "I intended coming over to the office before the meeting of directors took place. "

"It is the same old trouble about bonds, Judge Hildreth. There are not enough of them to go round. "

The Judge rubbed his hands in simulated pleasure. "Well, that shows good management, Peters, if the public are hungry for our stock. "

"The public are fools! " said the young man, hotly.

"Not at all, Peters. A discriminating public, you know, always chooses the best depositaries. " He chuckled softly. He had turned his eyes towards the window so as not to see the ghostly figure behind the young man's chair which had such a world of reproach in its face. "There is only one thing to do, Peters. We must water it a little, eh? "

"It seems to me we've been using the watering-pot rather too frequently. "

The Judge started. Had he detected a menace in the tone?

He temporized. His plans were not sufficiently matured yet. When they were he would crush this tool of his as surely and as carelessly as he would have crushed a fly.

"Nonsense, Peters! " he said pleasantly; "that is only a little clever financing to tide us over the hard places. Of course we will make it all good to the public—by and bye. "

"How? " The question rang out through the office like a pistol shot.

The Judge looked at the man before him in amaze. For once his face showed determination and an honest purpose.

"Will you tell me how we're going to do it? " he persisted with a strange vehemence. "I've been a fool, Judge Hildreth, a blamed, gigantic fool! I've let you hood wink me and lead me by the nose for years. I've done your dirty work for you and borne the credit of it, too; but I swear I'll not do it any longer. I thought at first—fool that I was—that everything you did was just the right thing to copy. My poor old mother told me you were the pattern I was to follow if I wanted to be an honorable man. An honorable man! Good heavens!

"Do you know where I've been these last months? I've been in hell, sir; in hell, I tell you! Every night I've dreamed of my mother and every day I've bamboozled the public and sold bonds that weren't worth the paper they were written on, and paid big dividends that were just some of their own money returned. And now you tell me to keep on watering the stock when you know we haven't a dollar put towards the 'Rest' and the money is just pouring out for expenses and directors' fees. There's barely enough left over to keep up the sham of dividends. You know it as well as I do. I've been an ass and an idiot, but I'm done with living a lie. Judge Hildreth, I came to tell you that if you don't do the square thing by these people who have trusted us, I'll expose you! "

His vehemence was tremendous and the words poured out in a torrent which never checked its flow. He had risen and in his excitement paced up and down the room. Now, overcome by his effort, he sank exhausted into a chair.

Judge Hildreth rose suddenly and locked the office door. When he turned again his face was not a pleasant sight to see.

"President Peters, " he said sternly, "this is not the age of heroics nor the place for them. In future I beg you to remember our relative positions. You seem to forget that I am the direct cause of your present prosperity, but that is an omission which men of your stamp are liable to make. I never expect gratitude from those whom I have befriended.

"But when you come to threats, that is another matter. You say you will expose me. To whom, if you please? *You* are the President of the Consolidated Company. Your name is associated with its business. Mine does not appear in any way, shape or form. You sign all papers, and it is you whom the public hold accountable for all moneys deposited in the institution. Any attempt which you might make to connect me with the enterprise would be futile, utterly futile. The public would not believe you, and you could not prove it in any court of law. "

The man, worn and spent with his emotion, lifted his head and looked at the Judge with dazed, lack-luster eyes.

"Not connected with the enterprise, " he repeated, "why, the whole thought of the thing came from you! and you have drawn thousands of dollars— —"

"I have simply given advice, " interrupted the Judge haughtily.

"Advice! " echoed the man, "and doesn't advice count in law? "

"If you can prove it; " said the Judge with a cold smile. "Do you ever remember having any of my opinions in writing, President Peters? The law takes cognizance only of black and white, you know. "

The victim writhed in his chair, as the trap in which he was caught revealed itself. Heavily his eyes searched Judge Hildreth's face for some sign of pity or relenting, but in vain.

"And if there should come a run on the funds? " he questioned dully.

"If there should come a run on the funds, " answered the Judge, "*you* would be underneath. "

The man's head fell forward upon the table, and the Judge, with a cruel smile, left the room.

* * * * *

Two office boys lingered in the handsome offices of the Consolidated Provident Savings Company after business hours were over.

"I tell you what it is, Bob, " said the eldest one, "I'm going to quit this concern. It's my opinion it's a rotten corporation; and I don't propose to ruin my standing with the commercial world. "

"Gee! " exclaimed the younger boy in delight. "You're a buster, Joe, and no mistake. The president himself couldn't have rolled that sentence off better, or that old piece of pomposity who conies to the secret meetings with the gold-headed cane. "

"That's Judge Hildreth. He's another deep one or I lose my guess. "

"Why, he's a No. I deacon in one of the uptown's swellest churches!"

"Guess he's a child of darkness in between times then, for I'll bet he does lots of underground work. I don't believe in this awfully private business. The other day, after old man Hildreth came, before the directors had their meeting, (he always does come just before that, to prime Peters, you know, ) what did he do but make Peters send for me to shut the transoms over his office doors, so that none of us fellows outside could hear what they were saying!

"I tell you I don't like the looks of things. This morning one of those heavy stockholders came in and wanted to take out all his money, and the president went white as a sheet. There's a flaw in the ready money account somewhere, I'll bet, and I'm going to leave before the bottom drops out of the concern. If you take my advice you'll follow."

The other boy laughed. "Bet your life I won't, then. Where'd you get such good pay, I'd like to know? I've had enough of grubbing along on $4.00 a week. No, sirree, I'll keep in tow with the deacon and get my share of all the stuff that's going, same as the other fellows do. "

"You won't do it long then, you mark my words. Did you see the president when he came into the office this morning? He looked as if he'd been gagged. I went into his office for something in a hurry afterwards and he was head over ears in Railway Time Tables. He jumped as if he'd been caught poaching. It's my belief he means to skip across the border. It's the only way for him to get out of the mess, unless he takes a dose of lead, you see.

"Well, here goes. I'm going to write my resignation with the president's best gold pen. You can do as you like, but it's slow and honest for me. "

## CHAPTER XIX.

Miss Diana Chillingworth was sitting in the old-fashioned porch of her old-fashioned house which opened into an old-fashioned garden in one of the suburbs of Marlborough, shelling peas. Everything about Miss Diana was old-fashioned and sweet. Her hair was dressed as she had been accustomed to wear it in her girlhood, and even the head mantua-maker of Marlborough, ardent worshiper at Fashion's shrine though she was, was forced to bow before her gentle individuality and confess that Miss Diana's taste was perfect.

She wore a morning dress of soft pearl grey, over which she had tied an apron of white lawn with a dainty ruffle of embroidery below its hem. The peas danced merrily against the sides of an old-fashioned china bowl. Miss Diana had an aesthetic repugnance to the use of tin utensils in the preparation of food.

Outside there were sweet lilies of the valley and violets and pansies, and the roses wafted long breaths of fragrance to her through the trellis work of the porch, while the morning glories hung their heads and blushed under the ardent kisses of the sun.

In the kitchen Unavella Cynthesia Crockett, her faithful and devoted "assistant" (Miss Crockett objected to the term servant upon democratic principles), moved cheerily, with a giant masterfulness which bespoke a successful initiation into the mysteries of the culinary art. All at once she shut the oven door, where three toothsome loaves were browning, and listened intently. Then she went out to interview Thomas, the butcher's boy, who came three times a week with supplies.

"The sweet-breads hez cum, Miss Di-an, " she said, appearing in the porch before her mistress.

"Well, Unavella, " said Miss Diana, with a pleasant smile, "you expected them, did you not? We ordered them, you know. They are very nutritious, I think. "

"Hum! There's some news cum along with 'em that ain't likely to prove ez nourishin'. Tummas sez the Provident Savings Company hez busted an' the president's vamoosed. "

"Dear me! I wish Thomas would not use such very forceful language, " said Miss Diana. "Do you think he finds it necessary? Being a butcher, you know? I hardly understand the words. Do you think you would find them defined in Webster? "

Unavella's eyes twinkled through her gloom. "I guess Tummas ain't got much use for dictionners, " she said. "He uses words that cums nearest to his feelin's. He's lost two hundred dollars, Tummas hez. "

"Dear me! How very grieved I am. But a dictionary, Unavella, is the basis of all education. Thomas ought to appreciate that. 'Busted, '" she repeated the word slowly, with an instinctive shrinking from its sound, "that is a vulgar corruption of the verb to burst; but 'vamoosed, ' I do not think I ever heard the term before. "

"Tummas says it means to show the under side of your shoe leather."

"The under side of your shoe leather, Unavella? " Miss Diana lifted her pretty shoe and held it up for inspection. "Do you see anything wrong with that? "

The faithful soul threw her apron over her head with a sob. "Oh, Miss Di-an! " she wailed, "it means the company's all a set of cheats, an' the biggest rogue of the lot hez lit out—run away—an' taken the money the Gin'rel left you along with him. "

## CHAPTER XX.

Miss Diana received the news in absolute silence. The brave daughter of a brave father, she would make no moan, but the sweetness seemed to have suddenly gone from the flowers and the light out of the sky.

Unavella looked at her in amazement. She was used to the stormy grief which finds vent in tears and groans. "It beats me how different folks takes things! " she ejaculated mentally. "Well, she'll need suthin' to keep her strength up all the more now she ain't got nuthin' to support her; " and, gathering peas and pods into her apron with a mighty sweep of her arm, she marched into her kitchen in a fever of sympathetic indignation and evolved a dinner which was a masterpiece of culinary skill.

Miss Diana forced herself to eat something. She knew if she did not, Unavella would be worried, and she possessed that peculiar regard for the feelings of others which would not allow her to consider her own.

"You are a wonderful cook, Unavella, " she said, with a pathetic cheerfulness which did not deceive her faithful handmaiden, who, as she confided afterwards to a friend, wuz weepin' bitter gall tears in her mind, though she kep' a calm front outside, for she wuzn't goin' ter be outdid in pluck by that little bit of sweetness. "I shall be able to give you a beautiful character. "

She lifted her hand with a deprecating gesture as Unavella was about to burst forth with a stormy denial.

"Not yet, please, Unavella; not just yet. Let me have time to think a little before you say anything. I feel rather shaken. The news was so very unexpected, you see, " she said with a shadowy smile, which Unavella averred "cut her heart clean in two. " "But everything is just right, Unavella, that happens to the Lord's children, you know. Things look a little misty now, but I shall see the sunlight again by and bye. In the meantime there is this delicious dinner. Someone ought to be reaping the benefit of it. Suppose you take it to poor Mrs. Dixon? She enjoys anything tasty so much and she cannot afford to buy dainties for herself. " Miss Diana would never learn the economy which is content to be comfortable while a neighbor is in need. "And, Unavella, if you please, you might say I am not receiving callers this afternoon. I am afraid it is not very hospitable, but I feel as if I must be alone. This has been rather a sudden shock to me. "

"You, you—angul! " exclaimed Unavella, as soon as she had regained the privacy of her kitchen, while a briny crystal of genuine affection rolled down her cheek and splashed unceremoniously into the gravy.

Up-stairs in her pretty chamber Miss Diana sat and thought. Ruin and starvation. Was that what it meant? She had seen the words in print often but they seemed different now. Ruin meant a giving up and going out, while the auctioneer's hammer smote upon one's heart with cruel blows, and one could not see to say farewell because one's eyes were full of tears. It would not be starvation—of the body. She must be thankful for that. The house and grounds were in a good locality and she had refused several handsome offers for them during the past year.

She caught her breath a little as she thought of the wide stretching field where her dainty Jersey was feeding, with its cluster of trees in one corner, under which a brook babbled joyously as it danced on its way to the river; the pretty barn with its pigeon-house where her snow-white fantails craned their imperious heads; the wide porch with its flower drapery, where she sat and read or worked with her pet spaniel at her feet, and where her friends loved to gather through the summer afternoons and chat over the early supper before they went back to the city's grime and stir.

Then in thought she entered the house. The room which had been her father's and the library which held his books. Could she sell those! She shivered, as in imagination she heard the careless inventory of the auctioneer. She had never attended an auction except once, and then she had hurried away, for it seemed to her the pictured faces were misty with tears and she fancied the draperies sighed, as they waved in the wind which swept through the gaping windows. There were the engravings which she loved and the pictures her father had brought with him from Europe, and the rare old china and her mother's silver service, and her store of delicate napery and household linen; while every table and chair had a story and the very walls of each room were dear. Had she been making idols of these things in her heart?

Miss Diana knelt beside the couch, comfortable as only old-fashioned couches know how to be. "Dear Christ, " she cried, "I am thy follower and I have gone shod with velvet while thy feet were travel-stained, and I have slept upon eider-down while thou hadst not where to lay thine head! "

She knelt on, motionless, until the twilight fell and the stars began to peep out in the sky. Then she went down-stairs and there was a strange, exalted look upon her sweet face.

"Unavella, " she cried softly, "I have found the sunlight, for I can say 'The Lord gave, and the Lord hath taken away; blessed be the name of the LORD. '"

"Oh, Miss Di-an! " wailed Unavella, "I b'lieve you're goin' ter die an' be an angul afore the moon changes! "

* * * * *

Miss Diana had been to see her lawyer and he had confirmed her decision. Her income was gone. With the exception of a couple of hundred dollars, coming to her from a different source, she was penniless. There was nothing left her but to sell.

When she reached home that night she looked very white and weary, but her smile was all the sweeter because of the unshed tears. Unavella had spread her supper in the porch. She ate but little, however. "I am sorry I cannot do more justice to your skill, Unavella, " she said with her gentle courtesy, "but I do not seem to feel hungry lately. "

"It's that li-yar! " muttered Unavella grimly, as she cleared the things away. "I never knowed a li-yar yit that didn't scare all the appetite away from a body. "

When her work was finished she came back to the porch where Miss Diana was sitting very still in the moonlight. "Miss Di-an! " she exclaimed impetuously, "don't you go fer to be thinkin' of sellin'! I've got a plan that beats the li-yar's all holler, ef he duz wear a wig."

"Sit down, Unavella, " said her mistress kindly, "and tell me what it is. "

"Well, I haven't said nuthin' to you before, 'cause I knowed it would only hurt you ef I wuz to let my feelin's loose about them thievin' rapscallions that dared to lay their cheatin' hands on the money the Gin'rel left ye; but I've been a thinkin'—stiddy—an' while you wuz comin' to your decision above I wuz comin' to mine below, an' now we'll toss 'em up fer luck, an' see which wins, ef you air willin'. "

Miss Diana smiled. "Well, Unavella. " she said.

"You decide ter leave yer hum, with all there is to it, an' me inter the bargain, an' go ter board with folks what don't know yer likins nor understan' yer feelin's, an' the end on it'll be that you'll jest wilt away wuss than a mornin' glory. I never did think folks sarved the Lord by dyin' afore their time comes.

"I decide to hev you keep yer hum, an' the things in it, an' me too. The hull on it is, Miss Di-an, *I won't be left*! " and Unavella buried her face in her hands and sobbed aloud.

"You dear Unavella! " Miss Diana laid her soft hand upon the toil-roughened ones. "If you only knew how I dread the thought of leaving you! But what else is there for me to do? "

"Gentlemen boarders, " was the terse reply.

"Gentlemen boarders! " echoed Miss Diana in bewilderment.

"Yes. You catch 'em, an' I'll cook'em. We'll begin with two ter see how they eat, an ef we find it don't cost too much ter fatten 'em up, we'll go inter the bizness reglar; " after making which cannibalistic proposition Unavella looked to her mistress for approval.

"Why, Unavella, " said Miss Diana, after the first shock of surprise was over, "I never even dreamed of such a thing! It might be possible, if you are willing to undertake it, it is very good of you. But we will not make any plans, Unavella, until I talk it over with the Lord. If his smile rests upon it, your kindly thought for me will succeed; if not, it would be sure to fail. I must have his approval first of all. "

She rose as she spoke and bade her a gentle good-night, and Unavella walked slowly back to her kitchen again. "Ef the angul Gabriel, " she soliloquized, "starts in ter searchin' the earth this night fer the Lord's chosen ones, there ain't no fear but what he'll cum ter this house, the fust thing. "

Up-stairs Miss Diana was whispering softly, as she looked up at the stars with a trustful smile. "Oh, my Father, if it is thy will that I should do this thing, thou wilt send me the right ones. "

CHAPTER XXI.

John Randolph did some hard thinking during the weeks which followed Richard Trueman's death. It was no light task which he had so cheerfully imposed upon himself. The boy was constitutionally delicate and fretted so constantly after his father that his health began to suffer, and it grew to be a very pale face which welcomed John with a smile when he returned from the office. The style of living was bad for him. He was alone all day, except for an occasional visit from the good-natured German woman who kept their rooms, and, although he was a voracious reader, the doctor had forbidden all thought of study for a year, even had there been a school near enough for him to attend, where John would have been willing to send him. He ought to be where the air was pure and the surroundings cheerful. John would have preferred to put up with the discomfort of his present quarters and lay by the addition to his salary towards the more speedy realization of his day-dream, but John Randolph had never found much time to think of himself; there were always so many other people in the world to be attended to.

"Dick, my boy, " he said cheerily one evening, after they had finished what he pronounced a sumptuous repast, "I have a presentiment that this month will witness a turning point in our career. I believe you and I are going to become suburbanites. "

The boy's sad eyes grew wide with wonder.

"What do you mean, John? "

"Well you see, Dick True, it is this way. As soon as I get my degree — earn the right to put M. D. after my name, you know, —I am going to take two rubber bags, fill one with sunshine and one with pure air, full of the scent of rose leaves and clover and strawberries—ah, Dick, you'd like to smell that, wouldn't you? —and carry one in each pocket; then, when my patients come to me for advice, the first dose I shall give them will be out of my rubber bags, and in six cases out of ten I believe they'll get better without any drug at all. You see, Dick True, the trouble is, our Father has given us a whole world full of air and sunlight to be happy in, and we poison the air with smoke and shut ourselves away from the sunshine in boxes of brick and mortar, only letting a stray beam come in occasionally through slits in the walls which we call windows. It's no wonder we are such poor, miserable concerns. You can't fancy an Indian suffering from nervous prostration, can you, Dick? and it doesn't strike you as probable that Robinson Crusoe had any predisposition to lung trouble? So you see, Dick True, as it is a poor doctor who is afraid of his own medicine, I am going to prescribe it first of all for ourselves, and we will go where unadulterated oxygen may be had for the smelling, and we can draw in sunshine with every breath. "

The pale face brightened.

"Oh, that will be lovely! I do get so tired of these old streets. But John, —"

"Well, Dick? "

"Why do you keep calling me Dick True all the time? "

John laughed. "Just to remind you that you must be a true boy before you can really be a True-man, Dick. I want you to be in the best company. Jesus Christ is the truth, you know, Dick. "

"Jesus Christ, " repeated the boy thoughtfully. "I wish I knew him, John, as well as you do. "

"If you love, you will know, " said John, the light which the boy loved to watch creeping into his eyes. "He is the best friend we will ever have, Dick, you and I. "

He opened several papers as he spoke and ran his eyes over the advertising columns. "H'm, I don't like the sound of these, " he said, "they promise too much. Hot and cold water baths and gas and the advantages of a private family and city privileges. Everyone seems to keep the 'best table in the city. ' That's curious, isn't it, Dick? And nearly everyone has the most convenient location. Dick, my boy, it's one thing to say we are going to do a thing, it's another thing to do it. I expect this suburban question is going to be a puzzle to you and me. "

And so it proved. Day after day John searched the papers in vain, until it seemed as if a suburban residence was the one thing in life unattainable. But the long lane of disappointment had its turning at length, and he hurried home to Dick, paper in hand.

"Dick, Dick True, we've found it at last! Listen:

"Two gentlemen can be pleasantly accommodated at 'The Willows. ' Address Miss Chillingworth, University P. O. Box 123.

"The University Post Office is just near the College, you know, Dick, so it is in a good location. Two gentlemen—that means you and me, Dick; and 'The Willows' means running brooks, or ought to, if they are any sort of respectable trees. "

The boy clapped his hands. "When can we go, John? "

John laughed. "Not so fast, Dick. There may be other gentlemen in Marlborough on the lookout for a suburban residence. I addressed Miss Chillingworth on paper this morning, telling her I should give myself the pleasure of addressing her in person to-morrow. It is a half holiday, you know, Dick. I like the ring of this advertisement. There is no fuss and feathers about it. She doesn't offer city privileges and promise ice cream with every meal. "

"But, John, " said the boy, ruefully, "we're not gentlemen. You don't wear a silk hat, you know, and I have no white shirts—nothing but these paper fronts. I hate paper fronts! They're such shams!

"Oh, ho! Dick, so you're pining for frills, eh? Well, if it will make you feel more comfortable, we'll go down to Stewart's and get fitted out to your satisfaction. But don't forget that you can be a gentleman in homespun as well as broadcloth, Dick. Real diamonds don't need to borrow any luster from their setting; only the paste do that. "

The next afternoon John strode along in the direction of 'The Willows' to the accompaniment of a merry whistle. It did him good to get out into the open country once more, and he felt sure it would be worth a king's ransom to Dick; but when he came in sight of the house he hesitated. There must be some mistake. This was not the sort of house to open its doors to boarders. "Poor Dick! " he soliloquized, "no wonder you felt a premonitory sense of the fitness of frills! Well, I'll go and inquire. They can only say 'No, ' and that won't annihilate me. "

He was ushered into Miss Diana's presence, and on the instant forgot everything but Miss Diana herself. Before he realized what he was doing he had explained the reason of his seeking a suburban home, and, drawn on by her gentle sympathy, was telling her the story of his life. Miss Diana had a way of compelling confidence, and the people who gave it to her never afterwards regretted the gift. With the straightforwardness which was a part of his nature he told his story. It never occurred to him that there was anything peculiar about it, yet when he had finished there were tears in his listener's eyes.

When at length he rose to go, everything was settled between them. John's eyes wandered round the room and then rested again with a curious sense of pleasure upon Miss Diana's face.

"I cannot begin to thank you, " he said, gratefully, "for allowing us to come here. I never dared to hope that my poor little Dick would have such an education as this home will be to him, but I feel sure you will learn to like Dick True. "

Miss Diana held out her hand, with a smile. "I think I shall like you as well as Dick, " she said.

\* \* \* \* \*

Weeks and months flew past and the household at 'The Willows' was a very happy one. Unavella was in great glee over the success of her scheme.

"I used ter think, " she confided to her bosom friend, "thet boarders wuz good fer nuthin' 'cept ter be an aggervation an' a plague; but I couldn't think o' nuthin' else ter do, an' I made up my mind I'd ruther put up with 'em than lose Miss Di-an, even ef their antics did make me gray-headed afore the year wuz out. But I needn't hev worritted. Two sech obligin' young fellers I never did see, an' never expect ter agin in this world. They don't never seem comfortable 'cept when they're helpin' a body. An' Mr. John's whistle ez enuff ter put sunshine inter the Deluge! I used ter think we wuz ez happy ez birds—Miss Di-an an' me—but I declare the house seems lonesum now when he leaves in the mornin'. He's alluz at it, whistle, whistle, whistle. 'Tain't none o' them screechin' whistles that takes the top off of your head an' leaves the inside a' hummin', but it's jest as soft an' sweet an' low! Sometimes I think he's prayin', it's that lovely. It's my belief it puts Miss Di-an in mind o' someone, fer she jest sets in the porch, when he's a' tinkerin' round in the evenings or dig-gin' in the gardin—he's never satisfied unless everything's jest kep spick an' span—an' there's the sweetest smile on her face, an' the dreamy look in her eyes thet folks' eyes don't never hev 'cept when they're episodin' with their past.

"An' the way they foller her about an' treat her jest ez ef she wuz a princess! I declare, it makes my heart warm. The young one called her his little mother the other night, an' Mr. John sez, sez he, 'Ye couldn't hev a sweeter, Dick, nor a dearer. ' He makes me think of one o' them folks in poetry what wuz alluz a' ridin' round with banners an' a spear. "

"A knight? " suggested her friend, who had just indulged a literary taste by purchasing a paper covered edition of Sir Walter Scott.

"Yes, that's what I mean. An' I sez to myself, —'ef they wuz like he is, an' wuz ez plenty in the Middle Ages ez they make 'em out ter be, then it's a pity we wuzn't back right in the center uv 'em, ' sez I. "

"Lady Di! Lady Di! " and little Dick came hurrying into the library where Miss Diana was sitting in the gloaming. "John wants you to come out and see if you like the new flowers he is planting. He says I must be sure to put your shawl on, for the dew is falling. "

Miss Diana's eyes grew misty as her little cavalier adjusted her wrap. "Why do you give me that name, Dick? " she asked. Only one other had ever given it to her before, in the long ago.

"What? Lady Di? " answered the boy. "Oh, we always call you that, John and I. Our Lady Di. John says you make him think of the elect lady, in the Bible, you know. "

And Miss Diana, as she passed the shelves, laid her hand caressingly upon the beloved books with a happy smile. God had sent her the right ones!

## CHAPTER XXII.

Marion entered Evadne's room one glorious winter's morning and threw herself on the lounge beside her cousin with a sigh.

"I don't see how you do it! " she exclaimed.

"Do what? " asked Evadne.

"Why, keep so pleasant with Isabelle. She works me up to the last pitch of endurance, until I feel sometimes as if I should go wild. It is no use saying anything, Mamma always takes her side, you know, but she does aggravate me so! Even her movements irritate me, — just the way she shakes her head and curls her lip, —she is so self-satisfied. She thinks no one else knows anything. It must be a puzzle to her how the world ever got along before she came into it, and what it will do when she leaves it is a mystery! "

"She is good discipline. "

Marion gave her an impetuous hug. "You dear Evadne! I believe you take us all as that! But I don't think the rest of us can be quite as trying as Isabelle. She does seem to delight in saying such horrid things. She was abominably rude to you this morning at breakfast and yet you were just as polite as ever. I couldn't have done it. I should have sulked for a week. I know you feel it, for I see your lips quiver—you are as susceptible to a rude touch as a sensitive plant— but it is beautiful to be able to keep sweet outside. "

"You mean to be *kept*, Marion, " said Evadne softly, "by the power of God. I have no strength of my own. "

Marion sighed dismally. "Oh, dear! I don't know what I mean, except that I'm a failure. It is no wonder Louis thinks Christianity is a humbug, though he must confess there is something in it when he looks at you. You are so different, Evadne! I should think Isabelle would be ashamed of herself, for I believe half the time she says things on purpose to provoke you. She doesn't seem to get much comfort out of it any way. I never saw such a discontented mortal. Don't you think it is wicked for people to grumble the way she does, Evadne? It is growing on her, too. She finds fault with everything.

Even the snow came in for a share of her disapprobation this morning, because it would spoil the skating, as if the Lord had no other plans to further than just to give her an afternoon's amusement! She is *so* self-centered! "

Evadne looked out at the street where the fresh fallen snow had spread a dazzling carpet of virgin white. "He is going to let me give an afternoon's amusement to Gretchen and little Hans, " she said. "Uncle Lawrence has promised me the sleigh and I am going to take them to the Park. Won't it be beautiful to see them enjoy! Hans has never seen the trees after a snowstorm. "

"That is you all over, Evadne. It is always other people's pleasure, while I think of my own! Oh, dear! I seem to do nothing but get savage and then sigh over it. I know it is dreadful to talk about my own sister as I have been doing—they say you ought to hide the faults of your relations—but it is only to you, you know. Do you suppose there is any hope for me, Evadne? " she asked disconsolately.

Evadne drew her head down until it was on a level with her own. "Let Christ teach you to love, dear, " she whispered, "Then, 'charity will cover the multitude of sins. '" She opened the book she had been reading when her cousin entered and took from it a newspaper clipping. "Read this, " she said. "Aunt Marthe sent it in her last letter. If we follow its teachings I think all the fret and worry will go out of our lives for good. "

And Marion read, —"To step out of self-life into Christ-life, to lie still and let him lift you out of it, to fold your hands close and hide your face upon the hem of his robe, to let him lay his cooling, soothing, healing hands upon your soul, and draw all the hurry and fever away, to realize that you are not a mighty messenger, an important worker of his, full of care and responsibility, but only a little child with a Father's gentle bidding to heed and fulfil, to lay your busy plans and ambitions confidently in his hands, as the child brings its broken toys at its mother's call; to serve him by waiting, to praise him by saying 'Holy, holy, holy, ' a single note of praise, as do the seraphim of the heavens if that be his will, to cease to live in self and for self and to live in him and for him, to love his honor more than your own, to be a clear and facile medium for his life-tide to shine and glow through—this is consecration and this is rest. "

When, some hours later, Evadne went down-stairs to luncheon, she felt strangely happy. Marion had said Louis must confess there was something in Christianity when he looked at her. That was what she longed to do—to prove to him the reality of the religion of Jesus. And that afternoon she was going to give such a pleasure to Gretchen and little Hans. It was beautiful to be able to give pleasure to people. She could just fancy how Gretchen's eyes would glisten as she talked to her in her mother tongue, while little Hans' shyness would vanish under the genial influence of Pompey's sympathetic companionship, and he would clap his hands with delight as Brutus and Caesar drew them under the arches of evergreen beauty, bending low beneath their ermine robes, while the silver bells broke the hush of silence which dwelt among the forest halls with a subdued melody and then rang out joyously as they emerged into the open, where the sun shone bright and clothed denuded twigs and trees in the bewitching beauty of a silver thaw. It would always seem to little Hans like a dream of fairyland and she would be remembered as his fairy godmother. It was a pleasant role—that of a fairy godmother.

She started, for Louis was saying carelessly to the servant, —"Tell Pompey to have the sleigh ready by half-past two, sharp. "

"Why, Louis! " she spoke as if in a dream, "I am going to have the sleigh this afternoon. "

"That is unfortunate, coz, " said Louis lightly, "as probably we are going in different directions. "

"I am going to the Park, " stammered Evadne, "with little Hans and Gretchen. "

"Exactly, and I to the Club grounds. Diametrically opposite, you see."

"But Uncle Lawrence promised me. He said no one wanted the sleigh this afternoon. "

"The Judge should not allow himself to jump at such hasty conclusions before hearing the decision of the Foreman of the Jury. It is an unwise procedure for his Lordship. "

"But poor little Hans will be so disappointed! He has been looking forward to it for weeks. "

"Disappointed! My dear coz, the placid Teutonic mind is impervious to anything so unphilosophical. It will teach him the truth of the adage that 'there is many a slip 'twixt the cup and the lip, ' and in the future he will not be so foolish as to look forward to anything. "

Evadne's lips quivered. "You are cruel, " she said, "to shut out the sunlight from a poor little crippled child! "

"My dear coz, I give you my word of honor, I am sorry. But there is nothing to make a fuss about. Any other day will suit your little beggar just as well. I promised some of the fellows to drive them out and a Hildreth cannot break his word, you know. "

"You have made me break mine, " said Evadne sadly, as she passed him to go upstairs.

"Ah, you are a woman, " said Louis coolly, "that alters everything. "

Did it alter everything? Evadne was pacing her floor with flashing eyes. "Was there one rule of honor for Louis, another for herself? No! no! no! How perfectly hateful he is! " and she stamped her foot with sudden passion. "I despise him! "

Suddenly she fell on her knees beside the lounge and cowered among its cushions, while the eyes of the Christ, reproachfully tender, seemed to pierce her very soul. "Love your enemies, bless them that curse you, do good to them that hate you, and pray for them which despitefully use you and persecute you, —that ye may be the children of your Father in heaven, for he maketh his sun to rise on the evil and on the good, and sendeth rain on the just and on the unjust. "

His sorrowful tones seemed to crush her into the earth. Was this her Christ-likeness? And she had let Marion say she was better than them all! What if she or Louis were to see her now? He would say again, as he had said before, "There is not much of the 'meek and lowly' in evidence at present. " "And he would be right, " she cried remorsefully. "Oh, Jesus Christ, is this the way I am following thee! "

"You do right to feel annoyed, " argued self. "It hurts you to disappoint Gretchen and Hans. "

"It is your own pride that is hurt, " answered her inexorable conscience. "You wanted to pose as a Lady Bountiful. It is humiliating to let these poor people see that you are of no consequence in your uncle's house. Christ kept no carriage. It is not what you do but what you are, that proves your kinship with the Lord. "

It was a very humble Evadne who, late in the afternoon, walked slowly towards the German quarter. "I am very sorry, " she said quietly, when she had reached the spotless rooms where Gretchen made a home for her crippled brother, "my cousin had made arrangements to use the sleigh this afternoon, so we could not have our drive. I am *very* sorry. "

And they put their own disappointment out of sight, these kindly German folk, and tried to make her think they cared as little as if they were used to driving every day.

"Did you notice, Gretchen, " said Hans, after Evadne had left them, "how sweet our Fraulein was this afternoon? But her eyes looked as if she had been crying. Do you suppose she had? "

"I think, Hans, " said Gretchen slowly, "our Fraulein is learning to dwell where God wipes all the tears away. "

"Are your eyes no better, Frau Himmel? " Evadne was saying as she shook hands with another friend who was patiently learning the bitter truth that she would never be able to see her beloved Fatherland again. "Are the doctors quite sure that nothing can be done? "

"Quite sure, Fraulein Hildreth, " answered the woman with a smile, "but there is one glorious hope they can't take from me. "

"A hope, Frau Himmel, when you are blind! What can it be? "

"This, dear Fraulein, " and the look on the patient face was beautiful to see. "'Thine eyes shall see the King in his beauty; they shall behold the land that is very far off. '"

And Evadne, walking homeward, repeated the words which she had read that morning with but a dim perception of their meaning. 'If limitation is power that shall be, if calamities, opposition and weights are wings and means—we are reconciled. '

## CHAPTER XXIII.

"Uncle Lawrence, with your permission, I am going to study to be a nurse. "

Judge Hildreth started. So light had been the footsteps and so deeply had he been absorbed in thought, he had not heard his niece enter the library and cross the room until she stood before his desk. Very fair was the picture which his eyes rested upon. What made his brows contract as if something hurt him in the sight?

Evadne Hildreth was in all the sweetness of her young womanhood. She was not beautiful, not even pretty, Isabelle said, but there was a strange fascination about her earnest face, and the wonderful grey eyes possessed a charm that was all their own. She had graduated with honors. Now she stood upon the threshold of the unknown, holding her life in her hands.

Louis was traveling in Europe. Isabelle and Marion were at a fashionable French Conservatory, for the perfecting of their Parisian accent. Evadne was alone. She had chosen to have it so. She wanted to follow up a special course in physiology which was her favorite study.

"A nurse, Evadne! My dear, you are beside yourself. 'Much learning hath made you mad. '"

"'I am not mad, most noble Festus, but speak the words of truth and soberness. ' I feel called to do this thing. "

"Who has called you, pray? We do not deal in supernaturalisms in this prosaic century. "

The lovely eyes glowed. "Jesus Christ. " What an exultant ring there was in her voice, and how tenderly she lingered over the name!

"Jesus Christ! " Judge Hildreth repeated the words in an awestruck tone. Did she see him cower in his chair? It must have been an optical illusion. The storm outside was making the house shiver and the lights dance.

"You must consult your aunt, " he said in a changed voice. She noticed with a pang how old and careworn he looked.

"Kate, " he called, as just then he heard his wife's step in the hall, "come here. "

"What do you wish, Lawrence? " and there was a soft *frou frou* of silken draperies as Mrs. Hildreth's dress swept over the carpet.

"Evadne wishes to become a nurse. "

"Are you crazy? " There was a steely glitter in Mrs. Hildreth's eyes, and her tone fell cold and measured through the room.

"She says not, " said the Judge with a feeble smile.

"Why should you think so, Aunt Kate? " asked Evadne gently. "Look how the world honors Florence Nightingale, and think how many splendid women have followed her example. "

"To earn your own living by the labor of your hands. A Hildreth! "

"All the people who amount to anything in the world have to work, Aunt Kate. There is nothing degrading in it. "

"Just try it and you will soon find out your mistake. If you do this thing you will be ostracized by the world. People make a great talk about the dignity of labor, but a girl who works has no footing in polite society. "

Evadne's sweet laugh fell softly through the silence. "I don't believe I have any time for society, Aunt Kate. Life seems too real to be frittered away over afternoon teas. "

"Are you mad, Lawrence, to let her take this step? Think of the Hildreth honor! "

Again Judge Hildreth laughed—that strange, feeble laugh. "Evadne is of age, Kate; she must do as she thinks right. As to the rest—I think the less we say about the Hildreth honor now the better for us all. "

He was alone. Mrs. Hildreth had swept away in a storm of wrath. Evadne had followed her, leaving a soft kiss upon his brow. He lifted his hand to the place her lips had touched—he felt as if he had been stung—but there was no outward wound.

The Hildreth honor! The letters in the drawer at his side seemed to confront him with scorn blazing from every page. He put forth his hand with a sudden determination. He would crush their impertinent obtrusiveness under his heel; then, when their damaging evidence was buried in the dust of oblivion, he would be safe and fret! Evadne knew her father had left her something. He would make special mention of it in his will—a Trust fund—enough to yield her maintenance and the paltry pin money which was all the allowance he had ever seen his way clear to make his brother's child. It was not his fault, he argued—he had meant to do right—but gilt-edged securities were as waste, paper in the unprecedented monetary depression which was sweeping stronger men than himself to the verge of ruin. He could not foresee such a crisis. Even the Solons of Wall Street had not anticipated it. It was not his fault. He had meant to make all right in a few years. What was that they said was paved with good intentions? He could not remember. He seemed to have strange fits of forgetfulness lately. He must see that everything was put in proper shape in the event of his death. People died suddenly sometimes. One never knew.

It would be safer to make re-investments. Yes, that was a good thought. He wondered it had never occurred to him before. His wisest plan was to have all moneys and securities in his own name. It would make it so much easier for the executors. It was not fair to burden any one with a business so involved as his was now. Of course he would make a mental note of just how much belonged to his brother. It would not be safe to put it in black and white— executors had such an unpleasant habit of going over one's private papers—but he would be sure to remember, and, if he ever got out of this bog, as he expected to do of course shortly, he would give Evadne back her own. It would leave him badly crippled for funds, but one must expect to make sacrifices for the sake of principle. Then, when these letters were destroyed, they would have no clue— he frowned. What an unfortunate word for him to use! A clue wag suggestive of criminality. What possible connection could there be between Judge Hildreth and that?

He fitted the key in the lock and turned it, then his hand fell by his side. No, no, he had not come to that—yet. He had always held that tampering with the mails evinced the blackest turpitude. He was an honorable gentleman. He started. What was that? A long, low, blood-curdling laugh, as if a dozen mocking fiends stood at his elbow, —or was it just the shrieking of the wind among the gables? It was a wild night. The rain dashed against the window panes in sheets of vengeful fury, and the howling of the storm made him shudder as he thought of the ships at sea. Now and then a loose slate fell from an adjoining roof and was shivered into atoms upon the pavement, while the wind swept along the street and lashed the branches of the trees into a panic of helpless, quivering rage. Could any poor beggars be without a shelter on such a night as this? How did such people live?

He caught himself dozing. He felt strangely drowsy. He straightened himself resolutely in his chair and drew a package of stock certificates from one of the secret drawers of the desk. He would see about selling the stock and making re-investments to-morrow.

It must be done, —to save the Hildreth honor.

CHAPTER XXIV.

Once more the Hildreth household was united, if such a thing as union could be possible, among so many diverse elements.

Isabelle's chill hauteur had increased with the years and a peevish discontent was carving indelible lines upon her face which was rapidly losing its delicate contour and bloom. Marion's pink and white beauty was at its zenith, and the social attentions she was beginning to receive only served to render her elder sister more than ever irritable and envious. Louis was his old nonchalant self, careless and listless, with an ever deepening expression of *ennui* which was pitiful in one so young. His European travels had not improved him, in Evadne's opinion.

She saw but little of her cousins. They passed their days in pleasure, she in work; but Marion, in her rare moments of reflection, as she thought of the strangely peaceful face of the young nurse, wondered sadly whether Evadne had not chosen the better part after all.

"Oh, Louis! " she cried one morning, and her voice was full of pain, "how you are wasting this beautiful life that God has given you! "

Louis stretched himself lazily in his arm-chair and clasped his hands behind his head. "Thanks for your high opinion, coz. Of what special crime do I stand accused before the bar of your judgment? "

"Oh, it is nothing special, but you are just frittering away the days that might be filled with such noble work, and you have nothing to show for them but—smoke! " She swept her hand through the filmy cloud which Louis just then blew into the air, with a gesture of disdain. "Now you will think I am preaching, but indeed, indeed I am not, only, it hurts me so! "

Louis laughed and threw away his cigar. "No, I will not charge you with belonging to the cloth, but I confess I should like you better if you had not entrenched yourself behind such a high wall of prejudice against all the good things of this life. You are too narrow, Evadne. "

Evadne folded her hands together as if she were holding a strange, sweet comfort against her heart. "The Jews said the same about Jesus Christ, " she said, "why should the servant be judged more kindly than her Lord? "

"But there is no harm in these things, Evadne. "

"There is no good in them. Life is so real, Louis! "

"Well, I own I am a light weight in the race. But I assure you such people are needed to balance matters. If every one was in such deadly earnest as you, Evadne, the old world would go to pieces. "

"But, Louis, it is dreadful to have no purpose in life! "

"The Judge has enough of that for us both, " said Louis carelessly. "Why should I choke my brains with musty law when his are charged to repletion? "

"Think how it would please Uncle Lawrence! " urged Evadne.

"True, " said Louis gravely, "but that is an argument which will bear future consideration. "

"Oh, Louis, " and Evadne's voice was choked with tears, "the time may come when you would give the whole world to be able to please your father! "

"But, Evadne, " said Louis gently, "a man must have freedom of choice in his vocation. My father chose the law for his profession, why should he rebel if I choose dilettanteism? "

"Because it is no profession at all. I am sure he would not mind what you did, if it were only real work. "

"Oh, pshaw! Always work, Evadne. I tell you I prefer to play. Miss Angel told me at the General's ball last night that she liked a man who took his glass and smoked and did all the rest of the naughty things. "

"She is an angel of darkness, luring you on to ruin. "

Louis shrugged his shoulders. "Possibly. If so, she is disguised as an angel of light. She sings divinely. "

"So did the Sirens. "

Louis laughed. "She has promised to go for a sail with me to-morrow. Better come along, coz, and keep us off the rocks. "

Evadne was silent.

"I like such a girl as that, " he continued. "She has common sense and makes a fellow feel comfortable. These moral altitudes of yours are all very fine in theory, but the atmosphere is too rare for me. "

"It is no real kindness to make you satisfied with your lowest. I want you to rise to your best. Oh, Louis, won't you let Christ make your life grand? It would be such a happiness to me! " She laid her hand upon his shoulder. Louis caught it in his and drew her round in front of his chair.

"Do you really mean that, little coz? Upon my word, it is the strongest inducement you could offer me. I feel half inclined to try, just for your sake, only you see it would involve such a tremendous expenditure of moral force! " and he lighted a fresh cigar.

\* \* \* \* \*

"I do wish you would not ride such wild horses, Louis, " said Mrs. Hildreth, as she stood beside her son in the front doorway, looking disapprovingly as she spoke at the horse who was champing his bit viciously on the sidewalk below. "It keeps me in a perfect fever of anxiety all the time. "

"Whoa, Polyphemus! Stand still, sir! Pompey, have you tightened that girth up to its last hole? Better do it then. Don't mind his kicking. It doesn't hurt him. It's just his way.

"My dear lady mother, if you knew what a pleasure it is to find something untamable where everything is so confoundedly slow you would not wonder at my fondness for the brute. As to your anxiety, that is ridiculous. A Hildreth has too much sense to be conquered by a horse and make a spectacle of himself into the bargain. *Au revoir.* Better take a dose of lavender to calm your nerves, " and Louis waved his hand to her with careless grace, as he gathered up the reins.

His mother looked after him with a sigh. "He is so fearless! What a splendid cavalry officer he would make! He makes me think of the regiment that went to the war from Marlborough. " Her eye fell casually upon Pompey who was shutting the carriage gates. "What a waste of precious lives it was to be sure, just to free a lot of cowardly negroes! "

It was late in the afternoon when Pompey went up town on an errand for Judge Hildreth. The street was full of men and horses hurrying to and fro but Pompey paid them but little attention. He was busy with his Lord.

Hark! What was that? The sound of a horse's hoofs ringing with a sharp, metallic clatter upon the paved street while children screamed and men turned white faces towards the sound and hurriedly sought the sidewalk.

On they came, the horse and his rider. Louis pale as death, Polyphemus mad with sudden fear and his own ungovernable temper. The bit was between his teeth, his iron-shod feet were thrown out in vengeful fury.

Pompey sprang forward.

"You can't stop him! " shouted the men. "It would be certain death! " But just beyond the street took a sharp turn to the right and a deep chasm, where extensive excavations for a sewer were being made, yawned hungrily.

The horse plunged and reared. Pompey had caught hold of the reins and was clinging to them with all his might.

\* \* \* \* \*

Mrs. Hildreth leaned over her son in an agony of fear. Louis was her idol. He opened his eyes wearily. His cheeks were as white as the pillow.

"Oh, Louis! " she wailed, "I knew that wretched horse would bring you to your death! "

"I am not dead yet, " he said, with a shadow of his old mocking smile, "although I *have* succeeded in making a fool of myself. How is Pompey? "

"Pompey! " ejaculated his mother. "I never thought of any one but you. "

* * * * *

Evadne stood in Dyce's little room, beside the bed with its gay patchwork cover. The iron-shod hoofs had done their cruel work only too well!

"Pompey, " she said wistfully, "dear Pompey, is the pain terrible to bear? "

The faithful eyes looked up at her, the brave lips tried to smile. "De Lord Jesus is a powerful help in de time of trubble, Miss 'Vadney; I'se leanin' on his arm. "

Evadne repeated, as well as she could for tears. "'Fear thou not, for I am with thee; be not dismayed, for I am thy God; I will strengthen thee, yea, I will help thee; yea, I will uphold thee with the right hand of my righteousness. '"

And Pompey answered with joyous assurance, —"'Though I walk through the valley of the shadow of death, I will fear no evil; for thou art with me; thy rod and thy staff they comfort me. '"

"The Jedge hez been here, " said Dyce with mournful pride. "He say he'll never find any one like Pompey. He say it wuz de braves' ting he ever knowed any one to do. He jest cry like a chile, de Jedge did; he say he never 'spect to find sech a faithful frien' again. "

"De Jedge is powerful kind, Missy. He say he'll look out fer Dyce ez long ez he live, " the husband's voice broke,

"I don't care nuthin' 'bout dat! " and Dyce turned away with a choking sob; "but I'se proud to hev him see what kind of a man you is. "

The night drew on. No sound was to be heard in the little cottage except the ticking of the wheezy clock, as Dyce kept her solitary vigil by the side of the man she loved. She knelt beside his pillow, and, for her sake, Pompey made haste to die. As the shadows of the night were fleeing before the heralds of the dawn, she saw the gray shadow which no earthly light has power to chase away fall swiftly over his face.

He opened his eyes and spoke in a rapturous whisper. "Dyce! Dyce! I see de Lord! "

The morning broke. Dyce still knelt on with her face buried in the pillow; the asthmatic clock still kept on its tireless race; but Pompey's happy spirit had forever swept beyond the bounds of time.

\* \* \* \* \*

The humble funeral was over. The Hildreth carriage, behind whose curtained windows sat Dyce and Evadne, had followed close after the hearse. The Judge had walked behind.

"So uncalled for! " Mrs. Hildreth said in an annoyed tone when, she heard of it. Your father never *will* learn to have a proper regard for *les convenances*. "

"Uncalled for! " ejaculated Louis. "I'll venture to say the Judge will never have a chance to follow such a brave man again. "

"He sent his carriage. That was all that was necessary. "

"Doubtless Dyce finds that superlative honor a perfect panacea for her grief, " said Louis sarcastically. "It is eminently fitting that Brutus and Caesar should have walked as chief mourners for they have lost the truest friend they ever had. "

## CHAPTER XXV.

"I'm afraid poor Evadne will be worn out with such constant attendance upon Louis, " said Marion some weeks after Pompey's death. "I don't see how she stands it. "

"It is hardly worth her while to undertake nursing, " said Isabelle coldly, "if she cannot stand such a trifle as this. "

"Why, Isabelle, just think of the strain night after night! You wouldn't like it, I know. I want Mamma to get a paid nurse, but Louis won't have any one near him but Evadne. "

"Of course *I* could not stand being broken of my rest, " rejoined Isabelle, "it is hard enough for me to get any under the most favorable circumstances, but probably Evadne sleeps like a log in the daytime. It is the least return she can make for having disgraced the family, to be of some use in it now. "

Marion laughed incredulously. "I should never think of associating Evadne's name with disgrace, " she said. "What *do* you mean, Isabelle? "

"Mamma says this nursing fad of hers upset Papa completely. He said the Hildreth honor had better not be mentioned any more. "

"Well, I don't know. It seems to me she is of a good deal more value to him now than the Hildreth honor. Dr. Russe says she is one of the best nurses he ever saw. That is a high compliment, for he is dreadfully particular. It is my opinion, Isabelle, that Louis is a good deal worse than we think him to be. Don't mention it to Mamma, for she is so nervous, but I heard Dr. Russo talking to Papa in the hall this morning, something about an inherited tendency and a derangement of the nervous system. I could not understand—he spoke so low—but Papa looked dreadfully worried after he had gone.

"Don't you think Papa looks very badly, Isabelle? And he seems so absent, as if he had something on his mind. I noticed it long before this happened. "

Isabelle laughed carelessly. "What a girl you are, Marion! You are always imagining things about people. For my part I have too many worries of my own. "

Upstairs Evadne was saying wistfully, "Don't you think your life should be very precious, Louis, now that two people have died? "

"Two people, Evadne? I know there was good old Pompey, —the thought of that haunts me night and day, —but who else do you mean? "

"Jesus Christ. "

"Oh! "

"Do you never think about him, Louis? "

"My dear coz, I find it wiser not to think. Every other man you meet holds a different creed, and each one thinks his is the right one. Why should I set myself up as knowing better than other people? The only way is to have a sort of nebulous faith. God will not expect too much of us, if we do the best we can. "

"A 'nebulous faith' will not save you, Louis, " Evadne answered sadly. "God expects us to believe his word when he tells us that he has opened a way for us into the Holiest by the blood of his Son. "

"That atonement theory is an uncanny doctrine. "

"It is the only way by which sinners can be made 'at one' with an absolutely holy God. Jesus said 'And I if I be lifted up... will draw all men unto me. ' His humanitarianism did not win the hearts of the multitude. The very men he had fed and healed hounded him *on to his cross*. "

"It is not philosophical. "

"I read this morning that 'the moving energy in the world's history to-day is not a philosophy, but a cross. '"

"The God of the present is humanitarianism. "

"Humanitarianism is not Christ. Paul says—'Though I bestow all my goods to feed the poor... but have not love, it profiteth me nothing. ' The love which he means is the Christ power, for no mere human love could reach the altitude of the 13th of 1st Corinthians. Real religion is not a creed, but a Christ. It seems to me the most important questions we have to answer are, what we think of Christ and what we are going to do with him.

"When Peter gave his answer—'Thou art the Christ, —the Anointed One, —the Son of the living God, —' Christ said, 'On this rock—the faith of thine—I will build my church. ' Humanitarianism, pure and simple, seems to me but an attempt to imitate Christ. It is beautiful as far as it goes, but it is not my idea of following him. "

"What is, Evadne? "

"When Jesus told his disciples to follow, he meant them to be with him. I do not think we can ever hope to be like Christ unless we believe him to be God and walk with him every day. If we have the spirit of Jesus in our hearts, we shall be model humanitarians, for we shall love our neighbor as ourselves. "

Louis caught her hand in his. "Begin by loving me! " he cried suddenly. "I love you, dear! These long days of watching have taught me that, although I began to suspect it some time ago. It is no use saying anything, " he went on hurriedly, as Evadne began to protest, "you must be my wife, for I cannot live without you! "

He drew a handsome ring, of quaint and curious workmanship which he had bought in Venice, from his finger, and before Evadne could recover from her astonishment, had thrust it upon hers. "See, you are mine, darling. Now let us seal the compact with a kiss. "

"Louis, you are dreaming! This can never be! " She struggled to free her hand but he held her fingers in a grasp of steel.

"It shall be, my sweet little Puritan! Do you suppose I will ever give you up now? I tell you I love you, Evadne! Love you as I never thought I should ever love a woman. Why, you can twist me around your finger. I am like water in your hands. "

"Louis, please listen! " implored Evadne, with a white, strained face. "This is utterly impossible, for—I do not love you. "

"I will teach you, dear, " said Louis cheerfully. "I know I have been a brute, but I will show you how gentle I can be. "

"Louis! " cried Evadne desperately, "you must let me go! I will *never* do this thing! "

She pulled vainly at the ring as she spoke. Louis' grasp never relaxed. When he spoke she was frightened at the recklessness of his tone.

"Take that ring off your finger and I go straight to the devil! You say you want to win my soul. Here is your chance. You can make of me what you will. I own there is something in your Christianity. I can't help sneering when I see Isabelle and Marion playing at it, but I have never sneered at you. Now, take your choice. Shall the devil have his own? "

His voice was quiet but she could see he was laboring under intense excitement. Evadne was in despair. What should she do? Only that morning Dr. Russe had said to her, —

"It is not the injury he sustained in the fall that worries me. He will get over that. But the shock to the nervous system has been tremendous. Humor him in everything and avoid the least excitement, as you value his life. "

She leaned over him and said gently, —"Dear Louis, you are not strong enough to talk any more to-day. I will wear the ring a little while to please you, but remember, this other thing you want can never be. "

He looked up at her, his face pallid with exhaustion, "Promise me, " he said faintly, "that the ring shall stay on your finger until I take it off. "

And Evadne promised.

CHAPTER XXVI.

Three years had slipped away and Evadne still wore her cousin's ring. A great tenderness was growing up in her heart toward him. She yearned over him as only those can understand who know what it is to carry the burden of souls upon their hearts by night and day but no thought of love ever crossed her mind. To Evadne Hildreth, love was a wonderfully sacred thing. The ring fretted her and she longed to be freed from its presence, but Louis held her to her promise. If he only waited long enough, he persuaded himself, his patience would be rewarded. Some day this shy, sweet bird would nestle against his heart. In the meantime he would keep the ungenerous advantage which his illness had given him. He forgot that it needs more to tame a bird than merely putting it in a cage!

Isabelle had been intensely curious but her questions had elicited no satisfaction from her brother, and Evadne had answered simply, "Louis took a fancy to put it on my finger: I am wearing it to please him, that is all: " and even Isabelle found her cousin's sweet dignity an effectual bar against her morbid inquisitiveness.

They had seen comparatively little of each other. Evadne was constantly busy, either at private or hospital nursing, and very short were the furloughs which she spent under her uncle's roof. Louis had spent the first winter after his illness with his mother in the South of France, now he was in Florida, but he wrote regularly, and Evadne answered—when she could. Sweet, pleading letters which he read over and over and honestly tried to be better: but it was only for her sake; he knew no higher motive—yet.

It was a perfect day. Down by the river an alligator was sunning himself, and the resinous breath of the pine trees swept its aromatic fragrance over Louis as he lay at full length in a hammock with his hands behind his head. He had thrown the magazine he had been reading on the ground and it lay open at the article on Heredity which he had just finished. His desultory thoughts were roaming idly over the subject, when one, more far reaching than the rest, made him start lip with a sudden shock of unwelcome surprise.

"By Jove! Can it be that I am a victim of it too? It looks confoundedly like it, although even my sweet little Puritan has not felt it a sin against her conscience to keep me in the dark. "

He thrust his fingers with an impatient gesture through his hair. "Now I come to think of it, the case grows deucedly clear. The South of France one winter and Florida this! Simple nervous prostration would seem to the uninitiated better fought in the exhilirating ozone of Colorado, or—the North Pole—than in this languorous atmosphere. 'An inherited tendency. ' Is this the pleasant little legacy which my respected ancestor has bequeathed to his only grandson? It skipped the Judge, but it caught poor Uncle Lenox, and now it has nabbed me! What a fool I have been not to surmise what this confounded pain meant between my shoulders! Grandfather Hildreth kept himself alive with nostrums until he was seventy, but he was an invalid all his life. He ought to be cursed for his contemptible selfishness in bringing so much suffering upon the race! There's none of the taint about Evadne, bless her! Russe told me the Hospital examiners said they had never passed such a perfect specimen of health. "

He stopped suddenly and bit his lips in pain. Would he not follow his grandfather's example—if he had the chance?

"What in the world is the meaning of all this? "

Louis had arrived by an earlier train than he was expected and only his mother was at home to greet him. The hall was in confusion, workmen's tools lay about and ladders stood against the walls. Mrs. Hildreth laughed lightly, as she laid her hand within her son's arm.

"Oh, they are only getting ready for the floral decorations, " she said, "we give a reception to-morrow in honor of your return. How well you are looking, Louis. I am so delighted to have you at home. "

"Thanks, lady mother. I do not need to ask how you have survived my absence. How is Evadne, —and the Judge and the girls? "

His mother laughed again as she drew him on the sofa beside her. She seemed in wonderfully good humor. "Rather a comprehensive question, " she said. "Sit down and we will have a comfortable talk before the others get home. Your father looks wretchedly but he says there is nothing the matter. I suppose it is just overwork and the usual money strain. Isabelle too is not as well as I should like her to be. Suffers from nervousness a great deal, and depression. There is a new physician here now, a Doctor Randolph, who we think is going to help her, although he is very young; but she took a dislike to Doctor Russe because he belongs to the old school. And now I have a surprise for you. Marion is engaged! "

"Engaged! Why, you never hinted at it in your letters! "

"It has all been very sudden. I wrote you there was a young New Yorker very attentive to her. "

"Yes, but that is an old story. There were two fellows 'very attentive' when I went away. How long since the present devotion culminated? "

"Just a week ago to-night: and they are so devoted! "

"A second Romeo and Juliet, eh? " —Louis' laugh had a bitter ring, —"By the way, what is his name? "

"Simpson Kennard. "

"Brother Simp! Rich, I suppose? "

"Oh, yes, very. In fact he is eligible in every way. "

"I see, " yawned Louis, "Possessed of all the cardinal virtues. It is a good thing his wealth is not all in his pockets, for they are apt to spring a leak. But Evadne—how is she? "

"Oh, she is always well, you know, " said his mother carelessly. "There they come now. "

"These Indian famines are a terrible business, " said Judge Hildreth as they lingered over their dessert that evening. It was pleasant to have Louis and Evadne back again. He too was glad to see his son so well. "I don't see what the end is going to be. "

"People say that about every calamity, Papa, " said Isabelle, "but the world goes on just the same. "

"Of course it does, Isabelle, " said her brother. "You see we can't waste time over a few dying millions when we have to give a reception for instance. "

"But that is a necessity, Louis, " said Mrs. Hildreth, "we must pay our debts to society, you know. "

"I am sure I don't see where I could economize, " sighed Marion. "That lecturer last night was splendid and I would like to have given him thousands but I hadn't a dollar in my purse. I never have. I spent my last cent for chocolates yesterday. "

Evadne smiled and sighed but said nothing. The lecturer the night before had felt his soul strangely stirred at the sight of her glowing face, and the plate when it passed her seat had borne a shining gold piece, but perhaps she had not as many temptations as Marion and Isabelle.

"I would have willingly filled you up a check with the cost of the floral decorations, Marion, " said her father with a twinkle in his eye. "They would have purchased a good many bags of corn. "

"But that is ridiculous! " said Isabelle. "What would a reception be without flowers, I should like to know? As it is, I expect it will be a poor affair compared to the Van Nuys' last week. We never seem to be able to do anything in proper style. You would better put your new Worth gown, on the collection plate, Marion, and appear in a morning dress to-morrow night. Louis would be the first one to be scandalized if you did! "

"Well but, Isabelle, I had to have something now. I have worn my other dresses so many times, I am perfectly ashamed. "

"Of course, sis, " said Louis gravely, "it was a most imperative expenditure. It is a strange coincidence that you should have chosen that particular make though. It has always been a fancy of mine that the Levite was robed in a Worth gown when he passed by on the other side. "

"The sufferings must be awful, " said Evadne, anxious to relieve Marion's embarrassment. "I saw in the paper to-day that— —"

Mrs. Hildreth lifted her hands in mock alarm. "Pray spare us any recital of horrors, Evadne! I never want to hear about any of these dreadful things. What is the use, when one cannot help in any way?"

"You forget, Mamma, " said Isabelle with a laugh, "that Evadne revels in horrors. What would be torture to our quivering nerves, to her atrophied sensibilities is merely an occurrence of every day. "

Louis gave a sudden start in his chair, but on the instant Evadne laid her hand upon his arm, and its light touch soothed his anger as it had been wont to soothe his pain.

Evadne Hildreth was climbing the heights of victory. She had learned to cover her wounds with a smile.

## CHAPTER XXVII.

"Who is that calf, Evadne, standing by the piano? " Louis put the question to his cousin the next evening, as he sought a few moments' respite from his duties as host at her side.

"That is Mr. Simpson Kennard. "

Louis surveyed the fashionably dressed, weak-faced, sandy-haired young man from head to foot. "He will never get above his collar! " he said in a tone of infinite scorn.

Evadne laughed. "You must confess it is high enough to limit the aspirations of an ordinary mortal. "

Marion fluttered up to them, her cheeks aglow with excitement. "Louis, where are you? I want to introduce you to Simpsey. He has just arrived. "

Evadne looked after her as she led her brother away. "Poor little soul. What a butterfly it is! Fancy having a husband whom one could call Simpsey! "

She started. Her knight of the gate was standing before her with outstretched hand. A great light was in his face. "Do you remember? " he asked, and Evadne's eyes glowed deep with pleasure, as she laid her hand in his. They would never be properly introduced, these two, "'Life is a beautiful possibility, '" she said, "I am proving it so every day, —but, oh, the awful suffering in the world! I cannot understand, —"

And John Randolph answered with his strong, sweet faith. "God understands, *we* do not need to. "

They were standing in an alcove partially screened by a tall palm from the crowd which surged up and down through the rooms. He took from his pocket a morocco case, and, opening it, held it towards her. What made the color flush her cheeks while her eyes fell beneath his gaze? She only saw a little square of lawn and lace, but the name traced across one corner was 'Evadne'!

"Did you leave nothing behind you at Hollywood that day? " he asked gently.

"My handkerchief! " she cried. "I missed it before we reached Marlborough. I must have left it at the gate. " But Evadne had left more behind her than she knew.

"I will keep it still, " he said, "with your permission. Will you give it to me? "

"Oh, Doctor Randolph! " Isabelle's voice fell shrill upon Evadne's silence, "they are calling for you in the other room to decide a knotty question—something about microbes. I told them I was sure you would know. Will you come? "

John Randolph put the case quickly in his pocket and smiled as he turned away. He thought he had read consent in her lovely eyes.

After the reception was over Evadne knelt by her window until the stars faded one by one from the sky. Then she turned away with a happy sigh. When he came to get his answer, she would know.

* * * * *

"Give that to me! " Isabella spoke imperiously to the servant, who was passing through the hall with a note in her hand. From where she stood she had recognized the clear handwriting of the prescriptions which the new doctor wrote. Her demon of curiosity overcame her. The tempter was very near.

The girl held the note towards her. "It is for Miss Evadne, " she said. "Miss E. Hildreth, you see. "

Isabelle gave a careless laugh. "Did you not know I had an E in my name also? Evelyn Isabelle. I know the writing. The note is meant for me. "

So the truth and the lie mingled! When John Randolph called that evening he was ushered into the presence of Isabelle.

"I am so sorry about Evadne! " she exclaimed, before he had time to speak. "She had an engagement with my brother. He monopolizes her whenever he is at home. " She laughed affectedly. "Oh, I cannot tell you when it is coming off, but she has worn his ring for years. They will not give us any satisfaction—deep as the sea, you know. It seems so strange to me, but then I am so transparent. She is a clever girl, but very peculiar. Does not seem to have much natural feeling, you know, but I suppose I am not fitted to judge, I am so emotional! "

John Randolph bit his lip hard. It startled him to find how sharp a pain could be.

*****

Day after day Evadne waited but her knight never asked for his answer. She began to meet him professionally, for his reputation was steadily increasing, but he made no attempt to resume the conversation which had been so rudely interrupted. He treated her with a delicate chivalry always—that was John Randolph's way—and once she had caught such a strange, wistful expression on his face as he looked at her and then at a patient's arm which she was deftly bandaging. She was puzzled. What could it all mean? Well, God understood.

The surgical ward in the new Hospital at Marlborough was filled to its utmost capacity and Evadne found her work no sinecure. The force of nurses was inadequate to the demand. Often she would be called from her rest to minister to the critical cases which were her special care, and she would go down to the ward saying softly, "The Master is come and calleth for thee, " and bending tenderly over the sufferers, would behold as in a vision the face of Christ.

"My dear Miss Hildreth! " the superintendent exclaimed one day, "how is it that you make the patients love you so? "

Evadne laughed merrily. "If they do, " she said, "it must be because of my love for them. " And the Superintendent answered in a hushed voice, "Why, *that* is the Gospel! "

They called her 'Sister, ' these rough men. She liked it so. She felt herself a sister to the world.

It was evening and the lights were turned low in the surgical ward. Evadne was making her round before going to her room for a sorely needed rest. John Randolph, who had come to pay a second visit to an interesting case in one of the medical wards, stood in the shadow of the doorway and watched her hungrily. Each one wanted to say something and Evadne listened patiently. To her the mission of a nurse meant something higher than gruel and bandages. She never forgot as she ministered to the body that she was dealing with a soul.

John Randolph, standing with folded arms in the doorway, heard her low, sweet laugh, as she strove to brighten up a lachrymose patient; and caught at intervals the name of Jesus, as she reminded one and another of the Friend whose sympathy is strong enough to bear all the weight of human pain, and once he thought he heard the sweet note of a prayer. He started forward. Evadne was bending over a man who had been badly crippled in a saw mill. His left arm was gone and all the fingers from his right hand. With the morbidness of those who delight in concentrating attention upon their own sufferings, he had pulled off the loosened bandage with his teeth and held up the stump for inspection, and Evadne had laid her cool, soft hands on either side of the unsightly mass of red and angry flesh and was holding them there while she talked!

"She gives herself! " cried John Randolph with a great throb of longing. "It is what Jesus did, in Galilee. "

A wave of passion broke over him. It was not true, this story. It could not be! How could her nature, sweet as light, ever be attuned to that of her cynical cousin? She was coming nearer, nearer. He would stay and meet her. He thought he had read his answer in her eyes. Now he would have it from her lips as well.

But then, there was the ring! Isabelle had been right. It was no lady's ornament, and he had seen the initials L. H. graven in the heart of the stone as their hands had met one day in dressing a wound. Evadne Hildreth was not one to wear a man's ring lightly and John Randolph bent his head and groaned.

"Sister, Sister, won't you sing before you go? "

"Oh, yes, Sister, give us just one song! "

The men raised themselves on their elbows in pleading entreaty, and Evadne stood in all her sweet unconsciousness before him and began to do their will. Soft and clear the music fell about him. The air was 'The last Rose of Summer' but the words were 'Jesus, Lover of my soul. ' When the song was ended, John Randolph, hushed and comforted, walked noiselessly down the stairway and out into the quiet street.

Evadne had sung her message, while she folded its leaves of healing down over her own sore heart, and human love had paled before the exquisite beauty of the love of God!

## CHAPTER XXVIII.

"John Randolph! "

"Rege! "

The two men stood facing each other with hands held in a vice-like grasp, all unconscious of what was going on around them in the street.

"Where did you come from? "

"Where have you been? "

John laughed. "In and around Marlborough all the time, except when I went to New York for my degree. "

"And never let us hear a word from you all these years! "

"You forget, Rege, your father forbade me to hold any communication with Hollywood. "

Reginald's face grew grave. "Poor father. Well he's done with it all now. "

"You don't mean that he is dead, Rege? "

"Yes—and little Nan. "

"Oh! " The exclamation was sharp with pain.

"I think she fretted for you, John. She just seemed to pine away. Every day we missed her about the same time, and they always found her in the same place, down by the green road. Then scarlet fever came. She never spoke of getting well—didn't seem to want to. The night she died she put her arms around mother's neck and whispered. 'Tell Don me'll be waitin' at the gate. ' That was all. "

John wrung Reginald's hand and turned away. Reginald looked after him with misty eyes. "I used to tell mother it would break his heart. I never saw any one so wrapped up in a child! "

"And your father, Rege? " John was calm again.

"Had a fit of apoplexy soon after. I think Nan was the only thing in the world he cared for. It had never struck him that she could die. We sold Hollywood and went abroad. Mother's health broke down—she was never very strong, you know. We spent one year in Italy and one in France, but the shock had been too great. She lies in a lovely spot beside the sea. "

"Not your mother too, Rege! "

Reginald's voice broke. "Yes, they are all gone. It was a great deal to happen in a few years. I am a wealthy man, John, but I am all alone in the world, except for Elise. Well, " he added more lightly, "I have learned not to rebel at the inevitable. It is only what we have to expect. "

"Elise! " echoed John wonderingly, after the first shock of grief was over.

"My wife, " said Reginald proudly. "You must come home at once and let me show you the sweetest woman in the world. "

"Not just yet, Rege I must pay a visit to Mrs. O'Flannigan, then there is the hospital, and the dispensary, and I promised to concoct a bed for a poor fellow in the last stages of heart trouble. But I will come to-night. "

"Always helping somewhere, John. What a grand fellow you are! "

"We are in the world to help the world, else what were the use of living? "

"I can't do anything, " said Reginald, "with this clog. " He looked contemptuously at his ebony crutch as he spoke.

John laid his hand upon his arm. "Rege, " he said in his old, tender way. "I think this very 'clog' as you call it, is a preparation to help those who are passing through the baptism of pain. "

* * * * *

Mrs. Reginald Hawthorne welcomed her husband's friend with a winning charm. She was very pretty, very graceful and very young. Reginald idolized her. John saw that as he looked around the sumptuous home whose every fitting was a tribute to her taste. They had just finished unpacking the things they had brought from Europe.

"Strangely enough, " said Reginald with a laugh, "I told Elise this morning that now I was going to start out in search of you! "

He had developed wonderfully. John saw that too. Travel and trial had brought out the good that was in him—but not the best.

The evening passed pleasantly. Mrs. Hawthorne played beautifully, and Reginald had kept ears and eyes open and talked well.

"How about the other life, Rege? " asked John when they had a few moments alone. "This one seems very fair. "

"All a humbug, John. You Christians are chasing a will o' the wisp, a jack o' lantern. You remember my fad for mathematics? I have followed it up, and I find your theory a 'reductio ad absurdum. ' I must have everything demonstrable and clear. This is neither. "

"Yet it was a great mathematician who said, 'Omit eternity in your estimate of area and your solution is wrong. '"

Reginald shook his head. "I have nothing to do with this faith business. I go as far as I see, no further. "

"God calls our wisdom foolishness, Rege. Jesus Christ put a tremendous premium upon the faith of a little child. "

"Things must be tangible for me to believe in them. Reason is king with me. "

"Without faith in your fellow man—and your wife—you would have a poor time of it, Rege; why should you refuse to have faith in your God? Is your will tangible, and can you demonstrate the mysterious forces of nature? You know you can't, Rege, you have to take them on trust; and if you had seen what I have, you would know that poor human reason is a pitiful thing! But I won't argue with you. Some day you will understand. "

Reginald Hawthorne went back into the room where his wife was sitting. "Elise, darling, you have seen one of the grandest men in the world to-night. The only trouble is that on one subject he is a crank. "

"Oh, Reginald, do you mean it! I thought he was splendid. And what a wonderful face he has! "

Reginald started. "Hah! Am I to be jealous of my old friend? But I might have known, " he added sadly, "no one could care long for such a wreck as I! "

The girl wife put her arms around his neck and kissed him softly, "You foolish boy! " she whispered, "you know I shall never love any one but you! "

And Reginald Hawthorne counted himself a perfectly happy man.

## CHAPTER XXIX.

Judge Hildreth sat in his library, alone. He had left home immediately after dinner, ostensibly to catch the evening train for New York, and had sent the carriage back from the station to take his family to the Choral Festival which was the event of the year in Marlborough, and then returning in a hired conveyance, had let himself into his house like a thief. When we sacrifice principle upon the altar of expediency, truth and honor, like twin victims, stand bound at its foot. He wanted to be undisturbed, to have time to think, and God granted his wish, until his reeling brain prayed for oblivion!

No sound broke the stillness. With the exception of the servants in a distant part of the house, he was absolutely alone.

He drew out his will from a secret drawer of his desk and looked it over with a ghastly smile. "To my dear niece, Evadne, the sum of thirty thousand dollars, held by me in trust from her father. " Then came a long list of charities. It read well. People could not say he had left all to his family and forgotten the Lord. If his executors should find a difficulty in realizing one quarter of the values so speciously set forth, they could only say that dividends had shrunk and investments proved unreliable. It was not his fault. He had meant well. Besides, he had no thought of dying for years. There was plenty of time for skillful financing. Other men had done the same and prospered. Why should not he?

But the letters must be destroyed. He had come to a decision at last. It was an imperative necessity. His hesitancy had been only the foolish scruples of an over sensitive conscience. The tremendous pressure of the age made things permissible. He was "torn by the tooth of circumstance" and "necessity knows no law. " So he entrenched himself behind a breastwork of sophisms. Long familiarity with the suggestions of evil had bred a contempt for the good!

He stretched out his hand towards the drawer. There should be no more weak delay. If a thing were to be done, 'twere well it were done quickly.

The horror of a great fear fell upon him. Again his hand had fallen, and this time he was powerless to lift it up!

The hours passed and he sat helpless, bound in that awful chain of frozen horror. In vain he struggled in a wild rage for freedom. No muscle stirred. Where was his boasted will power now? Hand and foot, faithful, uncomplaining slaves for so many years, had rebelled at last!

His brain seemed on fire and the flashing thoughts blinded him with their glare. The letters rose from their sepulchre and, clothed in the majesty of a dead man's faith, looked at him with an awful reproach, until his very soul bowed in the dust with shame. His will still lay upon the desk, open at the paragraph "to my dear niece, Evadne, " and the words "in trust, " like red hot irons, branded him a felon in the sight of God and men!

He remembered having once read a quotation from a great writer, — "When God says, 'You must not lie and you do lie, it is not possible for Deity to sweep his law aside and say—'No matter. '" Did God make no allowances for the nineteenth century?

The others returned from the Festival, and Louis passed the door whistling. He had had a rare evening of pleasure with Evadne. Towards its close, under cover of the rolling harmonies, he had leaned over and whispered "I love you, dear! " and Evadne had held out her hand to him with the low pleading cry, "Oh, Louis, if you really do, then set me free! " but he had only smiled and taken the hand, on which his ring was gleaming, into his, and settled his arm more securely upon the back of her chair; and John Randolph, sitting opposite with Dick and Miss Diana, had watched the little scene and drawn his own conclusions with a sigh.

The night drew on. The electric lights which it was Judge Hildreth's fancy to have ablaze in every room downstairs until the central current was shut off, still gleamed steadily upon the rigid figure before the desk, with the white, drawn face and the awful look of horror in its staring eyes. In an agony he tried to call, but no sound escaped the lips, set in a sphinx-like silence.

He must shake off this strange lethargy. It was not possible for him to die—he had not time. To-morrow was the meeting of the

Panhattan directors—they were relying upon him to work through the second call on stock—and two of his notes fell due, if he did not retire them his credit would be lost at the bank; and there was the banquet to the English capitalists, with whom he was negotiating a mining deal; and he must arrange with his broker to float some more shares of the "Silverwing"—and manipulate, manipulate, manipulate—

An agonized, voiceless cry went up to heaven. "Oh, God, let me have to-morrow! "

In the morning a servant found him, when she came to clean the room, and fled screaming from the presence of the silent figure with the awful entreaty in its staring eyes.

Louis hurried downstairs to learn the cause of the commotion, followed by Mrs. Hildreth, swept for once off her pedestal of stately calm.

Shivering with horror the family gathered in the beautiful room which had been so suddenly turned into a death chamber, the servants weeping boisterously, Isabella and her mother in violent hysterics, and Marion clinging with wide, frightened eyes to Louis, who found himself thrust into a man's place of responsibility and did not know what to do!

He sent one servant to the Hospital for Evadne—instinctively he turned in his thought to her, —another for the Doctor; while with one arm around Marion, he tried to sooth his mother and Isabelle.

And in the midst of all the wild commotion his father sat, unmoved and silent, his agonized face lifted in an attitude of supplication, his lifeless hands lying heavily upon the now worthless papers, since for him there would be no to-morrow!

\* \* \* \* \*

The stately obsequies were ended. The paid quartette had sung their sweetest, while Doctor Jerome, standing beside the frozen face in the massive coffin, had delivered an eloquent eulogium, and Mrs. Hildreth, clad in her costly robes of mourning, had been led to her carriage by her son. Everything had been conducted in a manner befitting the Hildreth honor.

\* \* \* \* \*

"Evadne! " Louis turned a white, scared face towards his cousin, who stood beside him as he sat at his father's desk. Upstairs Mrs. Hildreth and Isabelle were in solemn consultation with a dressmaker. In the drawing-room Marion was being consoled by Simpson Kennard.

"Well, Louis? " She laid her hand on his shoulder gently. She was very sorry for him.

"There is some awful mistake. Poor Father seems to have counted on funds which we can find no trace of. The estate is not worth an eighth of what he valued it at. There is barely enough to keep you, mother and Isabelle, alive! " He laid his head down on the desk while great tears fell through his fingers. The shameful mystery of it was intolerable.

"But, Louis, have you looked everywhere? There must be some explanation—"

Louis shook his head. "Everywhere, but in this drawer. I opened it but there is nothing but musty old letters. I haven't time to go into them now. Oh, little coz, I don't dare to look you in the face. All the money that was left you by your father is gone! "

"Don't tell Aunt Kate and the girls, Louis, There is no need that they should ever know. I have my profession and I am strong. Uncle Lawrence never meant to do anything except what was right, I know. "

Louis looked up at her and there was a strange reverence in his cynical face. He was in the presence of a Christliness which he had never dreamed of. "I am not worthy to touch the hem of your garment, " he said humbly. But he did not offer to release her from her promise. He had not learned to be generous—yet.

Evadne's dream was ended and rude was the awaking. The idea of helping her fellows had grown to be a passion with her and very fair had been the castle in the air of which she was the Princess. A home, not rich or stately but full of a delightful homeiness which should soothe and cheer those who, walking through the world amid a storm of tears, call earth a wilderness, while their desolate hearts echo the mournful question, —"Is there any sorrow like unto my sorrow. " She, too, had been lonely, —she could understand, and by the sweet influence of human love and sympathy lift their thought above the earthly shadows up to the love of God.

She had not dreamed of doing things on a grand scale. Evadne Hildreth was wise enough to know that comfort cannot be dealt out in wholesale packages, —she never forgot that Jesus of Nazareth helped the people one by one.

She had never questioned the terms of her father's will—if there was a will. She had supposed when she became of age there would be some change, but her uncle had made no reference to the subject and she had not liked to ask. He was always kind—he would do what was best. Some day she would be free to carry out this beautiful dream of hers. She could afford to wait. Now there was nothing to wait for any more!

How strange it seemed, when the need was so great and she longed to help much! Well, she was only a little child, —she could trust her Father. God understood.

That was what he had said, this strong, true friend of hers, that night he asked the question which he had never asked again. How gentle he was! —but it was the gentleness of strength—and how every one depended on him! She, herself, had learned to expect the helpful words which he always gave her when they met. Friendship was a beautiful thing!

## CHAPTER XXX.

John Randolph came up behind Evadne one morning as she was dressing the burns of a little lad who had been severely injured at a fire. She did not hear his step—she was telling a bright story to the little sufferer, to make him forget his pain, and the boy was laughing loudly. His face was very grave, but his eyes lightened as they always did when they rested upon her face.

"Mrs. Reginald Hawthorne is very ill. Can you, will you come? "

And Evadne answered with a simple "Yes. " They needed so few words, these two.

"I tell you I will not die! " The piercing cry rang through the handsome room and fell like molten lead upon the heart of the man who with strained, haggard face was sitting by the bedside. "You have not told me the truth, Reginald! There is a God. I feel it! You have always laughed and called me young and foolish, but I know better than you do, now. You said if our lives were governed by reason, we would meet death like a philosopher, and I do not know how to die! You used to laugh and say the whole thing was child's play and there was nothing to fear, and I believed you, —I thought you were so wise, but it was easy to believe you then with your arms folded close about me and the sunlight streaming through the windows and the shouts of the children outside, but now you cannot go with me and I am afraid to go alone. " The eyes, wild and despairing, burned fiercely in the pallid cheeks. "Do you hear, Reginald? I am afraid, I tell you; horribly afraid! You used to say you would lay down your life to save me. Why do you not help me now?

"What makes you look so strangely, if it is all nonsense, Reginald? why do you shut out all the sunshine and why is the house so still? You told me once you were going to die with a laugh on your lips. I am dying, Reginald, why don't you help your wife to die as you mean to do? A——h! "

Her voice died away in a low wail of terror and the delicate blue veins in her temples throbbed with feverish excitement. Reginald Hawthorne had crouched down in his chair and buried his face in his hands. The pitiful cry began again.

"To die, when life is so sweet! To be shut up in a coffin and buried in a cold, dark grave! You don't love me, Reginald. If you did, you would die too—with a laugh on your lips you know—then I should have that to cheer me, and we should be together, and I should not be afraid. But now you look so strangely, Reginald. Don't you care for me any more? Can you let them take me away from this beautiful world and stay in it all by yourself?

"I suppose you will give me a splendid funeral—you are so generous you know—but I will not care whether the prison is pine or mahogany if I am to be shut up in it all alone! And you will have a long procession, with plumes and flowers and show, but you will leave me in the dreary cemetery and you will come back to our home, where we have been so happy together—so happy, just you and I—but you see you are a philosopher and I do not know how to die!

"And some day you will forget me—men do such things they say—and another woman will be your wife and I will be all alone! "

"Sister! " The abject man in the chair held out his hands in an agony of entreaty, "Come here and help us—if you can! " and Evadne came swiftly into the room, and, sitting down on the side of the bed, gathered the pitiful little figure to her heart.

"It is not death but life, " she said gently. "This body is not *you*. The home of the soul is more beautiful than, any earthly home can ever be. It is those who are left behind dear, who mourn, not those who go. "

Elise Hawthorne laid her head on Evadne's shoulder like a tired child. "But I am afraid, " she whispered. "If this is true, and God is holy, I am not fit, you know. "

"Your Father loves you dear, for he sent his Son to die. The thief on the cross was a sinner, yet Christ took him to Paradise. The fitness must come from Jesus. His blood washes whiter than snow. "

"But I have done nothing to earn it. I have lived for myself alone. "

"We never can earn a gift, dear. God gives in a royal way. He says to you only 'Believe I have given you life through my Son. '" Evadne had taken the tiny Bible which she always carried from her pocket and was turning its pages rapidly. "Here it is. Will you raise the blind, Mr. Hawthorne, that your wife may see for herself? 'God so loved the world that he gave his only begotten Son, '—the best he had! —'that whosoever believeth in him should not perish, ' you see there is no death for those who trust in him. And then 'He that believeth on the Son *hath* everlasting life. ' It does not mean that we may have it after years of toil. The Israelites, stung by the serpents, had no time to reason or plan to live better, for they were dying, but they could turn their eyes to the brazen serpent which God had ordered to be lifted up in the midst of tho camp for an antidote to the poison. So Christ has been 'lifted up' upon the cross for us. He died instead of you. Why should you die forever when he has paid your ransom and set you free? "

"But I cannot touch him, —I cannot be sure it is true. "

"The Israelites could not touch the brazen serpent. They simply looked, and lived. There is just one condition for us to-day and it is 'Believe. ' Cannot you take your Heavenly Father at his word as you would your husband? Cannot you treat God the same? "

Mrs. Hawthorne looked wonderingly at her nurse. "Treat him the same as I do my husband! " she exclaimed. "Why, with Reginald, I believe every word he says. "

"And I with God, " said Evadne reverently.

"What charm have you wrought? " asked John Randolph in a whisper, as they stood together that evening beside a quiet sleeper. "This is the first natural sleep she has had. I believe it will prove her salvation. "

Evadne looked up at him, and over her face a light was breaking, "I have led her to Jesus, the Mighty to save. "

\* \* \* \* \*

The Hawthornes were going to Europe. The young wife's convalescence had been tedious and it was a very frail little figure which clung to Evadne the evening before they started. They had pleaded with her to go with them. "Give up this toilsome work which is overtaxing your strength, " Reginald had said, as they sat together one evening in the twilight, "and make your home with us. You have grown to be our sister in the truest sense of the word and we have learned to lean upon you, Elise and I. We can never hope to repay you, " he continued huskily, "but it would be such a pleasure to have you with us for good. "

Evadne looked at the pleading eyes with which Elise Hawthorne seconded her husband's wish and her lips trembled. "How rich God is making me in friends! " she said. "I shall never forget that this thing has been in your hearts, but I must be about my Father's business. "

And then John Randolph had come to make one of his pleasant, informal visits and they had sat together in a beautiful fellowship, talking of the things pertaining to the Kingdom.

"Doctor Randolph, " Elise asked suddenly, "what is your conception of prayer? Evadne says it means to her communion and companionship with Jesus. She says it is 'the practice of the presence of God. '"

John Randolph's face grew luminous. "To me it means a great stillness, " he said. "Did you ever think of the silences of God? 'Be still, and know that I am God, ' 'Stand still, and see his salvation. '"

"But are we not to ask for what we want? " asked Mrs. Hawthorne wonderingly.

"Oh, yes, but we learn to ask so little for ourselves when we love our Father's will. The trouble is, we, want to do the talking. God would have us listen while he speaks. "

"Then what does it mean to worship God? " she asked. "We cannot always be in church. "

John Randolph smiled. "We do not need to be. If our hearts are all on fire with the love of God, we worship him continually. "

When he rose to go he turned towards Evadne. "How goes life with you now, dear friend? "

The grey eyes, full of a clear shining, were lifted to his, "I am absolutely satisfied with Jesus Christ. "

Marion was married and living in New York. Louis had taken a small house, where he lived with his mother and Isabelle. He spent his days in the monotonous routine of a hank, and to his pleasure-loving nature the drudgery seemed intolerable, but he said little. Evadne never complained!

One day he went to see her at the Hospital and she was frightened at the pallor of his face. She led him to the superintendent's reception room—there they would be undisturbed. He staggered blindly as he entered the room and then sank heavily on a sofa near the door. He looked like an old man.

"Louis! " she cried in alarm, "what is the matter? "

He took a letter from his pocket and held it toward her. It bore her own name, and the writing was her father's!

"Can you *ever* forgive? " Then he buried his face in his arms and groaned aloud. The awful disgrace and shame of it seemed more than he could bear.

Interminable seemed the hours after Louis had left her, walking slowly, with that strange, grey shadow upon his face, and stooping as if some unseen burden were crushing him to the earth. She dared not let herself think. She must wait until she was alone. At last she was free to go to her room.

Down on her knees she read the passionate farewell words, which made her heart thrill, so full of tender advice and loving thought for her comfort. Through streaming tears she looked at the closely written pages of instructions, so minute that she could not err—and he had disliked writing so much! This was the weary task which had tried him so! And all these years she had never known. She had been robbed of her birthright!

Fierce and long the battle raged. When it was ended God heard his child cry softly, "Forgive us our trespasses as we forgive those who trespass against us. "

She had forgiven!

## CHAPTER XXXI.

Mrs. Simpson Kennard was sitting in her pretty morning room with her baby on her knee. She looked across the room at her sister who was paying her a visit. "I wish you had a little child to love, Isabelle. It makes life so different. I am just wrapped up in Florimel. "

"For pity's sake, Marion, " cried Isabelle peevishly, "don't you grow to be one of those tiresome women who think the whole world is interested in a baby's tooth! I certainly do not echo your wish. I think children are a nuisance. "

Marion caught up her baby in dismay. "Why, Isabelle, just think how much they do for us! They broaden our sympathies—I read that only the other day, and— —"

"Broaden your fiddlesticks! " said Isabelle contemptuously. "Easy for you to talk when you have everything you want! If you had to live in that poky little house in Marlborough, I guess you would not find anything very broadening about them!

"It is perfectly preposterous to think of our being reduced to such a style of living! " she continued, as Mrs. Kennard strove to soothe her baby's injured feelings with kisses. "Just fancy, only one servant! I never thought a Hildreth would fall so low. "

"But you and Mamma are comfortable, Isabelle. It is not as if you were forced to do anything. "

"Do anything! " echoed Isabelle. "Are you going crazy? "

"Well, see how hard Evadne has to work? and she is a Hildreth as well as you. "

"Evadne! " said Isabelle sarcastically, "with her nerves of steel and spine of adamant! Evadne will never kill herself with work. She is too much taken up with her wealthy private patients. You should have seen her driving round with the Hawthornes in their elegant carriage And I reduced to dependence upon the electric cars! I don't see how she manages to worm her way into people's confidence as she seems to do. I couldn't, but then I have such a horror of being forward. "

"'All doors are open to those who smile. ' I believe that is the reason, Isabelle. "

"Stuff and nonsense! " was Miss Hildreth's inelegant reply.

"She is a dear girl, Isabelle. Why will you persist in disliking her so?"

"Oh, pray spare me any panegyrics! " said Isabelle carelessly. "It is bad enough to have Louis blazing up like a volcano if one has the temerity to mention her ladyship's name. "

"How is Louis? " asked Mrs. Kennard, finding she was treading on dangerous ground.

"Oh, the same as usual. He looks like a ghost, and is about as cheerful as a cemetery. He spends his holidays going over musty old letters in papa's desk. I'm sure I don't see what fun he finds in it. It is so selfish in him, when he might be giving mamma and me some pleasure—but Louis never did think of anyone but himself. One day I found him stretched across the desk and it gave me such a fright! You know what a state my nerves are in. I thought he was in a fit or something, —he just looked like death, and he didn't seem to hear me when I called. He had a large envelope addressed to papa in his hand and there was another under his arm that didn't look as if it had ever been opened, but I couldn't see the address. I ran for mamma, but before we got back he was gone and the letters with him. Whatever it was, it has had an awful effect upon him, though he won't give us any satisfaction, you know how provoking he is. It is my belief he is going into decline, and I have such a horror of contagious diseases!

"If Evadne is so anxious to work, why doesn't she come and help mamma and me? It is the least she could do after all we have done for her, but as mamma says, 'It is just a specimen of the ingratitude there is in the world. '"

\* \* \* \* \*

The months rolled by and Evadne sat one afternoon in the superintendent's reception room reading a letter which the postman had just delivered. It bore the Vernon postmark.

She had seen but little of Mrs. Everidge through the years which followed her graduation. She had been constantly busy and her aunt's hands had been full, for her husband's health had failed utterly and he demanded continual care. Now her long, beautiful ministry was over, for Horace Everidge, serenely selfish to the last, had fallen into the slumber which knows no earthly waking, and Aunt Marthe was free.

"I do not know what it means, " she wrote, "but something tells me I shall not be long in Vernon. I am just waiting to see what work the King has for me to do. "

Evadne pressed the letter to her lips. "Dear Aunt Marthe! If the majority had had your 'tribulum' they would think they had earned the right to play! "

She looked up. John Randolph was standing before her with a package in his hands.

"I have been commissioned by the Hawthornes to give this into your own possession, " he said with a smile.

She opened it wonderingly. Bonds and certificates of stock bearing her name. What did it mean? John Randolph had drawn a chair opposite her and was watching her face closely.

"You cannot think what long consultations we have held on the subject of what you would like, " he said, "you seemed to have no wishes of your own. At last a happy thought struck Reginald, and he sent me a power of attorney to make the transfer of these bonds and stocks to you. It is a Trust Fund to be used to help souls. We all thought that would please you best of all. You are a rich woman, Miss Hildreth. "

A great wave of joy swept over her bewildered face. "So God has sent me the fulfilment of my dream! " she said softly. And John Randolph understood.

That evening she wrote to Mrs. Everidge.

"Dear Aunt Marthe, —The King's work is waiting for you in Marlborough. The work that we used to long for—the joy of lifting the shadows from the hearts of the heavy laden—God has given to you and me! "

\* \* \* \* \*

"Why should you not come to 'The Willows'? "

John Randolph put the question one afternoon, as they were enjoying Miss Diana's hospitality in the fragrant porch. Evadne had just finished a merry recital of their woes.

"We have looked at houses until we are fairly distracted, Aunt Marthe and I. One had a cellar kitchen, and I am not going to have my good Dyce buried in a cellar kitchen; and one had no bathroom, and another was all stairs; and they are all nothing but brick and mortar with a scrap of sky between. I want trees and water and fields. The poor souls have enough of masonry in their daily lives. "

"I believe it is decreed that you should come here, " he continued, after the first exclamations of surprise were over. "It is just the work our lady delights in, and she cannot be left alone. Dick goes to College next month and I must live in town. The house is beautiful for situation, and a threefold cord of love and faith cannot easily be broken. "

He looked round upon them, this man who found his joy in helping others, and waited for their answer.

"It would be beautiful, beautiful! " cried Evadne, "if Miss Chillingworth were willing. But the house is not large enough, Doctor Randolph, we shall need three or four guest chambers, you know. "

"Nothing easier than to build an addition, " said John, with the quiet reserve of power which always made his patients believe in the impossible.

Evadne laid her hand upon Miss Chillingworth's—"Dear Miss Diana, " she said gently, "you do not say 'No' to us; do you think you could ever find it in your heart to say 'Yes'? I know it must seem a terrible innovation, but we could never have imagined anything half so delightful, Aunt Marthe and I. The atmosphere—outdoors and in—is perfection! "

Miss Diana looked at the sparkling face and then at Mrs. Everidge with her gentle smile. "I find myself *very* glad, " she said, "since I have to lose my boys, but do you think we had better make any definite plans, dear, until we have talked it over with the Lord? "

And John Randolph said to Evadne with eyes that were suspiciously bright; "It is impossible for anyone to get very far from the Kingdom, when they live with our Lady Di. "

The talk had wandered then to different subjects, and John Randolph listened to the soft play of Evadne's fancy and watched the light in her wonderful eyes. Her nature, so long repressed in an uncongenial environment, in this new soil of love and sympathy was blossoming richly and he found her very fair. He had rarely seen her resting. Now the shapely hands were folded together in a beautiful stillness—and then the breeze had waved aside a flower, and a sunbeam, darting through the trellis, fell upon the stone in her ring and made it sparkle with a baleful fire!

"Poor Louis! " Isabelle had said, the last time he had been called to prescribe for her frequently recurring attacks of indisposition, "he will have to wait for promotion now before he can think of marriage. It is very hard for him. "

So again the truth and the lie had mingled.

## CHAPTER XXXII.

Very sweet grew the life at 'The Willows' and Mrs. Everidge and Evadne and Miss Diana found their hands full of happy work.

Unavella still reigned supreme in her kitchen. "'Tain't a great sight harder to cook for a dozen than six, " she had remarked sententiously, when the plan was unfolded to her, "it's only a matter uv quantity, the quality's jest the same. Ef Miss Di-an's a'goin ter start in ter be a she Atlas an' carry the world on her shoulders, she'll find I'm warranted ter wash an' not shrink in the rinsin'. I'm not a'goin ter be left behind, without I hev changed my name. "

Dyce kept the rooms in spotless order and waited upon the guests.

"Dear friend, " said Evadne one morning, as she watched her putting loving touches to the dining table, "you take as much trouble as if you expected Jesus Christ to be here! "

"So I does, Miss 'Vadney, " she answered simply, "I never feels comfortable 'cept when dere's a place fer de Lord, " and Evadne answered, "Dear Dyce, you make me feel ashamed! "

Many and varied were the guests who partook of their hospitality. The famine which no material wealth can alleviate is not confined to the dwellings of the poor. Hearts starve beneath coverings of velvet and loneliness often rides in a carriage. Many were the patients whom the world counted "well to do" that John Randolph sent to Evadne to be comforted. There was nothing to make them suspect that the keen intuition of the young physician had read their secret. 'The Willows' was simply a charming retreat where he sent them to try his favorite tonics of sunlight and oxygen; they never dreamed they were to be the recipients of favors which would not be rendered in the bill.

It was a beautiful fellowship in which they were banded together, for the Hawthornes had returned and were learning to find their pleasure in doing their Father's will. Dick True was in the brotherhood also, and never came home for his vacations without bringing with him "some fellow who needed a taste of love, " and the overgrown boys would glory in their strength as they lifted Miss

Diana from the carriage after a delightful drive, and learn a strange gentleness as they were unconsciously trained in the little deeds of chivalry which bespeak a true man.

Soon after Evadne's dream had materialized John Randolph had sent her a dainty little equipage to help on the work.

"You are too kind! " she cried, as she thanked him, "too generous! "

"Can we be that? " he asked, "when we are giving to a King? It is a theory of mine that a drive in the country with the right companion is better than exordiums. These poor souls have never learned to see 'sermons in stones, books in the running brooks, and God in everything. ' You must give me the pleasure of a little share in your beautiful work, my friend. "

"A little share! " echoed Evadne. "Is it possible that you do not know, Doctor Randolph, how much of it belongs to you! "

The beauty of the life was that the guests were taken into the heart of the living and felt themselves a part of the home. They never preached, these wise, tender women, but the beautiful incidental teachings sank deep into hearts that would have been closed fast against sermons. There was no stereotyped effort to do them good, they simply lived as Christ did, and the world-tired souls looked on and marveled, and rejoiced in the sunlight of the present and the afterglow which made the memory of their visit a delight.

"'Do not leave the sky out of your landscape, '" said Aunt Marthe in her cheery way, as Mrs. Dolours was wailing over her troubles. That was all—for the time, —Mrs. Everidge believed in homeopathy—but it set her hearer thinking, and thought found expression in questioning, until she was led to the feet of the great Teacher and learned to roll her burden of trouble upon him who came to bear the burdens of the world.

"'We are not to be anxious about living but about living well, '" said Miss Diana to a young man who prided himself upon being a philosopher "that is a maxim of Plato's but we can only carry it out by the help of the Lord, my boy. " And he listened to Evadne's merry laugh as she pelted Hans with cherries while Gretchen dreamed of the Fatherland under the trees by the brook, and wondered whether after all the men who had made it their aim to stifle every natural inclination, had learned the true secret of living as well as these happy souls who laid their cares down at the feet of their Father, and gave their lives into Christ's keeping day by day.

"You just seem to live in the present, " wealthy Mrs. Greyson said with a sigh, as she folded her jeweled fingers over her rich brocade, "I don't see how you do it! Life is one long presentiment with me. I am filled with such horrible forebodings. I tell Doctor Randolph, it is a sort of moral nightmare. "

> "Some of your griefs you have cured,
> And the sharpest you still have survived,
> But what torments of pain you endured,
> From evils that never arrived!"

Evadne quoted the words from a book of old French poems she had found in the library. Then she asked gently, "Why should you worry about the future, dear Mrs. Greyson, when it is such a waste of time? Don't you believe our Father loves his children?

"A waste of time. " That was a new way of looking at it! Mrs. Greyson had always prided herself upon being thrifty, and, if God loved, would he let any real harm happen? She knew she would shield her children. How blind she had been!

"Ah, but you have never known sorrow! " and Mrs. Morner drew her sable draperies around her with a sigh. "Just look at your face! Not a shadow upon it and hardly a wrinkle. You are one of the favored ones with whom life has been all sunshine. "

Mrs. Everidge laughed brightly. She had never pined to pose as a martyr before the world.

"God has been wondrous kind to me, " she said, "but there is a cure for all sorrow, dear friend, in his love. The great Physician is the only one who has a medicament for that disease. It is not forgetfulness, you know—he does not deal in narcotics—but he lays his pierced hand upon our bleeding hearts and stills their pain. Our memory is as fresh as ever, but it is memory with the sting taken out. "

"Ah, but you cannot understand—how should you? You have always had everything you wanted, and you have never lost anything or longed for what has been denied you! " and a toilworn woman, whose life seemed one long battle with disappointment, looked enviously at Miss Diana, over whose peaceful face life's twilight was falling in tender colors.

"Not quite everything I wanted, dear, " said Miss Diana softly, "but I have come to know that God himself is sufficient for all our needs. "

"Our dear Miss Diana has learned that 'we must sit in the sunshine if we would reflect the rainbow, '" said Aunt Marthe in her low tones. "It is a good rule, 'for every look we take at self, to take ten looks at Jesus. ' She lives in the light of his smile. "

Then through the open window they heard Evadne singing,

"Oh, the little birds sang east, and the little birds sang west,
And I smiled to think God's greatness flowed around our incompleteness,
Round our restlessness, his rest. "

And the weary soul folded its tired wings, all wounded with vain beatings against the prison bars of circumstance, and was hushed into a great stillness against the heart of its Father.

\* \* \* \* \*

John Randolph sought Evadne in the familiar porch which had grown to be to him the sweetest spot on earth.

"You are always busy, " he said with a smile, as he lifted the garment she was making for the little waif who was to have her first taste of heaven at 'The Willows. ' Satan has no chance to find an occupation for you. "

"But, oh, Doctor Randolph, what a drop in the bucket all our doing seems, when we think of the need of the world! "

"Yet without the drops the bucket would be empty, dear friend. God never expects the impossible from us, you know. I think Christ's highest commendation will always be, 'She hath done what she could. ' It is when we neglect the doing that he is wounded. "

After a pause he spoke again. "With your permission I am going to send you a new patient. " There was no trace of the struggle through which he had passed. This brave soul had learned to do the right and leave the rest with God.

Evadne laughed. "Still they come! Is it man, woman or child. Doctor Randolph? "

"Your cousin Louis. " His voice was very still.

"Poor Louis! Is it more serious then? He has been looking wretchedly for months. "

John Randolph examined her face critically. Could she call him "poor Louis" if she loved?

"His present trouble is nervous strain, aggravated by the unaccustomed confinement, and some mental excitement under which he is laboring. He must have a long rest, with a complete change of environment. If anyone can lift the cloud which seems to be hanging over him, I think it is you. "

Evadne shook her head sadly. "The only one who can help Louis is Jesus Christ, " she said.

CHAPTER XXXIII.

Louis Hildreth lay upon a couch in the cool library the morning after his arrival at 'The Willows. ' Evadne had been shocked at the change in him since she had seen him last. His eyes were sunken, while underneath purple shadows fell upon his pallid cheeks. He touched Evadne's hand as she sat beside him. It was his hand!

"What a splendid fellow Randolph is! " he exclaimed suddenly. "He is making himself felt in Marlborough, I tell you. Strange, how some men forge their way to the front, while the rest of us just float down the stream of mediocrity. No wonder we are not missed, when we drop out of the babbling conglomerate of humanity into silence, " he added bitterly. "Who would miss a single pair of fins from amidst a shoal of herring! "

"I think it is because Doctor Randolph is not content to float, Louis, " Evadne answered gently. "He must always be climbing higher. Like Paul, he is 'pressing towards the mark. '"

"He is a grand fellow! And the beauty of it is he never seems to think of himself at all. Most men would get to be top-lofty if they accomplished as much as he does every day. "

Evadne's lips parted in a happy smile. "I think Doctor Randolph is too much occupied with Jesus to have time to waste upon himself. "

"Upon my word, coz, you're a puzzle! You talk in an unknown tongue. Don't you know Self is the god we worship, and the aim of our existence is to have it wear purple and fine linen, and fare sumptuously every day? "

"It should not be! " cried Evadne. "Oh Louis, dear Louis, life can never be grand until we are able to say—'Self has been crucified with Christ! '"

\* \* \* \* \*

Weeks rolled into months and Louis was still at 'The Willows. ' His cynicism had come to have a strangely wistful ring. John Randolph's visits were frequent and they held long conversations together, these men, the one who had seized every opportunity and made the most of it, the other who had let his golden chances slip through his fingers one by one; then John Randolph would go bravely back to his life of toil, while Louis listened to Evadne's sweet voice as she sang in the gloaming, or watched his ring glisten as her deft fingers were busy with their deeds of love.

"How do you do it? " he exclaimed one evening when they were alone together. "You never rest! Your whole life seems to be centered in the lives of others, and there is nothing attractive about them, if there were I could understand. It looks like such drudgery to me. Tell me, little coz, what makes you give up all your ease to make these people happy? "

"When we love our Father it is our joy to do his will, " she answered softly.

"If I could live like you and Randolph I should be perfectly satisfied. I wish I had the courage to try. "

"Mere outward living cannot save us, Louis. Nothing can but faith in the atoning blood and the name and the love of Christ. Then—when we believe, you know—all things become possible. We make an awful mistake when we think we know better than the Bible. Nicodemus lived a perfect outward life, yet Christ said to him, 'Except ye be born again—of the Word and the Spirit—ye cannot see the Kingdom of God. ' We are running a terrible risk when we try to live without Jesus. "

"That is what Randolph says. He is a one idea man, if ever there was one, and yet he is so many sided! He is the most uncompromising fellow I ever knew. I should as soon expect to see the stars fall from the sky as to see him do a shady thing. You would be amused, coz, to see the lady mother and Isabelle joining forces to lay siege to his affections. "

What meant that sudden start and then the blush which flamed up over cheek and brow? Louis Hildreth closed his thin fingers over Evadne's ring with a long drawn sigh. He was beginning to realize that a hand, without a heart, is an empty thing.

Long after she had left him he lay motionless. This knowledge which had come to him so suddenly had a bitter taste.

\* \* \* \* \*

"You ought to get well, Hildreth, and you ought to be a very happy man, " John Randolph spoke the words suddenly as he rose to take his leave.

"I never expect to be either. When a man has all he has prided himself upon swept away from him, and all that he longs for denied him, how can it be possible? "

"'Count it your highest good when God denies you. ' Is that too hard a gospel? We shall not read it so in the light of eternity. It is only that Christ may become to us the 'altogether lovely' One. "

"Did you ever love—a woman? " Louis put the question suddenly, watching his friend's face with a jealous scrutiny.

"Yes. " The answer was as simple and straightforward as the man. He knew of nothing to be ashamed of in this beautiful love of his life.

"And her name was? —"

"Evadne. "

John Randolph spoke the name for the first time to another, looking up at the sky. When he turned to leave the room he saw that Louis' face was buried among his cushions and he drove away in a great wonderment. What could it all mean?

> "Knocking, knocking, who is there?
>   Waiting, waiting, oh, how fair!
> 'T is a pilgrim, strange and kingly,
>   Never such was seen before.
> Ah, my soul, for such a wonder,
>   Wilt thou not undo the door?"

Evadne sang the words softly in the twilight: sang them with a great note of longing in her pleading voice. She and her cousin were alone.

"Evadne, come here. "

She crossed the room and knelt beside his couch.

"Little coz, I have let the Pilgrim in. "

And Evadne buried her face in the cushions with a low cry. The crown of rejoicing was hers—at last!

\* \* \* \* \*

"There is only one thing wanting between you two. " Louis looked wistfully at John Randolph and Evadne, as they stood beside him, talking brightly of how he should help when he grew strong.

"And what is that? " Doctor Randolph asked the question with a smile.

Louis drew his ring from Evadne's finger and laid her hand in that of his friend. "Take her, Randolph, she is worthy of you. I would not say that of any other woman. "

With a great joy surging in his heart, John Randolph held out his other hand. She must give herself. He could not take her from another's giving.

A lovely shyness flushed into the pure face, their eyes met, and Evadne laid her hand in his without a word.

"Evadne! " The rich, tender tones fell throbbing through the silence, enwrapping the name in a sweet protectiveness. "Life is—for us—to do the will of God! "

THE END.

Lightning Source UK Ltd.
Milton Keynes UK
UKHW010642260421
382641UK00001B/67